Second Chance

The Adventures of Gianni & Pepina {Book 1}

Giuseppe Scarpine

Join Giovanni 'Gianni' Pisano, retired American doctor with drug and alcohol issues, bouncing back and forth between USA and southern France, attempting the daunting task of figuring out life. He finally meets Pepina Soler, a beguiling Catalonian woman who helps him overcome some bad habits as they embark on a journey of cooking, eating, gardening and travelling around the world.

Book Cover Design by Jessica Bell
Author photo by Giulia Ebrahimi
Art painting by Giuseppe Scarpine

For Zsa zsa

Contents

Cast of main characters:

I

Purple Haze

1

True eloquence means saying all that is necessary and only what is necessary.
Francois de la Rochefoucauld

Where the hell did I put that stepladder? How in the world am I gonna be able to trim that friggin' tree branch? I let this damn tree get too big since the last pruning.

Wait, what was I going to get in the storage closet? Right, stepladder.

Whew! The opium I smoked the night before is really spacing me out. I'm unable to hold a thought one moment to the next. Kinda like a goldfish, ha!

Another espresso with a wee shot of Grand Marnier should clear up matters. It's still morning. I believe it's Tuesday, but what the hell does it matter? Who would have guessed that I, a retired American doctor, would be spending a majority of his time at his flat on the southern coast of France tending fruit trees? Oh, did I forget to mention that I am an alcoholic? At least from a medical standpoint I can admit that.

I purchased my little hideaway in the 90s, a small community close to the shore, just a stone's throw from Nice, or as the Italians call it, *Nizza*. This is my base while I'm living between the States and Europe. I can catch quite a few futbol matches, attend Euro basketball games (better rules, but less talent than NBA), attend the opera, and eat some of the best seafood in the world while tending my fruit trees (what a gig!). I was an oddity as the only foreigner in the village at the beginning. But fast forward to the present day, and I have witnessed retirees from the UK, Germany and Holland making their way from those cold, dank winters for a wonderful life by the warm, sunny Mediterranean.

The location itself has an archaeological history that is striking. There is an area in Nice called *Terra Amata* (beloved land), an archaeological site that provided proof of very early human use of fire, perhaps 380,000 years ago. Fast forward to around 350 BC: The Greeks from Marseille founded a port settlement in the area and named it 'Nikaia' after Nike, the Greek goddess of Victory.

Like much of the Mediterranean, it has changed hands on multiple occasions. In the year 1561 the Duke of Savoy abolished Latin as the language of those in power. He established Italian as the official language of the government. From 1815 to 1860 it was ruled by the Kingdom of Piedmont-Sardinia, being re-annexed by France in 1860.

Present day, the Italian influence is prevalent. There are French citizens of Italian ancestry like Signore Materazzi, the wine merchant from whose large oak casks I refill my wine bottles. The fishmonger I frequent down at the bay for some live fish right off the boats is Gerlando, from whom, by the way, I occasionally score some really good Afghanistan blonde hashish. I am a dedicated patron of Nicolo's successful gelato store down at the shore. My postal courier Carmelo pays me a visit at least once a week for coffee and a dram of Sambuca, while filling me in on all the village gossip. These are a few of my paisans with whom I can speak the beautiful language.

The wine is beyond good here. I do have experience with quality vino from my many excursions throughout Italy and France. When back in the States, I have been known to spend an inordinate amount of time hitting all the wineries in California's Napa Valley. I have attended dozens of wine tastings: pinot noir, sangiovese, cabernet sauvignon, zinfandel, syrah and malbec. The list goes on. I haven't even mentioned the whites.

The rose in France is supreme while relatively inexpensive. I'm teased constantly by my longtime friend Henri, to the point of calling me a cheap bastard, for purchasing inexpensive wine. Look, I am not one to pay forty euro for a bottle on a constant basis when there is perfectly good grape for a fraction. Anyway, I digress. I could go on about the grappa, pastis, absinthe and cognac… the beat goes on.

My dear friend Henri is owner of Pensione Acacia in Nice. Prior to purchasing my flat, whenever I would hang out on the Cote d' Azur, I would reside at Henri's fleabag establishment. Over the years I became what Henri called his VIP Yankee guest. Stale morning croissants, tepid coffee, a rarely operational lift, plumbing that would incessantly rattle and fart—besides that, it was an ok place to crash. The five-pound weight attached to the room key I found a bit inconvenient, so Henri eventually allowed me to have my own private key due to my dedicated patronage.

To be kind, Henri is a rotund five foot five inch man of my age, with olive skin, big brown bug eyes and very hairy arms. He always wears suspenders with polyester pants hiked up over his voluminous potbelly. Henri is bald with a very faint landing strip of greasy hair on top in which you could count the individual hairs. Yet you can always see him adoringly stroke that paltry fleece back with either hand, as if the wind was blowing it, getting into his eyes.

Henri is more than glad to take care of my place when I'm back in the States. To begin with, it's only six kilometers away from his pensione in Nice—a mere ten minute, two-stop train ride or, as Henri prefers, his old usually broken down Fiat Spider as his prime method of transportation. Henri is more than glad to scavenge any remaining fruit off my mini orchard, as well as using my abode for an occasional tryst with one of the local ladies of the night by the shore, which I've yet to prove. I don't accuse or deny the old bugger. He is more than welcome, due to the unwavering friendship he has shown me over the years, pulling me out of some very dark places due to drugs and alcohol.

When I was not across the pond in Europe, my former coworker (Gustavo) was renting out my townhome in the City of Santa Barbara, California via Air B&B. As the saying goes, *if you are not making money while you're sleeping, you're not making money. What a gig!*

I have done my best in not letting greed take hold of my life. In the past, I witnessed many of my medical colleagues during the dot.com era lose their knickers, while just a few made a fortune day trading, so I know firsthand that not a single person is so rich that they do not wish to see their wealth multiply indefinitely. Greed is a monster that needs to be checked.

My buddy Gustavo is Argentinean. He grew up in Rosario, but received his early medical training in Buenos Aires before moving to the States. Gustavo is brilliant, an incredible IQ with common sense to match—the latter being equally if not more important. Like Mark Twain said, *Common sense ain't so common.* His father was an Italian officer in WWII with a background even Gustavo was sketchy on. He informed me after many years that he did some investigation, finding that his father spent a majority of the war campaign in East Africa (Etruria and Ethiopia). Gustavo spoke very easy-on-the-ears lilting Spanish, as well as Italian and English.

While what I initially thought would be an incredible future as star skilled cardiovascular surgeon turned out to be not too exciting, I retained until my retirement a humble, yet honorable existence as a general practitioner, settling into a daily tedium of patients with gout to hemorrhoids. I would send my patients off on referral to a specialist, shirking any additional effort. When I did work, I led a rather under-the-radar general practice with Kaiser Permanente.

Gustavo, on the other hand, was a well-known and highly touted urologist in Los Angeles. I'm sure that as a child, Gustavo, like me, did not envision his future tickling blowholes, probing prostates and encouraging men not to worry about erectile dysfunction. However, who is to argue regarding destiny?

Gustavo, being a dedicated workaholic, with my counsel,

relegated the AirB&B tasks of cleaning my townhouse, changing the sheets and vetting the guests to his daughter Valeria. She was a twenty-one-year-old college dropout with drug issues that I could relate to big time. Somehow, the responsibility and the generous percentage that I gave her seemed to even her out and she began to ponder an entrepreneurial career in the hospitality industry. For this, Gustavo was eternally grateful to me. Gustavo kept a very distant eye on her, to not interfere, but at the same time to exert some paternal care on his troubled daughter.

Valeria always spoke in an easy manner with me. She confided personal issues which she would never dare mention to her father. This baffled Gustavo. However, he was appreciative that if his daughter could disclose troubling personal or drug related matters, that it was best with his friend and former colleague. He was well aware of my drug and alcohol issues and had been there for me when I was down. Gustavo was long divorced, sworn to never marry again. He married an American woman who abandoned their daughter and only child when Valeria was just a toddler. I felt that Valeria was holding some deep pain for a mother she never knew, while possibly holding a grudge against her father for being raised by a single parent.

On the surface, I guess I am more fortunate than most, being in rather good physical shape, still able to play hoops when my sciatica isn't acting up. In regard to finances, I have been fortunate to be in the right place at the right time concerning real estate and stock investments, coupled with the fact that I have no children. Consequently, I have been tagged by marketers as having discretionary funds.

It's a wonder that my liver and kidneys haven't failed at this point due to alcohol abuse, to name one. That is where genetics plays a part. I had so many patients who lived the life of an aesthetic monk, but were plagued with all forms of cancer, cardio-pulmonary issues and respiratory ailments. Generally, a large percentage of those aforementioned patients had long family histories of those diseases.

But the sickness of my mind, memories of the past, recollections I cannot escape… They are like the fog while you are driving, the hope that in the next moment it will vanish and there will be clear sailing. But the fog is relentless, my miserable co-pilot, though I delude and numb myself from these memories with alcohol, opium and an inexhaustible supply of pharmaceuticals.

You name it, France has it. Drugs are very available along the southern coast all along the Mediterranean: Spain, France, Italy and Greece. There are just too many smuggling operations from Turkey, Afghanistan and Iran.

The Russians seem to have taken over a majority of the illegal activity lately, competing with multiple crime organizations in Italy and Serbia, pushing very cheap drugs to the European populace. Cocaine, fentanyl, heroin and methylenedioxy-methamphetamine, commonly called MDMA (Ecstasy), are available in crystal, powder and pill form. These are all easily available on the streets. Fentanyl is an unbelievably powerful synthetic opioid analgesic. It is classified as a Schedule II prescription drug that mimics morphine, but can be more than 100 times as potent. The actual increase in worldwide accidental death rates by fentanyl overdose is staggering.

As a young man, in what seems to be an altogether distant lifetime, I was married. Emily was from Edinburgh, Scotland. She had the hair of a goddess—bronze melded with orange sunset—hazel eyes, skin like triple cream. When she got the least bit of sun, she looked like a poached lobster with a few freckles splashed over her curvaceous body.

We met in college in my first year in medical school. Emily was a literature major and made a fine English teacher at a high school in Santa Barbara, California, where we settled. She was always there for me through medical school and during my internship. The late dinners, the massaging of my feet after pulling a 14-hour emergency room duty—Emily was strict with my career. She wanted so badly to assist with the burden of breadwinner after a few years of belt tightening.

The year was 1980. Carter was on the way out and Reagan was a freight train rolling for what was to be eight years of Neanderthal reverse Darwinism. Coal and oil, forward ho! Solar and wind… take a backseat.

But I tell you, Carter had implemented the MHSA (Mental Health Systems Act), which was a proposal to federally continue to fund community mental health centers. Reagan abolished that law soon after his entry into office. Old Ronnie, who came from a rather privileged, yet B-rated movie career, had no concept of mental illness. Anything beyond his scope of comprehension was un-apple pie America and communist. Opening up all the sanitariums, letting the mentally disabled loose, still is one of America's darkest moments for the downfall of lending a brother or sister a helping hand. This will forever be Reagan's grim legacy. Ironically, Reagan was shot out on the street by John

Hinckley, an undiagnosed schizophrenic, soon after … Karma, baby!

As a young lassie, Emily backpacked throughout Europe with her girlfriends and schoolmates from Edinburgh. I enjoyed hearing her stories: island hopping in Greece, surfing in Portugal, camping in Germany's Black Forest, hundred-kilometer hikes in Spain. Emily possessed real athletic ability. Even some Slavic countries which she mentioned had far more interesting skiing, such as Estonia, Slovakia and former Yugoslavia. With that said, Emily became one hundred per cent American. She loved California weather. She had no inclination to ever return back across the Atlantic. Emily would always say how American life was so much simpler, less rigid, and in many aspects I would quite agree.

However, my own personal feelings were quite the opposite. Always I gravitated toward the Old World, with a yearning for grasping languages and cultures of many peoples with centuries upon millennia of rich history versus an upstart country with a couple hundred years of history.

I always told my mother that I wanted to be a History Professor. I worshipped Arnold Toynbee's exhaustive 12-volume *A Study of History* or his adventurous *Between the Oxus and the Jumna,* as well as Will Durant's detailed *Life of Greece* and intriguing *Our Oriental Heritage*. But common sense dictated that I needed to make money, so attempting to exercise that virtue, I embarked on a future as a physician. Without totally surrendering to the initial future of preference, as an undergraduate, my minor was in the classics; three years of a smattering in classical Greek and Latin kept me linked to my interest. It also assisted me in my lifelong study of three languages - Spanish, Italian and French.

We were two young professionals pulling in a decent living. At that time, Emily and I decided to have a child. I was a remarkable seed planter. Emily was equally enthusiastic in her physical and quite vocal desire to bear fruit. Within no time (minus the condoms) we were expecting our first child. We wanted a boy. However, a healthy child would suit us fine.

Remember, it was the 80s. People smoked tobacco in abundance. The Scots were big tobacco consumers. That was Emily's Achilles heel. She would hide smoking cigarettes from me, but the smell of ashtray hair and fingers gave her away. I on occasion had a few meerschaum pipes that I dabbled with that reminded me of my father, but never had a taste for cigarettes. Emily was raised by a rather extroverted blue collar machinist/tool and die-maker father. Her mother was an introverted, depressed housewife who suffered from multiple miscarriages and depression. Hence, Emily was an only child.

Perhaps it was inherited genetics from her mother, or what we know now medically about the effects of smoking tobacco on a fetus, coupled with her inability to quit smoking during pregnancy—who knows? All I remember is one evening, leading up to a three-day Labor Day holiday. We treated ourselves to a romantic dinner aboard the incredibly huge, long retired luxury cruise ship; the HMS *Queen Mary* in Long Beach, California, Emily was electric—five months pregnant, with glowing skin, and those bewitching hazel eyes. Her physique gave off just a hint of muscle. Her perky pear-shaped breasts were just filling out. We dined in a fine ballroom - The Winston Churchill - with soft lighting. A light jazz band was playing a Miles Davis tune, "It Never Entered My Mind," when we arrived, which rounded off an atmosphere of utter relaxation.

We had just started our Caesar salad and while I was finishing off my vegetation, I remember holding the bowl up to my chin like a savage, getting that last slice of parmiggiano reggiano cheese dangling haplessly off the edge. That was when Emily excused herself to go to the ladies. As she stood up, she reached behind her backside and mentioned that her seat must be wet. At the next moment, I saw in her eyes the realization and the horror of what it was. The blood on her hand explained it all.

The emergency room at Long Beach Memorial was fortunately not far away. In the car, my darling Emily miscarried. As she was being taken care of by the hospital staff, I retrieved from the car a small, bloody, lifeless fetus that may have resembled a boy —a canceled potential human being. I placed it in a small box in the trunk of my car that previously housed an auto part. In a stupor, I walked back to the emergency entrance, holding the box, looking like I was dropping off a package. An emergency room nurse sat me down, saying that my wife was in good hands.

Other than that, I don't really remember what transpired that day. It's been over thirty years. What happened with the box? The nurse must have taken it. Anyway, Emily never recovered mentally. She was not the same person that I had known and loved. My loving partner who formerly inhabited her body was gone. The fear of following in her mother's path toward multiple miscarriages must have torn her apart. All the postpartum therapy and prescription drugs just drove her into a darker abyss. Three months passed. After an intense day's work at the clinic, I found my dear wife and friend at home, sitting in our car, in the garage. Emily committed suicide by overdose of sleeping pills.

There are so many variables in life…why didn't I do this? Why did I do that? What's up with your decision making? The one thing in life you cannot buy back is time. How can missing the last second shot in my junior year at an insignificant high school basketball game haunt me in my dreams till this day, but I can't remember the last time I told my dearest Emily I loved her?

The last three decades I have anesthetized myself with all manner of booze and drugs to eradicate, cleanse and download in my head the adolescent behavior of my former years, the constant struggle to reinvent myself. Perhaps that's why I have become so involved with raising fruit trees. Gardening is a delayed gratification process. You plant, but you can't see an immediate result. Perseverance and patient care are required to get results. Am I supplying the proper nutrients? Giving enough water? Consuming the sumptuous and delectable fruit is of course rewarding, but knowing that the tree will flourish and remain in good health is my main objective. I believe.

Looking back, was it because all I was consumed with was the paycheck? Working such long hours as a physician, when I should have been taking a leave of absence, nurturing Emily back to health? All the warning signs were there. *You fool, you idiot, you inconsiderate asshole. What the fuck state of mind was your head in? Stop It! Just stop….* This is my daily torture. *Please stop. Please cease to exist!* This merry-go-round is my hell. What penance, what cost can I employ to jump off this nightmare carnival ride?

The Psilocybin mushrooms that I scored recently at the Vieux Nice (old Nice) market did not dissolve my ego or cleanse my brain of past sins like advertised. I did experience one helluva psychedelic trip, finding myself laughing my ass off uncontrollably, while masturbating on the Mediterranean shoreline at 3am. All this while watching what I thought at the time was a meteor shower. But as I came down from that mind-bending alternate reality, I realized I had been staring at a couple of street lights across the bay. From that experience, I decided to stay away from those unpredictable *fungi* while remaining, faithfully, a dedicated alcoholic.

Soon after Emily's suicide, my mother passed away from a myocardial infarction. She did suffer from heart disease and was on Heparin (an anticoagulant). A neighbor found her outside, in her garden, doing what she loved. I can only hope for such a beautiful, fitting end. Mother never quite understood Emily's suicide. She was devastated by what happened to the daughter she never had. She was always a constant source of encouragement to Emily. However, she noticed as well that something had snapped, that she was powerless to have any effect on helping Emily get through her ordeal. Professional help also seemed to drive her into a deeper depression.

I was somewhat of a dimwit back then. Who the hell am I now? I look in the mirror, I see a stranger.

It has been over thirty-one years since Emily decided to leave this world. I have never remarried, never attempted to have another relationship. It has been four years since I left my general practice. I can honestly say the only bit I miss is the unlimited goodies from the pharmaceutical companies (tranquilizers, barbiturates and opiates). I'm somewhat better abstaining from those nasty buggers more now in my self-imposed leisure than when I was working. I never contemplated following Emily in suicide. My rendition of that one-time-only performance was more like a slow waltz toward my demise. For my daily intake of drugs and alcohol will surely send me toward the final life curtain… eventually.

Giardino dell'amore

2

We must cultivate our garden.
Voltaire

My village had a population of about eight thousand in the nineties when I purchased. Presently, it has shrunk to about five thousand inhabitants due to the departure of young people for the more densely populated cities, coupled with the fact that many of the older generation were simply kicking the bucket. My modest flat had a small side yard that geezers in the community said was always abandoned and neglected. It was a long rectangular strip of weed-infested land nine meters in length by three meters in width. I contemplated how much I could push the envelope to maximize the given space for my gardening project.

Aware of the fact that I was being an ambitious gardener, I had planted six fruit trees, one of which was not a dwarf specimen but a sweetly scrumptious sapote blanco (native to Central America). For those who share an enthusiasm for rare fruit as I do, you know that that tree can get quite large, with a canopy 10 meters high. The area for my gardening project was vastly neglected, with some sad excuses for overgrown iceberg roses, a few agapanthus Africana, dilapidated dandelions, spurge, wild purslane (which is delicious, raw or sautéed), crabgrass and an assortment of unidentifiable weeds.

It took me one spring to remove everything and start conditioning the soil with chicken shit, horse shit, earthworm castings, some fish emulsion that my pal Henri gave me, and last but not least, my secret weapon soup: recycled coffee grounds, black and herbal tea leaves that I constantly keep replenishing in five-gallon container. To an earthworm, coffee grounds are like a juicy T-bone steak. They flourish and benefit the soil in so many ways.

As a child, growing up in an untraditional small Italo-American family, my mother raised me solo. My father (who I'm named after) came to America as a child, was raised strictly, studied hard to accomplish the American dream and became an electrical engineer.

He passed away when I was only six years old. He died of what they said was a brain tumor. He is nothing more than a distant memory. The one thing that stands out is he always had a pipe hanging out of his mouth. I was always fascinated with his pipes, holding them in my hands. That's what I remember most. Mother kept a couple of his meerschaum pipes. I have them to this day. I am drawn to the feel, the smooth contours as I run my fingers across them. I rarely, if ever, smoke tobacco. Perhaps, in this way, subconsciously, it is in remembrance to a father I never got to know.

One other item that reminds me of my father is the scent of his hair. I remember always wanting to hug my father tightly quite often. He must have thought in all honesty that I was a very affectionate little boy. But in reality, I just was so attracted to the smell of his Vitalis Hair Tonic. The fragrance is masculine and gave me a sense of security. I was afraid that over the years the brand would change its scent. However, it is still identical today and why you will always find a bottle of it in my medicine chest.

My mother was a wonder woman. Whenever she had even a minute, you could find her humming opera under her breath while gardening. We always had a garden comprised of fruit, vegetables and herbs, never without a fig, guava or plum tree. As a young lad I tried my best not to have any of my friends come over to play because Mother would be always transplanting some bush from the front yard to the back, planting a row of bush beans, stringing up supports for a variety of tomatoes. My friends would always tease me about being a farmer boy, which caused many scuffles. I realized as I grew into adulthood that my genetics were such that I found myself biologically wired to have the gardening gene, which I have grown to enjoy and it keeps my mind off other unsavory thoughts. I recall reading somewhere what I believe is a Chinese saying:

'If you want to be happy for a day, have a friend over for a glass of wine.

'If you want to be happy for a lifetime, have a garden.'

I find that saying resonates with me in every sense, since alcohol and gardening take up much of my time. Salud!

As I glance back at my life, it's apparent that I have idolized my father out of some distant ancestral respect. In reality, the closest I came to a father figure was my Zio Gerardo (Uncle Jerry), who was my father's older brother and my only uncle. He was named after the Patron Saint of Potenza in Basilicata Region, Italia (Santo Gerardo).

Whether he took me under his wing out of a sense of duty, or whether he was just lonely and was in need of company, I never quite figured out. Uncle Jerry never married and was quite content with who he was. "Feel free to call me Jerry or Uncle," he told me and further said, "We are Americans. Always observe the laws where you live, young man."

I was drawn to Uncle Jerry's accent, vaguely reminiscent of my father. I would emulate Uncle Jerry's accent at times. This would always bring a frown to his face, always followed by laughter. Uncle Jerry was small in stature, only about five foot two inches, very wiry, but deceptively strong. He had an amazing full head of hair, olive skin, clear brown eyes, and the beak of an eagle. Uncle Jerry, like my father, was also an engineer, retired long ago. He spoke with great reverence regarding L'Ordine Figli d'Italia (The Order Sons of Italy), of which he was a member. He encouraged me to be a proud Italian of Neapolitan roots.

When I reached the age of ten, every spring and summer Uncle Jerry would whisk me away, telling Mother not to worry, that he and his nephew were going camping or to the museums or some such stories. Mother was elated that a male relative would lend a guiding hand during my adolescence. In reality, we always escaped to Santa Anita and Del Mar thoroughbred horse race tracks. Uncle Jerry occasionally would take me to Hollywood Park, but only for stakes races. He said Hollywood Park and Los Alamitos only ran dogs. This was Uncle Jerry's passion. His knowledge and zeal for the ponies was contagious.

Our first stop was Santa Anita racetrack and the Breeders Cup. After that meet was finished, Del Mar would start for a month of races in late summer. Uncle was very savvy about horses. The paddock area - where horses are saddled up - was my favorite place. I could watch the detail in which trainers would prepare the horses, giving last-minute instructions to the jockeys.

I became attracted, looking forward to the sights and smells of the racetrack: tilled earth, fresh-cut grass, cigar smoke, horseshit and the bright colors of the flags, the extra-long shiny brass trumpet heralding the beginning of each race. Uncle became excited and happy at the racetrack. So I was happy too. I sensed that the horses were happy because they loved to run. The horses couldn't wait to run. At a young age, I loved to run also, so I could feel their joy when I saw the wild excitement that blazed in their eyes. I would stand at the finish line, feeling the vibration in the ground through my feet, the thunderous approach of their hooves setting off small explosions in the dust.

Each summer meet Uncle and I always met up with a man about the same age as my Uncle Jerry. His name was Melvin. Melvin spoke funny. I liked Melvin's laugh. Uncle Jerry liked Melvin and said he knew *'ciccia di cavallo'* (horseflesh). Melvin had different names for things. I would point to a jockey mounting up in the paddock and say – "Look at that jockey, Melvin, in the green silks."

Melvin would reply, "That bloke's name is Pincay; he's havin a good run this meet." Or he would say, "That's Lambert. He's a real wanker!"

Sometimes I would ask Melvin if any good horses were running that day, or some such nonsense, just to get a reply from him. He would roar with laughter, saying, "All the Gee-Gees are grand!" Then he would point at one and say, "Except that one there; he's ready for the knackers!" while slapping Uncle Jerry on the back as both of them bent over with laughter.

Bloodlines, trainers, jockeys - you name it. I learned to translate all the data in a Daily Racing Form. Workout times for six furlong races, whether they were on the dirt or turf course. The turf. That was my favorite, I felt that horses liked turf too. The long races on turf were exciting. Especially the San Juan Capistrano handicap at Del Mar (the marathon mile and three quarters). Melvin said where he came from there were only turf courses, no dirt. He liked to say, "Gee-Gees runnin' on dirt? Bollocks!"

Uncle would depend on me to give him info from the Racing Form (the all-inclusive Bible for horseracing). I took pride in rattling off the dam/sire of a particular horse, their morning workout times, where they placed in their last race and the time period in between races. Uncle also gave me the responsibility when we drove in the car to be the navigator. I would intently study the Thomas Guide Maps the night before as to which freeways and roads to take. Uncle took pride in giving me these responsibilities. I, young and wanting to be praised, loved being able to display my knowledge to him.

One summer we didn't see Melvin at Santa Anita, Del Mar or the other racetracks. The next year he came and he was holding a cane - kinda leaning on it. Uncle Jerry and I were happy to see Melvin. His face was a little different. One side didn't move and hung down like he was disappointed. Melvin noticed me staring at him and said, "Krikey! I fell off me Gee-Gee! No worries, laddie." Only half of his face laughed, but it was a still a Melvin laugh. I laughed back because I knew he didn't ride horses. Uncle explained to me later that Melvin had been ill but he was much better now.

Uncle knew a few racing stewards, trainers and grooms. So many people loved Uncle at the races. They called him "Banana Nose" because he was the spitting image of Eddie Arcaro, a great Hall of Fame jockey whose nickname was Banana Nose. They were even born the same year -1916!

Uncle made the most of his pretend fame. I remember the Herald Examiner sports page man once yelled out to Uncle Jerry when he was talking with a trainer "Hey! Banana Nose! Any nags you like today?"

Uncle would then, with that sly smile, raise his right eyebrow in a high arch, and with his right index finger, he would point to his temple and gently tap, very slowly, three times… always three times. This was Uncle's signature and the racetrack folk loved it. They would bark such remarks as:

"Oohh! Watch out, Banana Nose is gonna clean up today," cried the graveled voice of the Star News sports paper salesman.

The 'TurfMaster Bookie' would yell, "Get the saddlebags ready for all the loot Banana Nose is takin' home!"

While I was in high school I didn't want or have time to go to the horse races with Uncle Jerry anymore. It was summer. I enjoyed surfing at Huntington Beach and hanging out with my pals. Uncle invited me every time, but I always made some excuse. Uncle Jerry would tempt me by tapping his index finger on his right temple three times slowly - always three times – and he would then announce, "I'm gonna clean up today, my boy!"

I would laugh and reply, "Enjoy, Zio. Ciao!" I never did once ask him about if Melvin was still there, even though it was on my mind each time to ask. Uncle Jerry was killed when I was 16 years old. A drunk driver hit his vehicle head-on while he waited at a traffic light.

As I mentioned, the space I had was limited for my fruit trees. It was difficult to choose but I had enough real estate on the side of my flat for six trees. To itemize my mini-fruit orchard collection, my choices are as follows:

<u>Mulberry (_morus nigra_):</u> These luscious berries are so juicy and the taste of them as soon as it hits my tongue reminds me of my childhood friend Willy. His family was from El Salvador. They owned a gigantic mulberry tree that we made a treehouse in. The stains were impossible to get out of my clothes and my mother would always scold me for ruining so many shirts. But her scorn would always turn to laughter when I brought an old glass milk bottle filled with the purple/black juicy wonders of nature.

The Persians prize this particular mulberry. They call it shahtoot (king mulberry). From my mini-orchard one year I brought two kilos of these mulberries to my pal Nicolo down at the harbor. Nicolo has a gelateria and has carved himself a rather lucrative business with the tourist activity (cruise ship and bus industry). Anyway, that year he made a 'King Mulberry Gelato' he charged an arm and a leg for. He had so many requests that Nicolo literally, on hands and knees, pleaded with me to go into business. He told me to get rid of all the other trees and plant only this type of mulberry tree. Nicolo was so discouraged when I informed him that I had no entrepreneurial desire and felt no need to reinvent myself from loser retired doctor to the next Franco-Italo version of Ben & Jerry.

Ciao! Nicolo & Gianni Gelato Voila!

Nonetheless, Nicolo was able to poach a small plot of land at his fiancée's parents' house to plant three mulberry trees. Now he just needs the patience of a saint for the crop to bear fruit. He did attempt to pass off a concoction of blackberries, raspberries and black currant juice. However, this pseudo 'King Mulberry Gelato' was immediately ridiculed as an imposter and Nicolo was forced to retract and rename.

<u>Chocolate persimmon (*diospyros kaki*)</u>: It is native primarily to Japan. Even so, my persimmon simply thrives in this Mediterranean climate with the Cote d'Azur ocean breeze. I found that the Japanese name for persimmon (kaki) is identical to the Italian and French name - perhaps due to the Latin description.

The two main persimmons are Hachiya and Fuyu. The former variety has an elongated shape that always kinda reminds me of a very large Roma tomato. It also must be soft when consuming. If you attempt to eat it before it ripens, your mouth will pucker up due to it being so astringent. The latter is semi-round. You may consume it when hard or soft. Both are utterly delicious. The Fuyu and Hachiya varieties may be dried for enjoyment until the following season. However, it's a lot of work and perseverance with the skinning and hanging the fruit out to dry. Humidity control is important lest they become moldy.

By contrast, the chocolate persimmon is a small fruit compared to its two big brothers. To the untrained eye, when ripe it displays an interior brown color. The dark chocolate meat found inside can fool the uninitiated into thinking that the fruit is rotten. This is the main reason you rarely see the chocolate persimmon offered at markets due to the fact that aesthetically it is not pleasing to the eye for most consumers.

The fruit is sweet with a taste of spice, similar to allspice. I also have one of these in my front yard back in the States. To have a laugh, I have had people walking by for an evening stroll and mention what a beautiful persimmon tree with so many tasty looking fruit. I would snatch one off the tree and cut it open and say. "Alas, they have some type of disease and the fruit is spoiled," showing them the dark brown chocolaty color inside. This would fool them sufficiently to discourage anyone from picking when I am not around. What a dick! Ha!

My **fig tree (ficus carica)** is very popular amongst the bird population in the neighborhood due to its diversity; I have been successful via grafting in adding a whole menagerie of various figs to a single tree, including plump black mission figs, brown turkey, striped panache, green kadota, longue d'Aout, strawberry and violette de bordeaux figs. I have found fig trees to be one of the most agreeable to various graft techniques: whip, tongue and chip-bud grafting.

In regard to grafting, I know a Filipino gentleman (Joe Dizon) who is a fellow member of the California Rare Fruit Growers Association. He has grafted sixty-four varieties of apple on one tree successfully. Obviously, he has apples all year round. Bravissimo Joe!

The neighborhood birds will start on one of my ripe figs, patiently pecking one by one the thousands of tiny seeds in each fig. Finally they leave a very thin skin hollow shell of a fig, flapping in the breeze before they begin to spear another. The green zebra, streaked panache, longue d'Aout and plump kadota are a few green variety figs. The remaining grafts are the dark Violetta di Bordeaux, Brown Turkey, Strawberry and Black Mission—all purple masses of juicy sweetness. I cook them with just a little pectin to make Mason jars full of fig jam to share with Henri and his employee Vivian, her husband the butcher Jean-Michel and Livia, who makes socca at the market in Vieux Nice.

In the summer, I really look forward first thing in the morning to freshly squeezed juice from my **<u>sanguinelli blood orange tree</u>** (**<u>citrus sinensis</u>**). I purchased this beauty in Spain one year when Henri and I spent some time in Andalucía. This beauty never fails me, year-in, year-out. When given a choice between a Valencia, Navel or blood orange I will go with the latter every time. It's not too bad with a splash of Bombay extra dry gin. I also make ice cubes from the dark nectar to cool off during the hot summers.

<u>Sapote blanco (Casimiroa edulis)</u> is a fruit which really requires one to have a sweet tooth. Its sweeter-than-honey with soft custardy texture is not for every palate. The varieties abound: Vernon, Yellow Gold, MacDill, Concha, Honey Chestnut, Sue Bell and Pike, with a few more that I don't recall. Even the most trained eye cannot tell the difference in these globular fruits. However, there are very subtle differences in flavor between the various cultivars. I have grown fond of the Sue Bell variety for its abundance of fruits and delicious somewhat mild sweetness, outside skin and all.

When these green beauties turn a light canary yellow, that's when they are juicy ripe! You will rarely see them in the market due to their delicate nature. They bruise extremely easily due to the paper thin exterior skin. These fruits hold a very tender spot in my heart for reasons you will find out as time goes by….

My **<u>Jujube tree (Sisyphus jujube)</u>** is native to Asia and is highly productive. At times it is called a Chinese apple, or Chinese date. You can eat them crunchy right off the tree or let them further ripen to become soft and chewy. And, like the fig, it can be dried and kept for enjoyment throughout the year. Like a true date, they have a similar smaller elongated pit to be aware of, or you will surely crack a tooth. I harvest these at the end of summer. They vary quite a bit in size. However, Henri pops these in his big yap one after another like they are grapes. In between my trees I have placed large terra cotta pots with excellent farm soil that a seedy Armenian friend of Henri's supplied to me.

So one day, I'm in my mini-orchard piddling around and I hear the faint sound of Reggae music approaching with the creaking of a vehicle with questionable suspension. Well, this very kind Kenyan young man (Joseph) showed up in front of my place with an old beat-up truck, full to the top with rich humus-filled soil. One of my gardening tools I use to dig and loosen the soil is called a mattock. When Joseph saw it he stared in wonder.

He said, "Sir, if my country could have this tool, we could prosper greatly. I am Kikuyu tribe. We are largest population tribe in Kenya."

I thanked him profusely for making the trip to my humble garden. I asked if he was partial to reggae music. He stated that it was not popular at all in his country, but he always found time to listen to as much as possible because he gravitated toward the message of love and brotherhood.

We proceeded to make innumerable trips with a single wheelbarrow to transport the whole lot of rich soil up the steps to evenly distribute it among the orchard. I noticed Joseph had signs of vitiligo on both arms, coupled with a patch on one of his cheeks that met at the base of his nose. He wore a Paris Saint-Germain futbol cap very low-down on his forehead, as if he was faintly hiding his face. During my medical practice I encountered many patients with this incurable condition that has no known prevention. Vitiligo affects the melanin pigment-producing cells of the skin, the melanocytes.

We were both sweating profusely. Joseph was displaying the power of youth with vigor and stamina. My tongue was hanging out after about fifteen minutes. I offered some water and soft drinks to Joseph, which he gulped as if his life depended on it, but he kept looking over his shoulder, saying he needed to return the truck promptly. As he was getting ready to take off, I shook his hand. I had a fifty euro note wadded up in the palm of my hand. Joseph pulled his hand away as if snake bit.

Startled, Joseph said, "Oh no sir, my friend already took care of me, sir."

"Look," I said, attempting to be as reassuring as possible. "Take it Joseph. This is not charity. I was not pulling my weight. You schlepped hard getting that wonderful soil up there. You even raked it out despite my continual protests. It's yours, you earned it. Drive safe, young man."

With that I turned around and walked back up the steps to

my garden without looking back. I listened to the truck engine rattle and wheeze. As the rickety suspension was limping away, I heard Joseph exclaim (over the sound of Bob Marley's "No Woman, No Cry"), "May peace be with you, sir!"

I planted in any crack of space that was left in my strip of land with loads of garlic, shallots and scallions throughout. I love the manner in which all allium shoots thrust straight up, like slender green javelins from the earth. When they get up to about knee height I snip the ends with scissors and drop the cuttings back down around the trees; the smell temporarily sends the bad bugs packing. But honestly, most of the time I take the trimmings and put them in my rice or add to my vegetables in a stir fry. Scattered indiscriminately throughout is stinging nettle, which re-seeds year after year. I really enjoy an occasional good cup of stinging nettle tea - sans booze, believe it or not. The leaves are loaded with vitamin A and C. It's also good in soups. The Germans guzzle stinging nettle tea, claiming that it works wonders for inflammation of the joints, which I am experiencing more as time goes by.

The terra cotta pots were strictly reserved for herbs: Lemon thyme, Greek oregano, Genovese basil, lemon verbena, rosemary, feverfew and dill. The latter is, in my view, one of the more underrated herbs in gardening. I really enjoy steamed brown rice mixed with buckwheat and fresh organic dill.

<><>

Nizza

3

On a fine spring afternoon Henri and I shuffled off to Stad Louis II Monaco, for a match between AS Monaco and Bastia (a French football club based on the island of Corsica). It was a whitewashed 4-0 Monaco victory with Fabien Barthez in goal as a human backstop. After David Trezeguet scored his second goal we returned to Nice, where I accompanied Henri back to his Pensione Acacia for a *pastis* or two or three. As we arrived, Vivian (Henri's housekeeper) was busy vacuuming rooms, changing sheets and all the tasks to keep Henri's questionable establishment afloat. I always look forward to seeing her just for the opportunity to plant a kiss on each of her rosy cheeks that remind me of soft, ripe nectarines.

"Monsieur Gianni! It is so delight to see you. Health is good, yes? Thank you for bringing back Henri; he late to pay me this month."

Vivian is a sweetheart. Her husband, Jean-Michel, is a local butcher who always graces me with the choicest cuts of veal that simply melt in your mouth. I believe Vivian also partakes in the choicest cuts as well on a daily basis. Let's say Vivian is pleasingly plump, for she has a derriere that dreams are made of.

In the meantime, Henri looked evasive as he was pulling out a bottle of liquor hidden in a locked drawer, grumbling that he was not late to pay this trollop, for it was the last day of the month, so in his estimation, he was not late paying her salary. Henri and Vivian always carry on with this type of banter. The name calling was all terms of endearment. Henri has helped Jean-Michel on many occasions with his butcher shop and with tutoring the couple's two children in mathematics. The friendship worked both ways, as Henri's ever-expanding girth was testament to his patronage at the butcher shop.

"Jean-Michel is wanting rematch of chess with you, Monsieur Gianni," Vivian said mischievously.

Two weeks ago, for once, I whipped her beloved hubby. The stakes were a delectable bottle of Bordeaux that I have yet to uncork. I look forward to an appropriate time to have that sit-down for a chat with the god of the vine – Bacchus - who I chat with on occasion.

Henri, still grumbling, could not locate the pastis, accusing some staff perhaps of pilfering the alcohol. He was able locate some superb Japanese whiskey. So we settled in to knock down a few. We were silent, enjoying a moment of quiet to savor our libations. Henri had noticed that I had absentmindedly pulled out my meerschaum pipe that really served more as a security blanket than actually smoking it nowadays. He smilingly stated, "Gio, I notice you are still poking and biting that pipe, yes? I have not witnessed you-ah. You have not put any tobacco for quite some time, eh?"

I gave Henri a look of irritation. "Listen Henri, I have been a bachelor now for more years than I can recall. The only thing I get to 'poke and bite' anymore is this damn pipe, so keep your observations to yourself."

Defending himself, Henri said, "Gio, you can get any woman you want. And, if you don't want the commitment, there are plenty of nice *putans* I can introduce you to. Very clean, yes."

Not liking the way the conversation was going, I tried to make a point. "How many times do I need to tell you, Henri? Put a cork in it! Besides, I keep only one mirror at home. A few years back when I turned 60, that's when I hit the wall: the balding pate, contracting TB (two bellies), the sagging jowls… Henri, let's face it. We all become caricatures of our former selves."

Henri was quick to reply. "It is all the more reason to enjoy this time. You deserve it. You worked hard most of your life. You are a distinguished doc…"

"*Was* a doctor, Henri," I interrupted. "Not a very reliable one. How many patients over the years had to re-schedule appointments due to my either being hung over or passed out from whatever the hell drug I was on at the time? I wrote prescriptions and rarely gave sound medical advice. The worst type of doctor - indifferent."

Not wanting to continue the conversation I said my farewells, then skipped across the lane for a 10-minute walk, crossing the Rue de Enfant, to take a shortcut across Albert Gardens to the weekly Friday market day at Vieux Nice (Old Nice). I didn't want to waste an opportunity to stock up on some of the local delectable treats as long as I was in town.

The market in Vieux Nice was still bustling. I wasted no time in picking up three varieties of exquisite olives: Nicoise, Kalamatas and big Sicilians, with assorted pickled vegetables. Historically, the olive tree was a gift to humans from the goddess

Athena, and what a wonderful gift olives are to life. Also, some confectionary candies, lovely tart apples and a smattering of marinated eggplant. Last, a fresh, crunchy baguette, one bottle of mediocre red wine and one rosé. I was set for a 10-minute train back to the shore.

As I strode down the Rue de Del Mar, a familiar scent infiltrated my nostrils… of course! What would a trip to the market in Vieux Nice be without a visit to the gypsy Livia and her wonderful tasting socca. Hot off a huge circular iron griddle, Livia served up a local scrumptious concoction of pancakes from the flour of dried and ground chickpeas, lightly dusted with fresh cracked ground black pepper. This paper-thin crepe-like pancake was quickly grilled, then slapped into a scrap piece of newspaper and served steaming hot. Back in the day, it was a cheap 10 franc treat.

Livia is - let me be kind - mature. She has a seductive look that borders on sleazy. You will always see her wearing long flowing skirts of multi-colors, many layers of loose fitting blouses and long scarves. Bangles on every appendage and so many earrings it makes you wonder how she keeps her head upright. Her skin shows signs of wear from the sun and wind, but she is proud of every one of her wrinkles that have remained the same over the course of many years. Livia has always seemed to me to be frozen in time. She has those eyes that look in you and through you. Those brilliant emerald green eyes. I have never in all my time knowing Livia been able to hold her gaze than more than a few seconds.

The socca grill was quite busy when I arrived. Livia was as busy as ever, hurling loving insults in gypsy French to her clients.

She had not noticed me until I was directly in front of her, with only the circular iron grill between us. I said in an altered low voice, "Getting slow, ol' girl."

Those eyes, those enchanting eyes, quickly flashed up at me. I felt as though I had been slapped by her glare.

"Gianni, you American pig bastard! Why are you taking so long to take me away?" she said as if we had been conversing all day.

"I bet you say that to all the lads."

I flipped a two euro coin, which she caught deftly in mid air, then dropped it seductively inside her flimsy blouse without uttering another word.

"Just serve up the socca and don't scrimp on the crushed black pepper. I have to take care of a few things quickly, ok? I'll catch you later."

Livia slashed the griddle with her custom razor sharp serving implement. I always marvel at its design. It can best be described as a machete/scimitar/bowie knife. She served up the steaming hot goody, flinging it into a piece of newspaper. During this whole ceremony she had not taken her eyes off me.

"You visiting Henri, eh Gianni?" she muttered.

"No, why?" I lied.

"Pensione Acacia should have been condemned ages ago. But I guess even vermin need shelter in this cruel world," she said dismissively.

"Listen," I said. "Henri sends all his tourists to your business: Australians, Canadians, the English and yes, American 'pig bastards' like me, for which you should be grateful."

I departed while we were both bent over laughing and Livia

was uttering something I couldn't quite make out in gypsy French concerning the placement of her lethal weapon in an anatomically impossible place in my body.

<><>

Theadora

4

The following morning, completely disoriented from taking a temazepam and smoking too much hashish the evening before, I awoke to the irritating screeching of my recent lodger—a baby Eurasian blue jay.

Let me explain: Three days ago, while walking down the lane to my wine merchant, Signore Matterazzi, to refill my bottles from his oak casks, I passed my spinster neighbor's front door (who lived opposite, farther down before you turn to the shoreline), which she uncannily swings open every time I pass to gossip about everything under the sun. Claudette is quite possibly one hundred years old, with masses of still thick silver-white hair that hangs halfway down her humped back. As far as I can tell, she has brown eyes, but they are so hooded with folds of wrinkled skin that I am amazed that she can see at all. But those eyes are as sharp as a peregrine falcon, with the ears of a fox to match, for there is not a thing that goes by in the village she does not know. Claudette's scrawny frame holds less meat than a banty rooster. Her disposition matches that of a barnyard fowl.

She nervously said, "Monsieur Gianni! Help, help you, please! Come, come, you please."

Claudette gravitated toward, perhaps, her childhood version of an antique time-forgotten dialect of Alsatian French that probably even most French find hard to grasp. At a loss for words and too late to beat a quick retreat, I followed her hesitantly into a rat's nest lair, into a maze of thin passageways. Decades of various hoarded periodicals were stacked up in her old, small family cottage, inherited for many generations. I slithered past stacks of boxes, papers and books. Inadvertently, I brushed against one shoulder-high pile of magazines, which promptly spilled onto the dirty floor in front of me. I bent down uncomfortably to reach them without upsetting the other stacks. Organizing the magazines as best I could, I noticed a *Mademoiselle* magazine, with a cover date of 1954, a 1944 *L'Ecran* magazine and a copy of Marx's *Das Kapital* (translated into French). Passing through her dollhouse-sized kitchen, it felt like one would have to wear ice skates to wade through the years of caked-up grease on the floor.

We eventually made it onto a rather long, unstable-looking balcony where if you stood on your tiptoes you could steal a look over the apartments to the turquoise blue harbor. The best I could make out from Claudette frantically explaining to me was that every time she ventured out on her balcony she had been getting accosted by a kamikaze pair of jays that are protecting their nest, it was located in an unruly ficus tree that hung over her balcony. She had a few peck marks on the top of her scalp that she kept trying to show me, thrusting her head into my chest. Doing my best to not look disgusted, I asked how I could help.

Anyway, with her broom, she attempted to exact some revenge on the aggressive birds. In her frantic swinging of the broom, a nest, or partial nest, had plopped down on the end of her balcony. I could see that it looked like the parents figured this old crow was too tough to tangle with, so they took off, nowhere to be seen. As I peered down into what was left of this intricately woven masterpiece of a nest I could see two of the young chicks were dead. However, when I made contact to pick up the nest, a third one stretched its skinny pink neck straight up between its two dead siblings, with beak wide open, looking for a morsel of food. Needless to say, I adopted this little critter and immediately hoofed it back to my place.

Claudette was chattering away, thanking every saint for the last millennia for being rid of them, saying they were a bad omen.

As I hurriedly shuffled back to my homestead with nest clutched to my chest, it reminded me of an experience I had while I was a college student that was somewhat related to this, which I will explain in due time.

Back home I placed the chick, who was just starting to form some pin feathers, in a rolled-up towel on top of my kitchen table. Back out in my garden, I scratched around the base of my fruit trees, which are always healthily composted and mulched. I quickly came up with about a half-dozen pincher bugs and some small red worms. The chick was ravenous; after consuming three pincher bugs and one red worm she abruptly turned an about-face, pointed her rear, which just had the beginnings of a tail, at me then promptly pooped off the edge of the towel, a big white bubble, with all the poop inside - cleanly wrapped.

"Well, I guess you are one fine, neat young lady."

Whether it was a male or female, I had no idea. But my gut said this little birdie was a wee girl and I named her Theadora - gift of God.

In a few weeks I could tell by the plumage that Theadora was a Eurasian blue jay (Garrulus glandarius). A corvid. The Latin scientific name 'garrulus' means a chatter-box, noisy. Glandarius indicates 'of acorns,' a prized food. Her plumage was beautiful, with a rust-colored head, black streak of a mustache under the beak, grayish-brown back, tops of her shoulders a crisp coral blue, and black-tipped wings.

To say she was intelligent was an understatement. When I was typing on my laptop she would hop down off my shoulder and start pecking the keys. On one occasion, I said no, and continued to type repeatedly the key N, then O. Holy Merda! Theadora, while perched on top of the laptop screen, jumped down, pecked the N key and proceeded to peck the O! Dumbfounded, my first inclination was *Am I high? No, haven't had any weed for a couple of days.* It was early in the morning, so I wasn't drunk… although it's not uncommon for me to be looped before noon.

So Theadora, being the brainiac birdie that she was, never repeated the task, much to my disappointment and despite constant encouragement. I believe she felt it a bit undignified to be wasting her time with such trivial pursuits when she could be outside spearing some juicy crickets with a rather formidable beak or stealing one of my pens or flash drive, only for me to find it a couple days later, hidden behind the toilet or inside one of my shoes.

Thea was a great companion and liked to perch on top of my head while I watered the fruit trees out front. The local old folks in the village would stare in puzzlement and cross themselves when they saw the crazy foreigner with a wild bird on his head while tending his garden. Children would point and stare in wonder at the semi-domesticated jay. I was afraid that Theadora would become accustomed to humans and possibly get too close to someone who did not think fondly of the oft-considered noisy pest.

On another occasion, I witnessed her expertly snatching a cigarette from the hand of a tourist passerby on the fly. She flew in a couple of wide circles about thirty feet in the air with a lit cigarette firmly clamped in her beak. I have never seen anything quite like it. She finally landed in my sapote tree to promptly drop it. Such was the mischievousness of Theadora.

Every evening, after a full day outside, she would return indoors to retire in the bathroom, perched on the shower curtain rod. I always had to have some newspapers spread inside the tub area, for she was a prodigious pooper. Theadora turned out to be a real benefit because Claudette would avoid me now after prior years of harassment, ending the normal interrogation I would routinely receive. This was a real blessing. She was convinced that I was now cursed by the cunning corvid and it was an evil spirit that had inhabited my soul.

Henri, on the other hand, was quite intrigued by Theadora. He was of the belief that nature was telling me that I should not lead a solitary life and that this trickster jay was leading me to develop some more meaning in my existence. Henri always had a bit of the philosopher in his mind and felt that all manifestations in life have many deep meanings. Henri, coincidentally, was also once married with no children, not unlike myself. However, his wife Fanny developed breast cancer, battling it for years, until she finally succumbed.

Henri also suffered from high blood pressure. I always kept a spare aneroid sphygmomanometer (old school blood pressure cuff) at his place to monitor his blood pressure periodically. There were many of the new digital ones coming on the market; all you had to do was place the cuff over your arm snugly with Velcro and push the button. Henri said he did not trust the newfangled gadgets and would always ask me to employ the old traditional way.

Henri

5

God is a comedian playing to an audience too afraid to laugh.
Voltaire

Speaking of Henri, I had a need to go into town to pick up a copper saucepan that I had ordered from a chef friend of mine a while ago, being too lazy - or forgetful - to pick it up. But honestly, the real reason was Henri had been leaving me messages saying that he had secured a new bottle of Normandy Calvados that he was eager for me to try. When I make a visit to Henri's, with the specific task of trying a '*new bottle,*' I usually bring something to eat so that we at least get some food in our stomachs before drinking. I had made some Soupe au pistou, a popular Provencal dish of bean soup with pistou, akin to pesto with garlic cloves, fresh basil and olive oil. But without pine nuts. I filled up my hefty REI stainless steel thermos with the steaming hot soup and would probably grab a baguette on the way.

When I arrived at the front entrance of Pensione Acacia, Henri was his usual affable self, busy chatting up two female British tourists. He invited them for a drink with his friend who just dropped in, but they begged off, saying they were late to meet some friends in Roquebrune-Cap-Martin. When they departed I told Henri that he was better off with the ladies down by the shore. He just laughed heartily, stating that he wouldn't waste good Calvados on the uninitiated. A beer would have been their style.

He excitedly hopped back to his small office to retrieve the bottle and two brandy glasses. Business was slow so Henri led the way up to his small balcony on the second floor that faced a back alley. We ventured up there to sit outdoors and enjoy his liquor.

Henri already had a small brazier going with an iron lid resting on top. There were about a dozen castana with X's carved on them. He had placed them on top of the hot iron to roast. So we settled in for a long bullshit, savoring the calvados and munching on hot chestnuts. After an hour or so I went off on a rambling diatribe regarding my life circumstance. I felt I could always speak my mind with Henri. He was a willing ear, as well as providing occasional sound judgment.

"Henri," I said. The calvados was loosening my tongue. "I could have snuggled into any one of a number of lifestyles, and been content with any; I could have been a fisherman in Spain or lived a life in Denmark, been a forest ranger in the Pacific Northwest, spent a life with a beautiful Belgian woman, been a politician… not really, screw that, ha! But well, I ended up being me."

Henri gave me a perplexed look. Then he looked inside his brandy glass as if he laid eyes on it for the first time.

He said, "Gio, Merde! Were you drinking absinthe before you arrived? What have you been smoking? What is all this nonsense you are saying, my brother? Physsshh! Look, let's thank all the heavenly deities that we are still above ground with our face in the sun, regardless of who we are or what we do. Don't you agree?"

I nodded. "Look, I agree with that point, Henri; don't get me wrong. But take yourself for instance. How about if you had sold the business a couple years back… remember? And left for Japan with Michiko? (In the not-too-distant past, Henri had a romantic relationship with a Japanese woman, who we found out was a top level powerful politician back in Japan. She was Henri's intellectual match. They could talk for hours on everything from Socrates to Kant) Just role play with me for a minute. In the final analysis, Henri, we are not chameleons… we are homo sapiens. We are who we are because it is most difficult to reinvent ourselves."

Henri was nonchalantly tossing the peeled shells from the chestnuts onto the balcony floor, then kicking the shells over the balcony's edge with his short legs. He looked directly at me with a mischievous grin and said, "Physsssshh, Gio! You are the greatest example of how one can change their life. You have contradicted the nutty theory you just expounded. Look at your situation: retired American doctor, growing incredible fruit. Cooking and eating like a king. Living ah… how you Yanks say… 'The life of … uh…"

I interrupted to say, "Life of kiss my ass, Henri."

Calvados is usually around 80 proof. Henri was starting to slur a few words here and there.

I followed up by saying, "Henri, let's get some food into our stomachs."

When I first arrived I thought Henri's eyes jumped out of their sockets, rolled on the ground for a while like a pair of hot dice at a craps table, then jumped back into his skull, when he spotted the thermos with the hefty round Pain Paysan (literally 'Farmer's Bread') tucked under my arm. He displayed extreme patience the whole time not to quiz me on what sumptuous stew or soup I had created. Henri loves hot food and I'm always glad to share my cooking with anyone who relishes good, wholesome food.

Pepina

6

It was an overcast Mediterranean day, I was weeding and hand trimming a few of my trees to keep them from getting quite unruly, when, out of the haze of my deep concentration on pruning, I heard from the bottom of my steps leading up to my front entrance, a peculiar-sounding female voice; my first inclination was to wonder if that was her real voice or if someone stepped on a cat. *Definitely odd kinda Portuguese-accented rural French,* I thought.

Once more, I heard more clearly… "You no cuta doze a branches let doze horeezont a branches ok? Sapot no like."

Additionally, "Doze two abranches no crass ovare each othare; sapot tree grow abranches no heet each othare."

At first, feeling quite taken aback by her direct instructions I quickly disregarded, I felt quite impressed that this cute apparition knew about sapote trees. Nobody in the village ever guessed what kind of tree this was due to it being native to Central America.

The best that I could guess looking down from my trees, she

was maybe five and a half feet tall, light brown thick, curly hair that reached just above her shoulders, heart-shaped face and the cutest pixie slightly turned up nose and deep chestnut brown eyes. My guess was she was about ten years younger than me.

She was accompanied by a tall, gawky-looking woman - typical tourist - with Pentax camera slung around her pencil neck, striped Bermuda shorts with bony knees and chicken legs supported by jeezus sandals with large hammertoes. This was all a bit too much for me to take in so early in the day. But I couldn't get over my sapote girl.

"Hey!" I shouted in English. "Why don't you step up here to my yard and give me a quick lesson on pruning? I do need some help and I could use some of your expertise."

Without hesitation, sapote girl loped up the eight semi-steep stairs that led to my mini-orchard. I quickly took in the sight of her well-endowed breasts bouncing in a low-cut short sleeve blue blouse made of silk. My imagination got the best of me, conjuring up visions of us together on a trampoline nude. She quickly brought me to attention as she graced the final step up, then waltzed a few more elegant strides.

She said energetically, "Ohhh, yoo speak eenglis a-too, huuhh? I speek a-englis bery good with no accent. I can say - cheez a cracka barrel - with no accent whatsaso eber!"

Keeping a solemn countenance without cracking up from her accent, I placed my hand over heart and introduced myself.

"My name is Giovanni Pisano and I most heartily invite you to instruct me on the finer art of tree trimming."

She gave a sidewise glance as if to say, *This idiot thinks he's a comedian, so I will just humor him.* She said in a slightly dismissive voice, "My name is Pepina, Pepina Soler. I teenk you will keel that sapot if you keep chop eet like dat."

While she was saying that I could observe that her eyes were quickly scanning my whole row of fruit trees.

"Dis oranji tree, she needs-a molt nitrogen, anda kaki, how you say?"

"Per-simm-on." I enunciated slowly.

"Pesimon, si. Dis soil looksa much clay you need break with gypsum anda mulch many better."

I was so entranced by her quick appraisal of my garden that I hadn't noticed her travel friend had followed her up. She had her lips wrapped around one of my late season plump and sugary kadota figs.

She said in a measured drawl that I guessed was an American accent from the South, "You don't mind that I taste one of your figs, honey… do ya? Hmmm?"

I don't know about you, but I do not take kindly to folk who eat first and ask later. I felt like telling Minnie the moocher to shove that fig up her culo sideways…however, that would not impress the object of my attention, this lovely, solidly built little signorina who is so knowledgeable about my passion – fruit trees!

While feebly trying to enchant sapote girl I was multi-tasking how I could extricate her from the moocher. My first thought: I had printed an article on grafting stone fruit earlier in the morning. I figured I would quickly write my name, e-mail and mobile number on the article to show off that I graft fruit trees, coupled with a way to give juicy sapote girl my contact info.

"Senyor Geeovah-ney, you poot thee white stoff in dirt, make it breathe… better. You know dat white stoff. Ah…pee-white?

You know peewhite. Look like-a stie-rofoom."

I quickly translated the mispronounced word to be 'Perlite.'

"Please call me Gianni. And yes, Pepina, I do need perlite, but it is hard to find. It's good for the soil, like you said."

Pepina added. "Good for breathe and good for water go een."

It's easy to surmise at this point that there was nothing more in my life that I yearned for than to have Pepina become my future gardening pal. And, if I was a fortunate man, much more.

I soon found out that my unexpected guests were sightseeing the French coast and were on their way to Eze to take in all the perfumery factories, museums and general history of the scent industry which Eze and Grasse are known for. Pepina stated that she and her friend were renting an AirB&B in Menton and were at the tail end of their short two-day vacation stay. Her friend was returning to the USA and Pepina back home to Barcelona.

As I tried my best to get her to stay and discuss my trees over some coffee, Pepina said they definitely had to go if they were going to stick with their schedule. Seeing that my hopes were fading, I gave Pepina the literature with my mobile number, email and address. She did not seem to want to give me her phone number nor volunteer her email.

With my hopes fading fast and not knowing what else to do without showing desperation, I kept a smile on my face and walked both of my guests down the steps to wish them safe travels. Quite unexpectedly, the usually present Theadora was, I guess, experiencing a bout of shyness, due to the fact that I rarely, if ever, have guests. However, just as we reached the bottom step, Theadora landed on top of my head - her favorite perch - and made quite an unusual chortle that I had yet to hear. Needless to say, both ladies expressed surprise; Minnie the moocher gasped with both hands covering her mouth, not quite knowing what to say, while taking a few steps backward. However, Pepina, I witnessed for the first time, broke into the cutest ear-to-ear smile. She extended her dainty digits forward, as if to beckon the birdie down from my cranium.

She said in a smiling softly lilting voice, "Oooh, Senyor Gianni, pleeez say mee who your amic, eh?"

It was then, I believe, that I became totally enamored with her.

In the most polite, informal introduction, I said, "Voila! Theadora, I would like you meet Pepina. Pepina, this is Theadora."

Thea hopped off my head onto my right shoulder. I reached across my left hand in an attempt to have her perch, as well as to show off to Pepina that she was trained properly by this handsome and intelligent man. But Thea ignored me to display her independence and with a gentle flap of her wings, she perched on Pepina's forefinger.

"*Deu meu! Valenta noia*" (My God, brave little girl).

I slowly realized that Pepina charmingly reverted to her native Catalonian, cooing sweet things to Theodora, ignoring us, while it seemed as though the two were having a short chat. Pepina would whisper a few words. Thea would then cock her head sideways, while moving her beak without making a sound. Minnie and I stood motionless, until suddenly, with a burst of wings, Theadora disappeared as quickly as she appeared.

"Senyor Gianni, you sorprise mee yes? He's a, she's good girl. Angel send to you. Good fortuna have you. Thank you anda I forget you me email."

Since I didn't have my phone, I set a land speed record that would've made Usain Bolt proud for flying back up my steps to fetch a pencil to write down her email, the whole time thinking that I would spoil my feathered friend with many treats (fresh mashed crickets with live mealworms were Theadora's favorite) for saving my ass. I repeated Pepina's email more than once to make sure it was correct, then once again bid them a fond adieu and pointed them in the right direction as they scampered off to the train station.

My head was swimming like a young school boy. What was I thinking? How could this lovely lady be remotely interested in a balding, potbellied geezer like me? Once upon a time, the ladies would occasionally turn their heads for a second look, or so I've been told. But, man must submit to what the gods have ordained: spring, summer, fall and winter. And I was definitely exhibiting a bit of a snowstorm in the midst of winter.

Since my marriage with Emily, I had not one solid relationship and settled into being a confirmed bachelor. Don't get me wrong, Henri and yours truly have had on a few rare occasions traveled, and to say we did not partake in some of the finest establishments throughout the old world would be misleading. We both are lovers of women. Henri, as a master painter, expresses his emotions through his brush strokes. Henri looks at all women as works of art. He is a lover of every part of a woman's anatomy.

"Women," Henri says, "are created with the finest brushstrokes of God's angels, while men… are created when they drop the paint."

I enjoyed listening to Henri go on and on about the shape of a woman's ankle, the uniformity of the toes, the arch of the foot, the length of her slender neck, her elegant hands or a plump, silky derriere. I would delight in and agree with his assessments.

My desire was on a much more primal physical realm, a lust to consume, but a longing for something meaningful that always seemed just out of reach. My mind never probed further to solve what that 'something' was… One of my many incessant dreams is one in which I am always running toward someone or something and just when I'm about to reach a destination that will resolve this longing, I wake up. The failure to capture what that something is assuredly throws me into a deep depression, followed by a long bout of drugs and alcohol.

During the first week after my encounter with Pepina there was no communication. I sent a simple 'hello' on the second week, with no response. I sent another 'hello' on the third week, beginning to resign myself to the fact that I would not be able to speak with her again. I would check my laptop multiple times a day. Check my spam to ensure I didn't miss anything. During the few weeks I had made two trips to Nice, making an excuse for some shopping or other that I could have easily purchased in my village. Henri sensed that I was acting different due to my encounter with the 'sapote girl.'

"Gio, listen, you have brought up the story of your encounter more than a couple times… obviously, this lady, this Pepina from Barcelona, she has a piece of your balls, yes?" Henri added with a sense of urgency, "Go to Barca. Send her a message that you are there."

"You know, Henri, I could tell her I'm attending some lecture of the medical association, etc.…."

"No, no, no!" Henri bellowed. "You buffoon. You oaf! Don't

you believe in destiny? Go to Barcelona. If you two are meant to be, the miracle will happen and you will see her. If not, then you can go to that place in the gothic quarter and give a big kiss to long legs Leticia for me, no? Then go enjoy good paella at St. Joseph's Boqueria."

"Merde Henri! Ok. Let me chew on that for a while. I need to think."

"Chew your pipe, Gio. Chew your knuckles. But get yourself to Barcelona and don't come back until this is resolved… one way or the other. Live this life!"

A few days later, I was home having my customary morning double espresso (with just a dram of Chivas Regal). I looked in my cup to find a filbert nut floating on top. Thea had been hanging out in this small park in the village that had a lone hazelnut tree. Some days she can really bust my chops: She stuffed a thrashed nightcrawler worm in my pipe; she killed a small baby fence lizard and dropped it in the front pocket of my pajama top; she placed some rubber bands in the toilet that I found floating. Lastly, I found my flash drive to my laptop in my tennis shoes by the front door, this all in one day.

I was beginning to dig up some respect for the old crone Claudette; maybe Thea was a curse, as the gossipy old biddy would remind me. But as time moved on, I saw less and less of Theadora. Some nights she didn't return. Upon returning, she would make a racket right before sunset, squawking and shrieking for me to let her in. She would shoot straight to her shower curtain perch in the bathroom and begin to groom her feathers meticulously, always for no less than fifteen minutes.

Such was the life of Gianni Pisano, retired doctor, drug-using alcoholic, part-time bird owner and full-time loser, lost in the fog, not knowing which path to turn in life.

II

Barcelona

7

riting was never a skill that I wished to develop. I got by in my education with making the fewest words count, in true Spartan fashion. With a working life of writing short, precise doctor prescriptions, I was not one to compose long missives over email. I believed in blunt, to-the-point communication with no frills. This challenged me. I had to think in a way that would encourage Pepina to write back. Show some grace. Be inviting. Show my humanity. I composed the following:

===

To: Pepina
Fr: Gianni
Re: Ciao!
Will be in Barcelona in two days.
Will stay for two days. Want to see you.

Maybe coffee or beer?
Best Regards,
Gianni

===

Having sent this brilliant Pulitzer Prize-winning correspondence, I couldn't believe that such a sub-arctic message would warm the heart of Pepina. What an imbecile, chowderhead clown of a man I had become. *Che sara.*

The following morning I awoke in a stupor, sprawled on my divan. Thea had her prolific beak gently halfway up one of my nostrils. I quickly shooed the pesky bird away. As I attempted to right myself, an empty bottle of Bushmills Irish whisky slid down, banging loudly on the tiled floors. The noise sent shivers down my spine as I grasped my temples. "*Madonna.*" My voice croaked. My mouth was dryer than a month-old bone. I stumbled over to the bathroom sink to stick my coconut under the cold water faucet. I had to pee intensely. I thought my legs were going to buckle, so I side-stepped over to the toilet and sat down. Thea alighted on top of the dripping faucet and was guzzling away.

With wet hair dripping into my lap, I proceeded to urinate for what seemed an eternity. Blindly reaching out just enough to grab a towel to dry what was left of my hair, I got up and proceeded with my routine of making a double espresso.

While it was on the burner, I was transfixed by the pretty blue flame of the gas. Still trying to shake my addled brain, as a matter of habit, I glanced at my laptop on top of the counter, within arm's reach. I tapped the enter key and gave my email a quick perusal. Feeling that my eyes were in need of toothpicks to prop them open, I attempted to focus my sight on the laptop screen… and to my astonishment, the inbox had a new message:

===

To: Gianni
Fr: Pepina
Re: HOLA!

Yes.
my fone 93 226 41 62

===

"Minchia! Bonjour Thea bella! Papa is off to Barcelona!"

Train is out of the question. Flying is the only way to go to Barcelona. The latest company, 'EasyJet,' formed in 1995 in the UK, provided cheap flights that took about an hour and a half. Practically identical to the same short flight as from my stateside residence to Las Vegas. I didn't want Pepina to get the impression that I was a cheapskate so I booked a reservation in the city center at an H10 hotel.

I arrived early in the morning and to my surprise the hotel immediately gave me a room. As soon as I settled in to my deluxe room, I took a few deep breaths, picked up my cellphone and called Pepina. After many rings the phone disengaged. I tried again with the same result. Was I being stood up? Surely, it was just a problem with the connections. Then, after a few minutes, I received a call from an unknown number. I answered and it was Pepina. "So sorry Senyor Gianni, my phone, she don work good."

I lightheartedly replied, "No problem, Pepina. Would you like to have dinner tonight with me?" I was thinking I could slide in an upgrade over the initial coffee or beer invite.

"No, Senyor Gianni. I have tonight a family, but let's do café. Where are you?" I gave her my location and Pepina said, "Oh, you city central. I take subway, ten minutes. Go to carrer de colom 17, Artista Barca Café. It has torta good and gelato.18:00 ok?"

It was a blazing hot day in Barcelona as I set off for my rendezvous with Pepina. The hotel served up an amazing breakfast with unlimited bacon, fried eggs, an amazing array of fresh local fruits, yogurt and pastries. There were even some cold meats: sopresatta salami, mortadella, and assorted cheese. I took a breakfast roll and made a killer capacollo panino to stash in my room for later, in case I got the munchies. I had the day ahead of me with some time to burn and with excess energy flowing in my bones. I decided to take a walk.

The address she gave me was in the vicinity of Los Tarantos, an incredible cabaret of local flamenco talent that I patronize every time I'm in Barcelona. It's also a short walk to the gothic quarter across Placa Reial. *Hint: Stick to the narrow side streets that only accommodated a horse and cart in that distant period.

If you stay off the touristy Carrer de Ferran, it's a magical walk through time.

The striking gothic architecture of a time long past. The polished centuries-old cobblestones snake their way through beaten footpaths. Without getting too spooky, I've always felt as if I knew these streets, some sense of familiarity. No! I wasn't on my way to the bordello, going to send my greetings to 'long legs Leticia.' If I did travel to that famous establishment it would be to only to send my regards of behalf of Henri. I wanted to be zoned in on making a good connection with Pepina. I circled back and took a seat in the 'Artista Café' about five minutes early.

Pepina arrived at 18:05 with a whimsical smile on her face that was similar to when we first met. She wore a flowing summer dress that had buttons down the front, slightly revealing her cleavage. The dress was adorned with so many colorful flowers. Her waist was cinched with a belt that accented her bosom and made me draw upon all the limited powers I possessed not to stare like a vulture. Her face was au natural and was in no need of makeup. She wore earrings that had some Spanish pattern with a matching necklace. I felt outclassed with my Levi's 501s, Asics tennis shoes and short sleeve shirt. What a dope!

"Hola, Senyor Giovanni! Bery good-a to see you." Her smile was radiant.

"Yes Pepina, very good to see you too. You look very well. Please, just call me Gianni." *Could I be giving any more stereotypical responses? C'mon Gio, don't fuck this up.*

Pepina said, "Gianni, iss hot today. You face is red. You use flatscreen for sun, no?"

I knew, of course, she meant 'sunscreen,' but I was not about to correct her, for I was enraptured by Pepina. After basic pleasantries, she proceeded to tell me most sincerely that she was the baby of the family, youngest of five girls. Her sisters (from oldest to youngest) were Alba, Jacinta, Estel and Flor.

Her mother was a professional musician who passed away when she was in her teens. Their home was always filled with music. The girls all loved to dress up and play roles in popular operas.

Pepina stated that she never married, had no children and had been taking care of her father most of her life. She worked days for an Information Technology Company. She had limited assistance from the state to provide professional care for her father in the mornings. Pepina cooked and cleaned afternoons and evenings and took care of her father's business affairs. Her father Donat had steadily been declining over the years due to dementia. Her sisters lent no help. All were married and most more than a few times. I surmised that Pepina was left to do all the heavy lifting regarding family matters.

Donat, politically and/or militarily, seemed to have done fairly good for himself during the Franco years, from what I could surmise from Pepina's open talk. The indifferent sisters were circling like condors waiting for the feast. I find that greed transcends all cultural barriers, does it not? I had so many associates over the years fighting it out in court with siblings over the parents' will. Toxic blood feuds would ensue.

Pepina told me, surprisingly, that she was in her fifties and still had dreams of travelling the world. She expressed a fondness for the opera and classical, electronic and jazz music. Talk about variety in taste! She was so genuine and forthright in her manner that I was deeply touched. I had no choice but to spill my guts, not leaving out any sordid details from my past. She knew more than perhaps even Henri concerning my childless marriage and the tragic suicide of Emily. My medical practice struggles, the drugs, alcohol and bouncing back and forth between two worlds, here and in the states: I laid my life story on the table with no frills. I felt it was only just to return Pepina's openly candid and frank story.

An hour had passed in the blink of an eye. Pepina asked how the fruit trees were and, of course, Theadora. Pepina mentioned that it was a nice coincidence that her father's name (Donat) and Thea's name both meant 'gift from God.' She spoke of her father with the deepest reverence and love. Pepina was devoted to her father and from what I could gather from Pepina, he doted on her above all the sisters.

I extended, when the situation permitted, my most hospitable invitation for her to visit again and we could possibly do some exploration. Since we both enjoyed hiking, perhaps we could visit Cinque Terra. Pepina explained how she loved to hike in the countryside whenever the opportunity presented itself. However, due to her father's ever-increasing health issues, it was rarely, if ever, possible nowadays.

Her job, she mentioned, was very tedious, but from a social aspect she continued. Each time she spoke, at the end she would give that little smile. A piece of me melted with each smile, until I felt like just a large pat of butter in a pan with the tiniest flame underneath. *Easy boy, you are incredibly out of practice in this thing called courtship. Don't belch or fart inappropriately.* I had to pee since she arrived, but I didn't excuse myself on account of cheating any time away from Pepina.

It was 19:15 and Pepina stood up and said the following day would be very busy because after work, she had to take her father for a checkup in a clinic just outside Barcelona to run some tests. I stated that I would be more than glad to assist in transporting her father to the clinic. However, she said their driver (Iker), who also functioned as gardener, would be taking them. Taking a nonchalant deep breath, I posed the question.

"Pepina, may I give you a call occasionally? Do you mind?"

Much to my surprise and delight, Pepina responded straightaway with a curious smirk, "Gianni, me so disappoint if you do not, eh?"

"I just thought with your father's health…" My voice trailed off. *Don't blow it now, Gio. You sound like an insecure schmuck.*

Pepina smiled adoringly and said, "No Gianni, you call, we talk."

She stood up abruptly, planted a kiss on each cheek, and then scampered off in a flash. The blood surged in my ears and I could feel my heart racing. In a semi-stupor, I strutted over to settle the refreshments. The cashier was a twenty-something young lady with a nose ring, tattoo on one arm of an orange butterfly, and blue-green standing hair. I was the only remaining client. She had a devilish grin on her face. I felt she sensed my awkwardness with meeting Pepina there. After I paid and received the change she said, "Thank you and good luck!"

I chuckled and replied, "Many thanks, I need it." She gave a universal sign language, thumbs-up! As I exited the café, I thought, *What a bonehead. I could have walked Pepina to the subway station…argh!*

To say my step was lightened would be an understatement. I found myself already across La Rambla at Saint Joseph's Boqueria, with no recollection of how I got there. My mind was so preoccupied with meeting Pepina. I kept playing our encounter over and over, role playing in my mind what I should have said at each juncture of our discussion. I was second-guessing my unabashed honesty and was wondering if I scared Pepina off with my personal and professional work issues. Anyway, the die was cast. I would see what it provided.

The kiosk that I frequent in Barcelona is coincidentally called 'The Kiosk,' and it was hopping busy. Henri can sit there at the counter for hours, bullshitting with the locals while consuming mass quantities of grilled calamari, octopus, dorada and an occasional patatas bravas, local fresh fungi or carciofi, washing it all down with glasses of fruity Sangria. I also can make quite a pig of myself at 'the kiosk;' they grill a sea bass there that's exquisite. I usually get an appetizer of six grilled sardinas and whatever fresh vegetables of the day are lightly grilled with cold pressed Andalusian virgin olio di olivo drizzled all over. And what would this meal be without a few bottles of Estrella Galicia beer, a nice 5.5% pale lager that goes well with frutta di mare? I topped off the finger-licking meal with a good, strong black café Saula.

I only wished that Pepina could have accompanied me. It is my belief that she likes to eat, and that is what I like. Nothing worse than a finicky eating woman who pushes the food around on her plate, picking, and always leaves a lot of any meal on the plate. Looks like I will have to wait until I get a chance to test my theory.

I paid for two days and had the following day completely free, and Barcelona was hosting Mallorca that day at Camp Nou. It would be a good chance to see upcoming kid Lionel Messi and company in action. But there was no way I wanted to face the maddening crowds. So I picked up a couple of six packs of beer and spent a leisurely afternoon in my underwear, watching the game in the comfort of my cozy luxury H10 hotel room. What a gig!

Upon returning home I was thinking that I had to strike while the iron was hot. I would call Pepina early in the morning before her work or at the end of the day. Her father's tests were not good, and his continued cognitive decline was deeply affecting Pepina's well being. She informed me that two of her sisters insisted that he be put in a professional medical facility. The third sister was dead set against the cost that would ensue from said care, even though money did not seem to be an issue for this well-to-do family. The fourth sister did not want to be involved and remained incommunicado. I visited twice during that summer to assist Pepina in finding an appropriate home for her father to be comfortable and safe. Upon each visit, Pepina would always casually ask me to bring one or two sapote blancos, "only eef a-ripe Gianni, heehee."

On another occasion, I called late one night and chatted for about an hour. One of the topics was when we first met in front of my place. I asked directly, "So you were traveling with the American lady, uh Minnie, to visit the perfume industry in Eze. Where did you meet her?"

Right away Pepina responded, "I have a person at work who say I know American lady. My work friend, she say American lady, he, no she likes to hike like you, Pepina, and see many places. So Gianni, I meet her on her visit. We have fun together. She walk all day. She laugh good too. She eat everything, Gianni... like me, heehahee! Gianni, her name not Minnie. You mix it up a-with somebody else? Her name is Linda. She is kind, intelligent woman."

I muttered to myself, "Remind me at some point to play you the song 'Minnie the Moocher' by Cab Calloway."

In regard to Donat's medical care, I researched a number of specialty homes that had been reviewed superior in patient care with a specialization in Alzheimer's and forwarded my findings to Pepina. It was now up to the family to interview with each location to get a feel as to which would best suit their father's needs. During this time and multiple visits to Pepina, I found that my hypothesis was absolutely spot on; Pepina was definitely a *mangione* (chow hound).

It was a pleasure to watch her consume a meal. There would be no conversation, just the sound of cutlery and breaking of bread - a solemn ceremony. She could mop up a plate of pasta with the best of them. A fish skeleton picked so clean that I could dry it out and use it for a comb. Shrimp consumed so surgically complete that only its transparent shell was left glistening. Pepina did not discriminate against any dish and she would call all food blessings.

During these encounters with Pepina she told me many stories of her childhood and her relationship with her sisters. Once we were having tapas at a café and she informed me of some episodes in her childhood.

"My seesters always cut my hair bery short. Called me Pepe. Dressed me most time in boy's shorts. Father never home. Busy with government. Mother have many concerts. Busy too. So my seesters always take care-a of me."

"Haha!" I chuckled and immediately realized that was an insensitive reaction. I quickly changed my tune and said, "Sounds like the inmates were running the prison. I'm so sorry you were treated so poorly by your sisters."

"Gianni, you no understand, I love my seesters. They juss play games. They bored. They do some fun with me."

Attempting the best I could to understand the family dynamic, I kept my trap shut and became a better listener.

"Another time, my oldest seester Alba, she send me to *tabacheria* for cigarettes many time. Maybe I seven years old. She say, 'Pepe! Last time it took you sixteen minutes, we will time you. See you can go faster.' I run so fast and come back. My breath so hard. My seesters all clap and say good boy, give me bowl of juicy orange slices. But, they were lemon slices. My face make funny look when I bite. They all laugh so hard. I laughed too."

"Pepina," I needed to ask a question, "do you still laugh when you think about it?"

Pepina answered directly, without hesitation. "They all are bery unhappy. My seesters all have bad stories in their life. Bad marriage. Bad health. None interest work. No interest een life."

Pepina was about to add more, but she furrowed her eyebrows as if to concentrate deeply, then continued, "They were more happiest when we young at that time... They grow up. They become sad. No more laughing."

Before we left that tapas bar, Pepina said she had one more

story to tell me that would make me laugh. I feel she sensed that I didn't understand the sense of humor that her sisters inflicted upon her. So I ordered another beer and said I couldn't wait to hear this story.

"Nothing like a good laugh, cara mia. I'm listening."

"Ok Gianni." With her hand on my knee, she continued, "You will laugh. There was a big market close to our house, ten minutes walk. On that day, second seester…"

"Would that be Jacinta?" I asked.

"Si Gianni. You right. Jacinta, she say me to help her. So in store she show me large box that was bery tall as I. Jacinta struggle with it. So she say, 'Pepe, please try leeft that box over your head.' Always I want to please her. I was shocked to see that I could leeft, but I could balance on my head to walk, ok. It was deeficult size, but bery light. She praise me to say what a powerful little boy I was, then Jacinta stuff money in my pocket to pay for it. She say she go to the apothecary for medicina. But, I to go directly home with the box. Also, she say to treat me gelato later if I do good job.

"When I go home, she waiting for me in house at bottom our grande entrance staircase. Jacinta clap for me, say how strong I was. In loud voice she scream for Alba, Estel and Flor to come downstairs fast, see how strong our little Pepe was to carry such a large box all the way from big market store. I stand with my chest out puff big. I think I was Herakles. All seesters downstairs fall over laughing bery long, bery loud. I thought laughing never end. Anyway, Jacinta treat me to pistachio gelato later. It was so good! Many years after, I realize that my seesters had me buy and carry all the way home (they were too embarrassed to do) a grande economy-sized box of Kotex."

Pepina paused with a mischievous grin on her face, looking at me in expectation of a response. I took the cue and said, "Your family sure has an incredible sense of humor. It's great that you can look at your childhood with such funny memories." Her sense of humor would take some getting used to. I was very fortunate that Pepina did not take a similar life path to her sisters. Her decision to assist her father and not marry was admirable.

<> <>

The Feast

8

On another one of my visits to Barcelona, Pepina took me out to dinner. The family decided to hire additional outside care for Donat since his medical condition warranted extra care. Since the evening weather was beginning to have a slight chill, Pepina wore brown gabardine slacks that accentuated her shapely figure. Flat, comfortable, nondescript leather walking shoes, a supple tan leather jacket zipped tight underneath her bosom, which set off alarm bells in my head. I pictured myself as a mouse, lying on my back with legs crossed, nestled softly between Pepina's golden globes. She wore a gold necklace that held a disk of some colorful Spanish design with matching smaller disk earrings. The jewelry was similar but more colorful to when I came for the first time to meet her in that little café by Los Tarantos. Pepina was always au natural regarding makeup. Occasionally she may have used lipstick. Her lips always looked luscious to me – like juicy sweet mangos.

She vehemently insisted that this dinner was her treat. She said, "You reach for pocket to get money, Gianni. This eez bad manners."

I obeyed her and said that I was looking forward to this meal. We ventured for quite a stroll to what looked like the first floor of a small apartment in old La Barceloneta, an intriguing small community by the shore with a population of about twelve thousand.

I was fairly accurate in my assumption that it was a personal apartment kinda converted into a place for maybe nine guests, not counting the cook, waiter and bottle washer. The owner, who lived above on the second floor, was a swarthy-looking gentleman with a beak on him that Theadora would be proud of. One of his eyes continually twitched as if he had something caught in it. Or possibly, medically speaking, he could have suffered from a small stroke. Steel-tipped cowboy boots poked out from behind his long, greasy apron. But he possessed an incredible booming baritone opera voice that belied his physical appearance. He was the size of that diminutive tenor Jose Carreras (boots included). I expected him, at any moment, to burst into a Verdi aria. His familiarity with Pepina was evident with some rapid Catalonian that sounded more like the gypsy French of Livia back in Vieux Nice. He addressed me in stilted Italian.

"Signore Giovanne, buona sera. Mi chiamo Pascual!"

Obviously ol' Pascual had some reconnaissance as to my arrival. So I happily greeted him with equal aplomb, and we were shuffled over to a table – the only table. It actually sat four. The other five seats were at a pseudo-counter in front of the indoor grill and were occupied by three women and two men who were obviously locals. You could watch the cook do this thing from anywhere in this cozy minuscule café.

After we were seated, Pepina told me that this was a private establishment. Street traffic was prohibited. We were both famished from our long walk. There was no ordering. The dishes just flowed immediately in waves.

We began with a nice piece of bacala cooked with a light tomato sauce, accompanied by large white cannellini beans. It was salty but tasted of the fresh sea. The beans must have cooked all day. They were firm yet melted in your mouth. The tomato sauce was loaded with fresh oregano and garlic – heavenly. This was followed by el pintor style baked snails, octopus grilled with paprika, a few "razor blade-a clams" (as Pepina would mispronounce razor clams), and a small side dish of sautéed *"novellons,"* a local mushroom. I noticed a thin red flush upon Pepina's cheeks, as she was nursing a sangria throughout the meal, while I had three estrella beers down my gullet before the last dish.

Literally bursting, we cleansed our palette with a slice or two of delicate bellota Iberian ham. As the meal progressed, I noticed Pascual's eye no longer twitched, so I marked it off as a nervous tick from perhaps meeting a new customer. I nonchalantly undid the button on my waistband without Pepina noticing. My stomach had been experiencing the strict law of nature, gravity. As soon as I hit sixty, my belly was protruding at a rate that was difficult to head off.

Being a Baby Boomer myself, I found it hard not to reach in my pocket for at least the tip. However, uncannily, as if reading my mind Pepina thanked me for restraining myself from paying. After I gave my best to Pascual and the crew for an unforgettable meal, we escaped to walk off the gluttony. I detected Pepina slipping a hundred-euro note to Pascual as we departed. After a nice walk by the shore we stopped at a small bar. Por moi, a digestivo-sambuca and café, for Pepina just a café con leche.

Her knowledge of fruit was not limited to their growth on trees or bushes, but their own unique flavor, and the tartness, sweetness and texture of each. It was a joy to hear Pepina speak with such emotion. Walking through a vegetable market, listening to her exclamations of joy at such a lovely fresh bundle of bok choy, rhubarb, endive, rapini and Swiss chard. Equally scolding the merchants who displayed some wilting red leaf lettuce or asparagus past its sell-by date.

This was Pepina. This, I believe, was who Pepina had always been, with no pretenses. My love for Pepina grew exponentially with each encounter. We had yet to progress beyond hand holding and gentle brief kisses. But was I dissatisfied? Hell no! To my disbelief, it was hard to fathom the depth of emotions that I was experiencing. I was unable to compare to what I felt for Emily. That seemed another incarnation. I was living in a different age, immature, with an idea of what love was supposed to mean. Alas, a medically clinical definition. What I felt for Pepina was new, fresh and guiltless, with a scent of a child's playfulness.

I noticed as time passed since I met Pepina, I had not delved too far into my vast array of private pharmaceuticals. My drinking still remained unchecked, but somewhat controlled. Was I finally, at such an advanced stage of existence (geezer-hood)… high on life? What an epiphany!

<><>

Homecoming

9

On the highest throne in the world, we still sit only on our own bottom.
Michel de Montaigne

During the last month of summer, the five sisters, after much haggling, finally made a decision on the facility location, and Donat (their father) would be moved two weeks after his 92nd birthday. Prior to Donat's move to the care facility and two days after his 92nd birthday, Pepina received a call at work from the state care worker that her father had fallen unconscious. Before she could get to the hospital in all haste, her dear father Donat passed away. He never regained consciousness; it was a massive stroke.

I attended the funeral (sans invitation). To my surprise, it was held with a bit of pomp and circumstance, being requested as a family only funeral. However, a few dignitaries from the Catalonian government made their presence felt with overt condolences to the family. France unexpectedly dispatched one obscure antiquated retired minister to pay respects on behalf of the country.

I took a count of the sisters - all attended. I noticed each one arrived separately dressed in black, each with a personal driver.

They were all so covered up with veils and dark sunglasses I was unable to distinguish any features, with the exception of one, who I presumed was the oldest. She required a bit of assistance walking from who I assumed was her most recent husband.

At the end of the funeral I saw that she had removed a black head scarf to reveal dyed jet-black hair that belied her age. Her chin looked like it was put in a pencil sharpener. She bore no resemblance to Pepina. Who was I to comment? Perhaps Donat dabbled in more than government affairs. Possibly they were half sisters?

The other three remained cloistered. One common denominator was all sisters (with exception of Pepina) had enough ice on their fingers to support the entire Municipality of Catalonia for a year. If those diamonds were real, I couldn't imagine their worth!

Pepina understandably was very distant and I respected her space. After the ceremonies and Donat was laid to rest, Pepina very directly told me that it was very thoughtful of me to attend. She said to give her a couple of weeks or so to take care of the family estate. She also informed me that she had resigned from her employment since it was obvious that it was not her livelihood. This was another aspect of her personality that I just admired: no filters, get to the point, and here are the facts.

Back at home I continued to call often to see how matters were progressing and if there was anything I could do. Pepina was always polite.

One afternoon she said to me, "Gianni, you bery nice-a to me. How say you American … uh, jusss cool it."

Well, that's very direct, I thought and replied quickly, "Yes, cara mia. I weel jusss cool it!"

"Hey-a, Gianni, have fun my accent? Hahahee hee."

"No, no, no just a term of endearment, Pepina. Not make fun," I defended myself.

"Iss ok Gianni, bullshit iss ok."

Hmm? My sapote girl definitely can see thru the bullshit all right.

"My apologies, cara mia. I w …"

"Gianni, lissen. I go to you. You awayz come here-a. I go Nica' aereoplane."

Dumbfounded, I stumbled to search for the correct words, not to fuck it up. "Ah, um, absolutely Pepina. Sure, yes, come to Nica. Uhh, when…?"

"Dema', ah… scuse me. Tomorrow. I have a-teecket."

"*Bravissima, mon cheri!*"

"Gianni?"

"Yes, Pepina."

"I'm have hotel in Nica, ok? No problem."

Much to my chagrin, I replied, "I agree Pepina, no problem."

Back at the ranch, with Pepina arriving, I performed some basic duties in tidying up the place, which translated as scraping off the bird shit as much as possible in all the obvious places, washing a couple days' worth of dishes piled up in the sink, vacuuming and changing the towels in the bathroom.

Theadora was on another one of her excursions to who knows where. I had not laid eyes on her for at least a couple days. I beseeched all deities from past, present and future to hear my pleas to send Thea back home soon. While tidying up the place I performed a Hare Krishna dance, coupled with a pseudo-whirling dervish, chanted Nam Myoho Renge Kyo, praised Allah and sang a hymn I recalled from the Book of Mormon musical comedy before exhausting my limited polyphony of religious favors. In summary, I desired a reunion with the three of us together: Pepina, Thea, and yours truly.

I contacted Henri to say we would swing by to have a drink when Pepina arrived. Henri was chomping at the bit to meet my mystery lady. Most of the summer had been dominated by my conversations about Pepina. Henri always listened with interest.

He said, "I must meet this Iberian goddess who has transformed my dear friend into an upright man."

It was only eight kilometers from Nice Cote' d'Azur Airport to Henri's Pensione Acacia. Henri offered his ancient Fiat for me to pick up Pepina. He said it had been rebuilt and ran like a clock, which translated as he got the homeless Albanian mechanic in his neighborhood to change the oil. Henri helps quite a few poor souls with food and work when he can offer. He is a true compassionate man. He would have been a much better doctor than me.

I accepted his offer, knowing it would make him happy to contribute in some way. I was surprised to see the car in such fine condition, freshly washed and with the top down on a fine, sunny day. The flight was on time and Pepina was anxious to check in to her hotel first. I suggested we could swing by Henri's first for a drink and then proceed. Pepina was delighted to meet a friend of mine, especially Henri, whom I have discussed on more than a few occasions during our late night phone conversations and our meals together.

When we arrived at Pensione Acacia we entered through the double glass doors and proceeded to the little cafeteria where Henri's guests receive their frugal continental breakfast. The floor tiles had been amazingly cleaned and waxed; the tables were festive, with a few modest flower bouquets at each. The smell of fresh baked bread, roses and some type of light, yet to be defeated lavender scent filled the air.

On the middle table were some of my favorite fresh pastries with juicy ripe figs resting on top of a custard filling and flaky crust. The locally famous almond cookies also adorned the table. Coffee, tea, orangina and mineral water were offered. Henri and Vivian were standing at attention for a big, sincere, "Bienvenue a Pepina!" Henri had a white towel folded over his right arm as if we were attending a Michelin five-star venue.

Pepina squealed with delight and immediately skipped over to give Henri a big hug and planted a kiss each on his plump cheeks. In my conversations with Pepina, I may have mentioned Vivian and her husband Jean-Michel possibly once or twice. However, Pepina immediately hugged and thanked Vivian by name, asking how the husband and two children were, while thanking them so much for the lovely reception and treats. I was speechless. This was beyond friendship. I felt a family warmth that had been alien to me for what seemed a lifetime.

Vivian and Pepina were already tucked away at a table in the corner, each with a cup of tea. Vivian was showing photos of her two children on her mobile phone while Pepina was already scarfing down one of the fig pastries.

"Vivian, your children so precious," Pepina said. "I have no children. I have niece and eh… nephew. They all big now."

"The children are so much work, Pepina," said Vivian on a serious note. "It is a joy to watch them grow. But I worry about future time. I never plan to have children. Jean-Michel loves them. He educates them, has much patience. He is more better parent than me. He works very hard at the butcher shop, but he always makes time for children. Henri also is their godfather."

Pepina, who was working on the almond cookies, added, "I look ahead for good time to meet Jean-Michel and children, Vivian. Gianni say he enjoy to play chess with Jean-Michel, yes?"

"Oh, you do not want to disturb them." Vivian made the sign of the cross. "They go in room, lock door. Too serious. Men! Physhhh!" Both Vivian and Pepina began to laugh loudly.

"Henri," I said, "you really went to a lot of trouble for…"

Henri interrupted innocently with both hands imploring. "I had no idea, Gio. Vivian arranged everything. I came back from the fish market and voila! All was prepared."

I knew Henri was full of horseshit, but I accepted his answer with a wry smile. "Well, I can't thank you both enough."

Henri became animated. With his voice lowered, he said "Gio, this Pepina. What a lovely creature. You play cards good. She is a winning hand. I mean that in the best of ways. You staying clean with drugs, no? You look well, Gio. So what are your plans for the day?"

After profusely thanking Henri and Vivian for such a thoughtful and lovely visit, I escorted Pepina to the Hôtel Le Royal Promenade des Anglais on the Promenade Anglais. I thought to myself, Zut alors! This must have set her back a pretty penny. When we arrived Pepina exclaimed, "Ah Gianni, dees hotel. No. Too much. Iker, she make aeroplane/hotel reserve to me. I not crazy woman. Bery espensive." (Iker was the family driver/gardener.)

Iker was a he. Pepina always reverses the he/she pronoun, so I just adjust accordingly.

"Iss ok Gianni. I stay. Comm back two hours, we go walk beach and eat, huh? Dema… tomorrow we see fruit trees, Theadora too, eh?"

"Wonderful plan, cara mia. Be back in a couple of hours."

Using Henri's car I zipped down the lower corniche to my casa for a change of clothes. But not before I did some shopping to cook for Pepina. Still no sign of Theadora; when she does show up it's usually just before sundown. I had in mind an unorthodox meal for Pepina. I needed to pick up some sticky Japanese rice for my rice cooker, a bottle of dry Japanese sake, two very fresh spada steaks (swordfish) and a few other related items. What I had in mind for my initial homemade meal for Pepina was a gamble.

When I returned to pick up Pepina back at the hotel, I saw her seated in a royal high back chair in a stunning lobby, with grand chandeliers, large Persian rugs and rococo furniture. She was very intensely reading a newspaper. She didn't look up until I was standing above her. Finally she looked up with the grandest smile.

She said, "Gianni, iss soo good see you. Gianni, iss soo early. Less walk, yes?"

I smiled back at her lovely face. Rubbing my hands together, I said, "I know. The market in Vieux Nice is on. It's a three kilometer walk. Let's go."

It was a warm afternoon. Pepina was wearing Marmot hiking shorts, a form-fitting Patagonia long sleeve shirt and new Salomon walking shoes. Her legs looked sleekly oiled. My warped mind reminded me of an old French joke: What do French women put behind their ears to attract men? Answer: Their ankles.

A solitary necklace adorned her beautiful neck with a silver owl. I complimented her attire.

After I expelled the lewd joke from my mind, we commenced our journey with an invigorating walk, crossing over on the Promenade de Anglais to walk along the shore where there was a fresh gentle offshore breeze. Then, we headed to Boulevard Jean Jaures, west on Rue Rosseti and voila!

The market was fairly busy, with merchants shouting out the quality of their merchandise. I spied Livia from afar, but she had her back to me quite a distance away, with many patrons waiting almost in a full circle around her renowned socca business. Pepina was like an innocent little girl, looking at the florists' individual cut flowers and marveling. She motioned to me to look at three long-stem flowers that were of different colors. I was unable to impress my girl with the names of those flowers, but the name was on the tip of my tongue. Pepina shouted excitedly, "Dees gladiators are beeeg! Look at dee colairs Gianni!"

Friggin' gladiolas! Why couldn't I remember that damn name? Now I know I will remember that name. Haha! *Gladiators!*

"Ahh, yes! Beautiful gladiolas, Pepina. What striking colors."

Pepina picked up a large Valencia orange and smelled it as if it was ambrosia. A boisterous vegetable merchant was rather animated, indicating to Pepina that his daikon (Japanese radishes) 'were the largest and she was welcome to try.'

"Oh Monsieur," Pepina said mischievously, "truly the only theeng that I have seen larger… is your nose."

To which customers who were within earshot laughed hilariously and applauded Pepina. Brava! This sapote girl was not one to play with.

We eventually meandered over to Livia. The crowd had thinned out by this time; she only had one customer. One of her gypsy colleagues had just delivered a tray with three cups of mulled wine. Livia knows I favor this beverage at the market. It's a warm, heady local red wine with cloves, nutmeg, citrus fruit and other various spices. How she anticipated our arrival was a mystery… as were all things Livia.

I introduced Pepina, who stated that she loved socca and that she would like to see it in Barcelona, stating she and the locals would be dedicated customers. They exchanged pleasantries and I was so happy that Livia was thoughtful and kind to both of us, for I have seen her in action sometimes and she is one to be respected. I let the two get acquainted while I nosed around nearby.

After a quick visit with the knife sharpener, I ventured back to Pepina and Livia. After some small talk, we bid Livia a fond adieu. Pepina had already taken a couple of steps across to the olive merchant, asking where the particular olive she was munching on was grown. The olive merchant was ever so glad to engage Pepina in conversation, heaping many samples on her of his vast olive display.

I attempted inconspicuously to make my escape but Livia quickly ensnared me with those penetrating eyes before I could take another step and said to me, "Gianni, I don't know how you deserve such a fate." Livia was holding one of the wine cups, which I guessed was Pepina's. She was peering down into the cup, turning it slowly one way, then another. "I see this is a blessing for a long, happy life. Even though it pains me for reasons I don't understand. Gianni, she will, how do you Yanks say - fit you like glove."

I was speechless. I stood momentarily uneasy. Without making eye contact, I turned and began to walk away. However, my mind walked, but my body turned back to Livia. I said, "Thank you, Livia. Thank you very much for your kindness. Believe me."

It was a joy to watch Pepina jump from booth to booth. At one vendor I got a beer and Pepina an acqua minerale frizzante. The beer flavor was so intense, as if it was the first I'd ever tasted. As we stood at the counter, Pepina was so happy that I brought her to the market so that she could take in all the treats and see such interesting people. I told Pepina, "This day was marvelous with meeting Henri and Vivian, a wonderful stroll along the shore to the market, and you have made your mark with all the locals with your outgoing nature and…"

"Gianni," Pepina interrupted me, "you no worry, eh… wha Livia say you back there."

Feigning that I didn't have an idea what Pepina meant, I began to speak.

"Gianni!" Pepina quickly said before I could utter a word. This time her face turned from my smiling princess to a stern yet patient friend. "When I talking with olive man. I know Livia, she a-speak to you, yes? I know dat Livia, she a witch. I mean I don know her in the poissonly. Buuu… I know he read dregs of vino in coppa. Don tell wha she say. If you do, she jink us."

I tried to compute what was just said as lightning fast as possible. Pepina was correct in that Livia is a witch; she did foresee the future by reading the lees in the wine cup. By saying 'he' I knew Pepina meant 'she.' Lastly, that Livia could 'jink' us. Or more correctly, 'jinx' or curse us.

"Yes, cara mia. I want to apologize for hesitating. I do want to always be truthful with you. I promise."

"Gianni, yoo too serioso. We have witch in Espana too. Many more in Italia. Iss ok. OK?"

With that said Pepina finished her bubble water, then proceeded to let go of a belch that sounded as if someone stepped on a bullfrog.

I replied with a quick, "A salud!"

Not to be outdone in the burping department, I attempted to summon one up after polishing off my beer, but with no result.

As we set off for the train station, we passed L'Opera de Nice. There was a bulletin posted. The following week there was a performance of *La Traviata*, a classic by Giuseppe Verdi, based on the novel by Alexander Dumas. It is the lamentable story of Violetta, who is madly in love with Alfredo. The father of Alfredo makes Violetta leave him so as not to sully the reputation of his son. In the end, Alfredo sees the error of his way. Too late, he begs Violetta's forgiveness as she lies dying of tuberculosis.

Pepina was sad that she would be unable to attend but she encouraged me to go and added that we should attend the theater whenever possible. She added that her father would take her to Gran Teatre del Liceu and Palau del la Musica Catalana on many occasions. Pepina said these remained golden memories to her that she would always treasure.

We set off to the train station for a ten minute train ride for one euro ninety. Pepina was chomping at the bit to see if there were any ripe sapotes and to generally check out all the fruit trees, as well as a wee visit with Thea. I warned her that there were no promises with the birdie since I had not seen her for two days.

Pepina said, "See, you worry person. He be there. Lots fruit on trees... Theadora be hooome. You weel see!"

We arrived at the homestead. I purchased some lovely spada (swordfish) earlier and I was going to test Pepina's tastebuds. The fish filets would be boiled ever so lightly in Japanese miso soup, with chopped scallions. Untraditionally, I added some potent wasabi in the miso to cook with the fish as opposed to separately. I could get real miso from an international store in Nice. It's great because miso has live active cultures of good bacteria you can keep in the refrigerator. I had pickled some eggplant I grew the summer prior in vinegar, coriander and dill, and there was a separate small bowl of sticky Japanese rice. Also, a small wakame seaweed salad with sesame seeds. What would this fare be without a small glass of hot sake (rice wine) to wash it down? This was a gamble. I was hoping Pepina would enjoy my eccentric first meal made by pseudo-chef Gianni.

While I was preparing the meal, Pepina was continually looking out the front door or the side window, as if to will Theadora back home. I had already passed inspection of the fruit trees with flying colors. I was a bit taken aback in a good way when I gazed out the side window and saw Pepina busy with a hoe, vigorously working the soil, turning it over while pulling out the odd mustard or creeping rye grass that may have tried a feeble comeback. I noticed that she placed a few big jujube in her pants pocket while polishing off a small, juicy sapote. She had already consumed a chocolate persimmon because I saw the stem part on the potting bench that was left after she picked it clean. But hey, at the moment I felt this work that I had put into growing these incredible trees was all for Pepina. I said at one point when I was ready to serve up the meal, "If you keep eating all those fruit, you are not gonna be able to eat dinner cara mia"

She thought I was making a joke. "Hah! You cook Gianni, I eat your food. Hee-hee."

Prior to serving up the food, to accentuate the atmosphere I softly played a CD of meditative Japanese shakuhachi flute music.

Well, Pepina was, as usual, non-conversant during the meal. While I ate, I kept one eye on Pepina as she methodically speared the swordfish in the miso soup, complementing it with the occasional pickled eggplant planted on top of the steaming bowl of Japanese rice. She siphoned up the wakame salad while tasting miniscule sips of sake between them both. When almost the entire meal was literally licked clean, she finished by raising the medium-sized ceramic soup bowl with pictures of samurai to her mouth and drinking down the miso soup. After smacking her lips, Pepina gradually came out of her trance and looked up and said, "Good Gianni. Japonese iss berry delish. Me dreaming to go Japan Gianni. Add more of… whas-a picant (spicy) stuff in the broth?"

"That was wasabi, cara mia. Yes, Japan is a wonderful country and I would like to take you there. We can hike through some of the most enchanted forests. Go to many onsen (hot springs). And, of course, dine on some of the most exquisite seafood in the world!"

"Ah! Gianni, Less do it. I dream Japan sometime. I wanna eat real sooshi. I wanna go ka-pooki theatre. I wanna wear-a eskimo-no, si?"

"Of course, Pepina. We can go to Kabuki theatre. And you can wear a kimono and they will make up your face with white rice powder and dark red lipstick like a geisha girl. For sure."

Pepina's eyes lit up and she began clapping, squealing with delight. "Reeely Gianni! Reeely!"

I suggested, "How about a café con leche and then we can walk down by the quay side to digest."

"Si, Gianni. First we do dishes, after walk." I hate dishes, but if I could do dishes with Pepina, I was assured it would be fun.

We laughed about the vegetable merchant at the market and his rude gesture with the big radish. She remarked that all men naturally like to boast. We gradually shifted conversation, talking about how her sisters were handling their father's death. I felt Pepina had not yet mourned her father's passing and was handling it in a stoic manner. Perhaps later, the tears would come. And hopefully, I would be there for support.

As we were finishing the dishes, I handed Pepina the last dish for her to dry. But instinctively, I held her outstretched hand and gently pulled her close to me. With my back up against the sink, I slowly moved one hundred eighty degrees, as if we were slow dancing. We had switched places and now she had her back lightly leaned against the counter. I slowly bent forward and planted the slowest, loving kiss to her ready lips. There we remained. Being so close, the heat from her pillowy soft breasts sent me into rapture. We were both breathing so hard we would soon need to be on ventilators. Eventually, Pepina whispered, "Caro Gianni, where is my café con leche?"

With great difficulty, I detached myself from Pepina's warm embrace. At arm's length, we both looked at each other and began to laugh uproariously for I don't know how long. Our laughter was interrupted by a phone call on my mobile. I recognized the number immediately from the States. "Excuse me Pepina. Yes Valeria, how are you? How's business?"

"Hey Gianni. That's the reason I'm calling. Gotta minute?"

"Sure, what's happening?"

"Well, remember that Danish couple that stayed at your place last year for a week? They wrote that incredible review about their stay on AirB&B? You probably don't remember or care. Anyway, they just re-booked through AirB&B again, this time for three weeks! They enjoyed the place so much last year. Of course, I have yet to confirm without checking with you first. Were you planning to return soon? Dad misses you, but I know him and he is just jealous and wishes he had your lifestyle."

Oh man. What a gig. They could rent that place for a couple of months if they wanted. I was not going anywhere at the moment. I replied without hesitation, "Sure, sure, Valeria. That's fine, I'm glad. Three weeks is absolutely fine. So Gustavo misses me, huh? I bet. Your father is a workaholic. But anyway, I would rather talk about you. How's life treating you? Are you still researching the hospitality industry? You ok financially?"

Valeria jumped in. *"Basta*! Jeez, Gianni! You are sounding more like Dad. I'm good, yeah, you know. I have been, like, clean for five months now, like, you know. Going to the gym, swimming. It's a bitch some days, ya know. I dream about getting high all the time. Sometimes, like, I don't want to wake up because I'm enjoying the dream so much and… well, like you know as well as me, right?"

She had me there. I knew exactly what Valeria was talking about. The drugs. They consume you 24/7. As the saying goes, "Only those who the scorpion stings can tell each other how it feels." They become your friend, your enemy and your demise if you don't control.

But as much as I wanted to relay to her that my life had recently returned to some semblance of decency—a real relationship, with a woman that has grasped my heart with tender caring hands—now was not the time to go into detail. Our talk would continue at a different time.

"Yeah, Valeria. You got that right. Nailed that on the head. You know me well. The struggle is continuous. Don't give up fighting, ok?" No response on her end. "So please confirm that booking. Call me anytime when it's got nothing to do with the property ok? I like to know, young lady, how things are going. Sound ok to you?"

"I'll take care of it. Ciao!" CLICK. She hung up abruptly before I could get another word in edgewise.

Pepina had kept herself busy tidying the place up while I was talking on the phone and was in the bathroom out of earshot. I told her it was my friend's daughter who managed renting out my place on AirB&B in the states. Pepina casually said, "Eh, si. Valeria. How her father Gustavo?"

It took a while to sink in, but I recalled mentioning them

both when we met at that café near the flamenco theatre in Barcelona.

"Good memory, cara mia! Yeah, they are both well. Valeria is on a good path to get her life back on track and Gustavo is just work, work, work. Valeria has return tourists from Denmark who want the place for three weeks. They enjoyed the place so much last year. So I approved it."

"Bravo Gianni. You are business man. No?"

After coffee, we began to set off for a nice evening passeggiata. As I reached the front door to depart we heard the loudest litany of screeches, squawks and chirps. As I opened the door, Theadora burst on the scene faster than a cruise missile. Instead of her usual direct flight to the bathroom onto her shower curtain perch, she circled around the little flat like a B-52 bomber jet on a flight path. The whole time Pepina had the brightest smile on her face, jumping up and down on her toes applauding Thea, exhorting her on. "*Ole` ole` bona noia Ole* (good girl)."

Thea on the last go-round alighted on Pepina's outstretched hand and began to peck it rather roughly with that stout beak, but Pepina did not care or show any discomfort. After a few chirps, Pepina whispered something indecipherable. Thea unusually cocked her head sideways in a way I have never seen, preened her tail feathers briefly, then blasted off to her usual hangout, roosting in the bathroom to give her wings a good grooming before lights out for a restful night's sleep.

Pepina gazed at me with feral eyes, like an excited school child. She whispered, "Gianni, I felt he wass coming-a." Pepina was animated from the sudden encounter. She continued in a low whisper. "He was a-outside when we eat. Diss girl iss good omen, good fortune for you, Gianni."

I couldn't argue with that. I bowed and with my arm outstretched to the front door, I led Pepina outside for our walk. It was sunset while we headed to the harbor. As we passed the old goat Claudette, she was leaning on her broom giving us a sideways glance. I picked up our pace until we disappeared around the lane down to the shore. I reminded Pepina that it was Claudette who was responsible for my situation with Theadora.

Pepina said, "She give you mal d'ull (evil eye), Gianni. I feel it."

I said, "I think Claudette is at least one hundred years old. I've felt her malocchio (evil eye) many times before. I hope it does not jink us…"

In a serious tone Pepina replied, "I like sound 'malocchio' better than mal d'ull, Gianni. And I teenk you mean jinx."

I stopped walking, looking puzzled at Pepina when she corrected my pun on her pronunciation. She gave me a wink of the eye. We laughed together all the way down to the shore.

After a wonderful stroll with a picturesque sunset, Pepina thanked me wholeheartedly for such a wonderful evening and said she should be getting back to the hotel. Without looking too dejected I agreed and led the way to the station. Pepina said it was fine and that she could take it from there, but I insisted that I would take her all the way and that I needed the exercise.

As we began to make our walk back I heard a familiar horn blast from the fishing vessel of Gerlando, who provides fresh-caught fish to me as well as some excellent hashish from the Middle East. I wanted to ignore but we could both hear Gerlando yelling for me. As Gerlando tied off his small craft to the wharf he got a little creative with his talk, not knowing exactly who my lady friend was.

"Gio *sa va*! Good timing, my brother. I have some wonderful…uh, some smoked fish for you to try. I am sure you will find it pleasing, yes!"

I responded with an exaggerated smile and a wave, telling Gerlando maybe some other time and that we were in a hurry as I was guiding Pepina back for our return. I could see resignation in his eyes as we scampered off.

When we reached the entrance of the hotel Pepina jumped up one stair ahead of me, spun around so fast and unexpectedly held my face with both of her petite hands, kissing me multiple times on my face, my eyes and topped it off with a smooch on the top of my schnozola.

"You good boy Gianni. What we-a do tomorrow?"

After a brief chat regarding the following day's activities, we said our good nights with one more kiss.

Lastly, Pepina said, "Iker's little brother a fisherman all his life; he sometime too has smoke fish. Be careful Gianni, some smoke fish, you be trouble with policia, is illegal and bad for you, yes?"

Why didn't I just level with Pepina when Gerlando was offering me some fine hashish or quite possibly opium? Instead, she busts me attempting to be secretive in my shady dealings. Get your act together, asshole.

After admitting the truth I made a promise to myself and

Pepina for no more bullshit and deception.

On the way back I swung by Henri's. I had dropped off the Fiat Spider earlier in the day without really thanking him. Henri was dozing in a chair behind his office desk as I peeked through the double glass doors. I went through and Henri awoke in a haze, looked at me quizzically and stated, "Gio! I didn't expect you this evening. Where is your angel Pepina?"

When I informed Henri where Pepina was staying on the Promenade Anglais, he exclaimed, "Merde Gio. That is absurd!"

"Baby steps, Henri, baby steps. I don't want to rush this. I am still in disbelief that I have met Pepina. Anyway, the family driver made the reservation. Pepina is not a show off, definitely frugal. Henri, what the hell, this thing called life; such a cruel sense of humor. Finally, I find the one that I want to spend my life with. Here I stand, already in the sunset of my existence…"

Henri abruptly interrupted, "Ah Gio, but what a lovely sunset indeed." He continued, "What is a day, Gio? It is comprised of a sunrise and sunset. In between we can enjoy life's pleasures. A day is birth and death. Our life is the same; we live from our sunrise and we renew our lives after a glorious sunset. We continually launch ourselves into a beginning and an end. But there is no end, Gio! Don't you see? That is the mystery of this universe which we shall never grasp. It is, after all, mystic."

Henri stood with great difficulty. I could hear a few bones creak. He walked tentatively around his desk, rocking back and forth and side to side to gain some momentum forward, stopped abruptly in front of me, then proceeded to give me the greatest bear hug.

"Gio, Gio. For so many years I have witnessed you, my

brother, torn between two worlds, yes? Sometimes here, sometimes in America. But your mind was somewhere between, left in the vast ocean." Henri spread his arms out wide. "Come Gio! Let us drink to a new beginning. Let us drink deep to cleanse our bodies and minds of impurities. You will cast off all thoughts of life's trials and tribulations. Rid yourself of all failures. For tonight you begin anew, Gio!"

Henri the philosopher was on his game tonight. He reached under his desk and pulled out a bottle of Martell cognac Cordon Bleu. About a hundred twenty-euro bottle. I thanked him from the bottom of my heart for his unfeigned kindness and said I had time for one drink only.

Needless to say, you guessed it, we finished the bottle, swearing oaths of fraternity. I believe we even sang a few bawdy French ditties. I woke up at three in the morning. I had fallen off the chair that I passed out in. Henri was slouched in his chair behind his desk, snoring like a wild grizzly bear.

I had to piss like a race horse. I ran to Henri's little bathroom in back of his office with sink, toilet and bidet. I thought I was going to rip the porcelain off his toilet from the force of my urine; after about a couple of minutes I finished, washed my face, rinsed my mouth and proceeded to use the hotel phone to call a cab. It's only six kilometers home, but this boy was in no shape to walk, and the trains and buses were all closed at that early hour. I had a nice day planned with Pepina. I didn't want to show up hung over. I sure as hell wasn't doing a very good job of that.

<> <>

Epicurian's Delight

10

The following day was a simple gourmet paradiso with Pepina. I cooked again. This time for starters, a big plate of fresh mussels steamed with a little dry chenin blanc wine, chopped garlic and parsley from my small organic herb garden, a dollop of creamery butter. I threw a whole dried cayenne pepper that I had grown the year prior to give it a kick. Then a simple farfalle pasta primavera with red bell pepper, zucchini, tomato and rapini, complemented with fresh oregano, purple basil, crushed black pepper and rosemary that was all from my garden.

The olive oil I used was from one of Henri's Greek guests (Spiros) at the pensione who owned an olive oil company and supplied to the top notch restaurants in France. The guest gifted Henri with six liters of this Eleusian nectar from the Peloponnese. Kindhearted Henri gave two liters to Vivian and Jean Michel, two liters to me and kept the remaining two for himself.

The first thing Pepina exclaimed with the pasta primavera was the quality, fragrance and peppery boldness of the olive oil. Yes, she is my dream girl: great sense of humor, loves to eat, good taste in music, knows quality when she tastes it, knowledgeable gardener and is beautiful to boot! I didn't fare as well with the wine selection; I elected to go with an inferior Rose that I supplemented with a few mulberries, a slice of chocolate persimmon and a slice of sapote blanco in each of our glasses. The presentation was aesthetically exquisite. The taste was not so pleasant. Pepina scooped out and polished off the fruit in the blink of an eye; the vino she left for me.

Pepina returned early the following morning to Barcelona to finish some legal matters with her sisters. I was invited in a week or so. Pepina lightly stepped around the fact that she wanted to formally introduce me to her family. At her father's funeral I did not meet or talk to anyone during that somber ceremony. I received some peculiar looks but nobody approached me.

I accompanied Pepina to the airport for her return flight to Barcelona. I grabbed the train for a ride back to the homestead. I entered a carriage that had only three occupants. They were all young men, I guess around the same age - in their early twenties.

All three seemed to wear clothes two sizes too large. One had tattoos fully covering his neck, with a few Chinese characters haphazardly on his face, not at all stylish like the Maori of New Zealand. The second young man had a rather large nose ring and orange wool cap. The third had all silver upper teeth with a backwards baseball cap.

Nose ring was screaming at neck tattoo. Their street slang was practically incomprehensible. I did catch something like a robbery and I also caught mention of two thousand euro. Silver teeth was threatening to kill nose ring. All three were totally oblivious to my presence.

I played the role of the disinterested passenger, gazing at my cell phone. Neck tattoo stood up and pushed silver teeth up against the doors while nose ring was laughing hysterically. Nose ring's behavior was indicative of someone on methamphetamine. Silver teeth was telling nose ring to 'shut the fuck up.' At the next station the doors opened, and another young man entered the train sporting spiked Mohawk hair with a lit cigarette hanging from his lip. The carriage instantly took on the fragrance of a skunk from the marijuana he was obviously smoking.

The original three became silent when he entered. Mohawk, still standing, flashed a couple of quick hand signs. Neck tattoo slowly walked up to Mohawk and handed him what appeared to be a tightly packed roll of euro notes.

At the next stop all four simultaneously bolted out the exit. While feigning to be on a phone call earlier, I had sneakily taken a photo of the terrible trio before the ringleader made his entrance. I was able to snap one of with all three when they were arguing.

I would scour the papers and ask around about any local crime on the day.

Back home the following night I had an alarming dream. For the first time in my clouded memory, Emily appeared. She was getting ready to run at a track and field stadium that resembled the Los Angeles Coliseum, filled with screaming fans to maximum capacity. I was standing about one hundred meters away at the finish line. She was in shorts and tank top with the number six, which was her lucky number. She was in top physical condition. A horn sounded and she got down into the blocks to run, as if in a sprinting competition. However, there were no other competitors.

Off to her side was a little dwarf wearing only a thong. He was wheeling a small cannon toward the starting block area. He raised one arm and with the other arm pulled a thin rope attached to the cannon. A huge explosion with billowing smoke flew from the end of the cannon.

Emily leaped out of the blocks, fast as a cheetah. She was coming upon me very quickly. But strangely, as she ran I could see her hair flowing behind her; it was turning grey, wisps of it falling out rapidly. Her musculature was changing, as if she was aging with each forced step. As she approached closer and closer she looked cadaverous, as if she was one hundred years old with no teeth. With five meters to go, she outstretched her right arm and in her hand was one of those septodont self-aspirating syringes with the thumb ring (the type dentists use). It was aimed right at my heart. I believe I screamed as I shot up spring-loaded out of bed, drenched in sweat. *What the fuck was that?!*

Was this from some bad drugs I used in the past? Holy shit, that was petrifying. I discarded my soaked night clothes. As I was throwing cold water on my face in the bathroom, Thea hopped off the shower curtain and sat on my back as I was bent over the sink. I slowly stood upright; she jumped back up on her perch. I looked at her stupefied, as if to find the answer from her to that bizarre episode. She gave a short squawk, lifted one of her legs up into her soft feathery belly and went back to sleep.

<> <>

Fashion

11

A cynic is a man who knows the price of everything, but the value of nothing.
Oscar Wilde

I came to the decision that I should go shopping for some new fashionable attire for my meeting with Pepina's family. She had not yet given me the date as to when that would occur. In the meantime I figured I would try to look smart.

I paid a visit to Simone, the local barber in the village, to get a trim of what was left on my ever-receding potato head. Simone was a very well conditioned middle age Italian man, six feet tall with black curly locks (vainly permed and dyed). His eyes were a deep blue, and he had a Roman nose and real elephant flappers for ears.

Simone occasionally accompanied Henri and me to a futbol match. However, Henri had sworn off any future excursions with Simone due to his wildly fanatic behavior, including fisticuffs against the opposing team's fans. Otherwise, he was a very meek and mild-mannered family man. Simone was an Olympique de Marseille supporter. He would never answer why he didn't ply his profession in that old port town. One is better off just not talking football with him.

As Simone was trimming my sideburns, he mentioned that the folks in the village were saying I was giving refuge to a trickster spirit. I held my tongue and did not want to give a rash reply. But Simone's words were spaced out far apart from each other, as if he didn't comprehend them.

"Gio, you still have that, uh… jay?"

Eventually I replied. Taking a deep breath I said, "I see Claudette's gossip has reached your ears, eh Simone? That ol' witch keeps herself occupied by making up stories about spooks and specters. Thea is a harmless bird that she almost killed. She knocked their nest out of a ficus tree with that damn broom of hers. There were a couple more of them in the nest that didn't make it."

"Zut alors Gio! You even have a name for the jay? Thea?"

"Just finish your business with what's left of my hair. I think I prefer to talk futbol with you."

Now he came to life. Fully animated, he began to scream, "Merda! Did you hear Marseille? Physssh! They have fired that imbecile coach? Physssh! Blah, blah…."

There was one thing that always unnerved me about Simone. It was that he had this one wonky eye that constantly looked as if he was keenly interested in something to his left. I can't to this day explain why, when I look Simone in the eyes, I always fall for looking to his left, as if there is something vitally important over there that he is talking about. Oh, also his racist chants to opposing teams. Only those two points I disliked about him. Other than that, Simone was ok in my estimate.

To say I went overboard clothes-shopping would be an understatement. Back in Nice I decided for once in my life I would splurge ridiculously on fashionable overpriced men's wear. At this point, one would be accurate in stating that I was totally enamored with Pepina; it went without saying. I wanted to make a good impression for her and the four sisters. At least I could dress properly, even if they thought I was a schmuck.

Henri gave me an address on Avenue Jean Medicin. He said although the clothes were pricey, there was a tailor there – Ludovico - who years ago used to stay at Pensione Acacia until Henri helped him find a home in Nice. Ludovico moved to France due to almost no work and constant earthquakes in his hometown of Potenza, Italy. Henri stated that Ludovico was an honest man and that he would tailor the clothes to perfection for me.

Meanwhile, I acquired a Kiton Sport Coat Jacket Cashmere (1,900 euro), Bruno Cucinelli Pants (325), Salvatore Ferragamo cap toe oxford brown shoes (406), Attolini tie (139) and Luciano Barbera shirt (124). I had to keep reminding myself that this was for Pepina as well as myself. I chose earth colors. My coat highlighted variations of a brown and yellow check. Dark tan slacks, mustard shirt with geometric yellow tie. The brown leather shoes finished off the ensemble.

I learned a lot about fashion with Ludovico's passionate descriptions of various fabrics and designs. Ludovico reminded me of what I thought an ancient hoplite would look like: very noble, but very rough from life's hard trials and tribulations during decades of ancient wars. He was middle aged and lucky if he was five foot four. Large strong hands resembled groups of bananas with veins popping out like cords of wire. Piercing steel gray eyes (perhaps some Etruscan roots there). More importantly, his eyes held a powerful conviction of judgment. He wore a couple days worth of beard, but curiously had a clean-shaven upper lip.

Let's face it, men's high fashion was really not my cup of tea. Outdoor hiking attire was my speed. However, I was always open to new ideas and my encounter with Ludovico made the trip worthwhile. Ludovico was quite the gentleman. His dialect used similar phrases to what I grew up hearing with my mother and Uncle Gerardo's Neapolitan accent. He was delighted to meet a friend of Henri's, about whom he sang the highest praises. He also informed me while taking my measurements that the jacket and pants would be ready in three business days.

I really liked Ludovico and the feeling must have been mutual because at one point while he was going over my tie selection he said from now on to call him 'Lou,' just like Lou Reed the musician from New York. Lou explained that he always wanted to live in New York, but those plans had never been realized due to life's unforeseen obstacles.

He knew instinctively that I was going to great effort to impress a woman; he prodded me for some details. I relented from his inquisitiveness. I stated that it was indeed for a beautiful woman from Barcelona. Ah! The floodgates opened and Lou informed me of so many of his exploits with Catalonian women, who in his estimation are rivaled by no other for their beauty and temperament.

Lou desired more details, but I begged off, saying I had another appointment and that we would continue our stimulating conversation in a few days when the clothes would be ready for a final fitting. Lou passionately added that upon my return, that he had some incredible grappa that he would treat me to, made by his brother's small 'biologico' vineyard in the south of Italy. Lou saw my eyes light up like a fireworks pinwheel on the Champs-Elysees. I left feeling enriched from meeting a kindred spirit.

***Side note** - *This 'grappa' issue is a matter that will go solidly into the memory banks of ol' Gio Pisano!*

***Sub-side note** - *Medically speaking—perhaps equally from a psychological standpoint—isn't it interesting how detrimental causes that we make to injure ourselves seem to be the very causes which we tend to gravitate toward?*

Sub-Saharan Note- *But, hey! Grappa from an organic small label in the south of Italia… a salud!*

<> <>

The Farm

12

A few days had passed when Pepina called to inform me that all of her family would be together in two weeks on 11 September for 'Diada Nacional de Catalunya' (National Day of Catalonia). The family always gathered on this day with their father. This would be the first year that they would be one family member short following the death of their father Donat. There would be street entertainment, concerts, and political demonstrations with lots of flag waving for Catalonia. Pepina also mentioned that any time prior to that day she would like to invite me to see her 'jardin.' I jumped at the opportunity and asked her when I could come.

We agreed that I would arrive two days before the National Day holiday. That way I could book at least two days at the hotel to see Pepina's 'jardin' and attend their family day, with introduction to the four mystery sisters. I was at my wit's end to meet four women who were related to Pepina. They were all married, so no possibility on setting up a blind date for Henri. I laughed to myself, to think Henri would even contemplate being in a relationship.

Henri nowadays envisions himself as a modern day Romeo, a real Casanova. He knows every working girl in the harbor, and knows them by name. Henri loves to say, "In France we have so many delectable and mouthwatering dishes. Our taste for variety is worldwide. My variety of taste for women is international. For how can I only eat one dish all my life?"

Pepina made a point of recommending some gardening clothes for me to pack. *Gesu salvi mi*, she is gonna put me to work. But I bet it's going to be a blast! In my mind's eye I can imagine her little garden filled with zinnias, dahlias and heirloom roses. I can see a few tomatoes, large leaf fronds with yellow zucchini blossoms, various herbs scattered about. I also see a beautiful fountain with sea nymphs dancing about, accompanied by the lilting sound of a soft stream.

I arrived in Barcelona on the agreed-upon date and time. The address she gave me was in the Pedralbes district of Barcelona. This would be the first time that I had received an invitation to Pepina's home. She always politely refrained from allowing me to come to her residence due to her father's ill health and the fact that she was so busy taking care of him, which at times was so unpleasant due to his disease. I grabbed a taxi from the airport.

Normally I would have used the metro or bus system. Both France and Spain have incredible public transportation. Why the good ol' USA is so dependent on every individual being a solitary nomad in their solitary car, commuting every day on massive freeway systems and toll roads is utter lunacy! But hey! That's why I spend a majority of my existence in the Old World. They care about people!

A typical American spends a vast majority of their brain space on 1) What am I going to do about my medical care? 2) How much education can I afford? 3) Why is an automobile a necessity? Car insurance, registration, tires, smog certification, price of petrol and maintenance are very taxing expenses to a vast number of US citizens.

To be prompt the taxi was my best bet. When the cab pulled up to an incredibly stunning gated villa the driver, before shifting the car into park, glanced back at me to give me a close scrutiny, then said, "You sure dees is address, Meester?"

I was about to answer the dickhead. But, just then, a generic voice came over the loudly crackling intercom system that said, *"Entrar."*

The gates immediately opened to an incredible horseshoe driveway. The villa was a three-story structure. The main entrance was likened to a stunning glass atrium-style greenhouse. Inside this glass enclosure were a multitude of potted flowers. There was a car in the driveway, a shiny black Mercedes GL350 with black tinted windows. I paid the taxi driver. He seemed reluctant, in no hurry to depart, fiddling with something inside the glove box, so I told him to shove off. "Vamos!"

Pepina was waiting for me. She was accompanied by an old man with a slight humpback and enormous sweeping eyebrows that could have hired out to be a pair of used wisp brooms. He also looked like he had not shaved in about a week. He was smartly dressed out and had some very beautiful handmade shoes that must have set him back a penny or two. Pepina welcomed me with open arms and a peck on each cheek. She introduced hairy to me.

"Gianni, dees is our dear Iker. Iker do hello to Senyor Gianni."

In heavily-accented Catalonian, Iker responded like a well trained servant, "Hello, Senyor Giovanne, I am to meet you-a, so pleased."

Pepina rattled off something in machine-gun Cat to Iker. He jumped to and grabbed my small luggage and tossed it into the boot of the Mercedes. Pepina said, "Less not throw away time; we go now."

I was a bit perplexed as to why we were driving off somewhere, but Pepina headed me off on my obvious question by mentioning, "My jardin ees not een here. One hour we drive. Gianni, you evare go to Montserrat? My jardin before Montserrat."

"Whatever you say, cara mia. I'm all yours."

The drive was lovely on a bright, sunny day. The time passed so swiftly as I chatted away with Pepina while Iker drove expertly. We were driving on a road that paralleled the train, but after a dozen kilometers we moved onto a country road that passed some old farm homes.

I was mesmerized by the rolling hills and rich farmland that must have sustained people throughout the centuries. In the far distance, coming up I saw acre upon acre of lush green strange-looking orange trees in perfect rows - meandering hills were filled with them. As we drew even, I could see orange fruit loaded in the trees. These were not oranges, but persimmons. I spied, farther down the spacious property, many rows of grapevines that snaked their way, some half shaded and some glistening in the afternoon sun.

I exclaimed to Pepina, "Oh look! What wonderful Fuyu Persimmons! Jeez, look at all of them."

Iker said something to Pepina. I noticed the car was slowing down. I didn't mean for them to stop on my account due to my excitement and acting like a weekend tourist. Maybe Iker said he needed to take a leak. Pepina said in a subdued voice. "We stretch legs Gianni. I wanna you meet some friends."

Iker drove slowly to gradually stop on a gravel driveway in front of an old rustic-looking farmhouse frozen in time. The structure itself was all stone from the surrounding hills. The roof was laid with all new terracotta tiles. It was two-story and on the second floor was a large balcony with black wrought iron in the old Spanish fashion. Dozens of pots hung from the balcony and took up a good portion of the floor space. Pink and white fuchsia, geraniums, zinnia and dahlias poked their heads out from the pots, making a striking contrast against the stone building.

There were two donkeys lazing about the farmhouse and I spotted a couple of chickens with pants pecking away at the dirt. At least that's what I call them. I don't know what breed they are, but I have seen them before on many occasions and enjoyed how all their feathers continue down their legs, giving the impression that they are wearing pants.

Behind the farmhouse in the distance there was another more recent small home. There was a good sized pond on the side of the farmhouse. You could see mallard ducks, coots and a few other water fowl floating on the surface. They would occasionally duck down under the murky water, popping up here and there. It was a tranquil scene.

As I was taking in the beauty of the place, a middle aged couple came trotting out of the farmhouse with a young lady. They were holding hands and bowing and kissing Pepina. Iker had totally disappeared. We met halfway between the farmhouse and the parked Mercedes.

Pepina first introduced me to the gentleman by the name of Argi, then his wife Erlea and lastly to their daughter Berezi. I recognized that Berezi was a rather tall Down syndrome girl in her early teens. Argi was a man in his mid-fifties. You could see years of sun and outside life etched on his face. But that didn't stop his sincere smile that was missing quite a few teeth. His clothes were as weathered as his face. Argi's wife Erlea had on a long brown skirt that touched the earth; her breasts were pendulous in an equally long sleeve brown shirt. She had mousey hair and stunning blue eyes with a dainty pouting mouth. Erlea was possibly quite a few years younger than Argi. But they both emanated a pure country life. Berezi was a sweetheart; the whole time we were standing and chatting, she had her head lovingly rested on Pepina's shoulder. I could tell right away Pepina was like a great auntie to Berezi.

They were all carrying on in a tongue that I could not put my finger on, which was puzzling.

"They are dee caretakers of dees farm Gianni. They are Basque. They ask to me... what you theenk of my jardin?"

With my jaw resting rather loosely on the gravel driveway, I decided it was time to close my mouth to keep out the flies buzzing about. I looked seriously at Pepina and offered my wise-ass, sarcastic reply.

"Well, it needs a lot of work. When do we begin?"

Pepina matter-of-factly replied, "Iker show you. You change clothes and shoes, we go for tour, ok?"

Iker had buggered off. But when I turned he was standing right up against me, so close I bumped into him and almost tripped. I thought, *Wait a minute, how the hell did he appear out of thin air?* Iker had my bag in hand and led me into a room in the farmhouse to change into gardening clothes that Pepina had instructed me to bring.

On the way to change my clothes, I followed Iker along a small faux river path to the farmhouse. I dodged a menacing goose who tried to nip me. In my attempt to avoid the goose I inadvertently stepped on a lizard with a stunning blue tail that was basking in the sun and killed it. Iker gave me a peculiar look and said, "Step on lizard, good fortuna, si mucho." I reserved judgment on his remark with a simple nod of the head.

I brought along my trusty Merrill boots from REI in the States. I have yet to find better sturdy hiking footwear. I also brought a Columbia long sleeve shirt, Kuhl pants, a pair of gardening gloves and my cap to protect the balding coconut.

When I came back outside, Pepina was waiting in an electric golf cart. I ambled aboard and we took off up a trail running alongside the persimmon orchard, up and over a hill headed toward the grapes, which were all dark purple, black and dusty. The harvest season should be over by this time of the year. Pepina mentioned that the leftovers from these particular grapes (Pomace - stems, skins and seeds) would be used for making a type of Spanish Brandy local to the area. Pepina slowed down the cart so we could converse.

I said nonchalantly, "You are one sneaky sapote girl. I am still trying to take this all in. How often are you able to come out here?"

Pepina smiled that beautiful heart-shaped smile of hers. She measured her words and said, "The last few years no much, father needing much of care." She softly bit her upper lip before continuing. "Before spent my time here, dees is my home. My house is house behind. Berezi and I have much fun always. Her name means 'special' in Basque. We work hard weeth fruit a-trees. Her mama and papa have-a deeficul time for Berezi on farm. But I know Berezi mind, heza a good girl. Berezi need to be busy work and take care good weeth animals. When I stay here, Berezi be with me, all day all-a night."

We were going uphill rather steeply, with grapes on both sides of us bursting with ripeness. Pepina stated years ago, they experienced the grape leaf phylloxera. The vines suffered to the point that they were going to eliminate the whole crop, but Argi and Erlea created a concoction and had them sprayed after pruning in late winter with a secret recipe they created: a mixture of cinnamon, chamomile, various botanic herbs and urine. All the fruit pickers would chip in to piss into large containers provided by the farm. It worked so well, the entire vineyard was saved. Pepina mentioned that Donat graciously gifted the house to the Basque family. He helped many of the farmers in the area for years during hard times.

We now crested the top of the hill. The geography changed to a more rocky landscape and a rather modest I would guess three acre orchard of Quince trees (Cydonia oblonga).

"Pepina!" I exclaimed. "This is incredible. Che cazzo! I love quince and wish I had room to plant one. Unbelievable."

Pepina became more animated at my excitement.

"Si Gianni, Argi and Erlea make a tasty marmalada con quince. The people in village-a always buy it ebery year. Essa bery good! Believe me. Why say bad word Gianni, eh."

We jumped out of the cart. There were two poles with a small circular wire net to pick fruit in back of the golf cart. The poles had another long six-foot extension that attached. We each wore a double strap burlap bag that we slung around our necks to throw the sun-ripened quince in. We had a joyous time in the late summer sunshine. The quince tree branches grow vertically, shooting up to the sky. Only when the fruit, which generally grows on the ends of the branches, ripens do the branches, under the weight of the fruit, begin to bend down horizontally, making them easier to snatch.

One of the irrigation lines looked as though a critter had chewed through it, thirsting for water in the warm Spanish summer. It was causing a bit of flooding. I spied a farm hand crouched down by the water line attempting to repair. As I approached he stood up and greeted me.

"Hola." He had an air of resignation and as many wrinkles on his face as a spider web. He exhaled a long breath and mumbled, "*Jodido conejo.*" I introduced myself and complimented him on this very productive quince orchard. He looked at me askance while continuing to mend the savaged irrigation line.

Pepina mentioned the rabbits were numerous and that she loved to cook a good rabbit stew with potatoes, shallots, carrots, green beans and zucchini. As she was explaining the recipe to me, she could see that I was salivating in anticipation of such a meal. I could see she was having fun with me, explaining all the juicy details. One way she prepared the rabbit was to soak it overnight in a dry red wine, usually a sangiovese.

I noticed a few owl boxes on poles extending at least five meters high to keep the rodents in check. I've heard from others in the States that a single barn owl family can consume two hundred rats and mice per month. The '*rabeets,*' Pepina said, were plump and sweet in her '*jardin*' from all the delicious organic food they ate. The rabbits and ground squirrels only eat the fruit that falls to the ground. The nasty culprits that ravage the fruit trees are the fox-tailed squirrels and the rats. They can easily climb the trees, take a bite or two off a fruit, then move on to the next one, ruining a good percentage of the crop. After filling our bags up with large yellow quince we made it back to the cart.

Pepina made a U-turn and we traveled back the way we came. However, she took a sudden left on to a very small trail that I failed to notice on the way up. It meandered for a while. We were in scrub chaparral land now, dotted with holm oak (Quercas ilex), Spanish red oak (Quercus falcata) and coyote bush (Baccharis pilularis). I saw a few spikes of multiple blossoms reaching up to the sky of an unidentifiable Salvia bush (possibly Salvia leucophylla). I could see coming up soon was the home that Pepina said was where she resided while at her *jardin.'* As we pulled up to the modest little cottage, Pepina stopped and looked at me with a stern countenance.

"We look only couple minutes ok? Ok Gianni?"

"Ok cara mia, only couple of minutes. Dees 'tour' I'm enjoying bery much!"

Pepina ignored my idiotic reply, like water off a duck's back. She led the way up a beautifully handmade cedarwood porch, with a hitching post for the donkeys. The door, I quickly noticed, didn't even have a lock on it. As I entered, it was as if I was punched in the face. The simplicity, the wood and the fragrance. *Mio Dio*, the fragrance!

My senses were in overdrive. Hanging all about from the solid oak beams were hand-tied bundles of every herb you could think of. I walked from one end of the thousand square foot room to the other, pointing and naming each one.

There were dozens. But I was unable to name two; one was Lovage (levisticum officinale), which I am totally unfamiliar with and is used on meats and liqueur flavoring. The other was Chervil (anthriscus cerefolium), widely used by the French on fish, salads, soups. It reminds me of anise, which I adore.

My lovely Pepina was an apothecary from the remote past. With tears welling in my eyes, I looked at Pepina and we spoke, not in words, but in a deep understanding of how life is in constant flux. Ebbing back and forth, unpredictable. Pepina interrupted the silence.

"I know you Gianni, yes? You no know me yet, huh? I mean I done-a know all you dees time. But I know all you last time."

Instinctively, I knew what Pepina meant. It came hard to me to verbalize what I felt.

"Yes, yes. Pepina, I can feel what you say. I want to 'know you all this time,' with all my heart. I'm convinced this is not the first time we have met. Why don't I know you last time?"

Pepina gave me a matter-of-fact reply. "Many, many much drugs Gianni. Your head too many, how you say… roadblock?"

I could summon no words. Pepina continued, "We now go Gianni. We here too long a-already."

As we were leaving, I kept looking over my shoulder to take in as much of the place as possible. I knew this room as if I had built it with my own hands. The niche in one corner with two chairs and a modest table, all handmade in maple wood. An enormous hearth with wood stacked like soldiers alongside. A custom-made butcher block table that looked roughly hewn from a giant oak.

We climbed back into the cart. Pepina raised her brows and

said, "I cheat you Gianni. Thea, he… she remind me. Tell me about you; birds sacred Gianni. They messengers from God, they are. We return to Barca now."

In the waning light of evening, we smiled at each other. The light made her face glow. And my heart bawled I LOVE YOU! Still, my voice remained silent. I thought of my college days, studying Latin and Greek; a quote which I never forgot from the ancient Greek tragedian Euripides, who famously said, "A slave is someone who cannot speak his thought." I remained mute, but a contentment passed between us.

What Pepina said got me thinking. When I was a boy I found a puppy and brought it home. As I was a responsible youth, Mother did not question this adoption. I always made sure my dog had the best of care, with proper food, and he always had his shots. We could run together forever. That animal was the only dog I ever owned.

During my student days when I was departing to take a college final in physics, I decided to take my dog for a quick run so that he would not be locked up in my flat all day. By this time, he was quite gray in beard and knew of days gone by. But Jake never lost his libido, continually on the hunt. We were having a run in the park when he spotted a bitch cocker spaniel across the street and he flew like a javelin right into an oncoming Datsun 240Z.

The driver immediately came to a stop. He was so devastated you would have thought that it was his dog. After telling the driver to fuck off, I carried Jake, whose back was broken and who had no control of his hind legs. Totally distraught by the accident and with the looming mandatory final exam, I shuttled my dog to the nearest vet to care for with the promise that I would return in no later than four hours.

To this day I don't even recall attending that final exam. My only thought was Jake being cared for and in no pain. Needless to say, I rushed back to the veterinarian.

The front office staff looked at me with surprise and stated that Jake was no longer there and that the vet had put him down due to the seriousness of his injuries. Without a single word, I walked out of that office back to my car. I do remember one of the veterinary staff members came to my car. She asked me before I departed if I was all right. I was too numb to reply. I was about to put the key in the ignition when she produced an invoice for seventy-two dollars for their services.

The following two weeks were quite different without my canine companion. Trying to adopt a pragmatic approach to the experience, I was preaching to myself out loud one evening that at this stage I could move forward without being a pet owner. That's when, outside my side door from the kitchen, I heard a bird making an unusual sound.

My cheap apartment was right next door to a beautiful home that had an extensive backyard with an English country garden motif, very colorful with a wide variety of bushes and trees. Just a couple of steps from my side kitchen door, under a hydrangea bush, I spotted a young chick that apparently fell out of its nest from a nearby sycamore tree.

It had just a bit of downy fluff on top of its colorful head, and signs of its feathers forming maturity. I gathered up the little creature and brought it inside. It was not an ordinary bird, for it had already formed sharp talons and a pronounced curved beak. It had to be, coincidentally, about two weeks old.

After close scrutiny in some nature books in my modest private library, I came to the belief that I may have found a merlin or possibly a kestrel. I would know better after the plumage developed. I also quickly realized this birdie was in need of fresh meat, which was its natural diet.

By researching its dietary habits I found I would have to buy mice from the pet store and supplement with insects such as large grasshoppers, which were plentiful in the neighborhood. Also, luckily where I was living there was no shortage of small fence lizards. When I was out of all of these, I could get beef heart, chopped into tiny pieces, from the butcher.

All of these were consumed voraciously and in no time this bird filled out into quite a spectacular diminutive raptor. Within a few weeks I was able to train it to come to my fist by whistling and offering a small piece of meat. No sooner had it gained confidence in flying than it flew out the side kitchen door where I found it and never returned.

I feel that animals have much to teach us regarding life and the less discussed topic of death.

As we were getting into the car for our return to Barcelona I heard a pitiful scream. We saw Berezi running from behind the farmhouse toward the car. The shrill desperation of her cry moved something inside me. "Scusa me Gianni, I have small talk with Berezi," Pepina said. They disappeared back behind the farmhouse.

Meanwhile, I relaxed in the car. Iker went out for a smoke. Or at least I thought he did. One minute he was there, and then, unless he crawled under the car? The 'small talk' finished about twenty minutes later. As Pepina got back in the car she apologized for taking so long.

I said "No worries. I'm so glad you spoke with Berezi. But it looks like we have to wait now for Iker."

Pepina tilted her head, baffled. "No, Iker here; he finish cigarette." The driver side door swung open swiftly and I could see Iker flick his cigarette butt between thumb and forefinger quite some distance before sliding gracefully into the front seat. What the fuck…?

Once we were back on the main road Pepina confided in me regarding her girl talk with Berezi. "Berezi is confused, but she ok. One of workers on farm, they have daughter who is Down syndrome, same age. Berezi don't know if ok to love her…Gianni?"

"Yes, Pepina."

"She say that when she is with friend, her heart flaps its wings." I looked at Pepina. By this time she had big pools of tears overfilling their banks. The current was running tributaries downstream to a heart-shaped beautiful landscape.

"Yes my dear, it doesn't get any better than when the wings begin to flap." I was holding Pepina tightly now, my heart steadily flapping on her chest.

The ride back was quiet. Iker (Senyor Enigma) looked like a new man. Had he trimmed his eyebrows? Yes, I kept stealing a glance from my backseat into the rear view mirror to catch his pair of newly groomed tumbleweeds that shadowed his eyes. I mentioned in a hushed voice to Pepina as we were comfortably chauffeured, "You know, Pepina, I can get a car at the airport and drive us around instead of asking poor Iker to drive us about."

Pepina looked at me incredulously and said, "No, no, no Gianni. Why you take job from poor Iker? She was like leetle brother a-to Papa. She he weel always have-a job with family."

"That is fine, cara mia, I would not want to take his job. I just thought I could kidnap you and take you to faraway places and enjoy you all myself…huh."

Pepina's eyes lit up like a Christmas tree. "Reeely Gianni! Where do we a-go? Tell me Gianni. Pleeez tell me."

Startled by her boisterous reply, I became equally excited. "Look, Pepina. You mentioned before that you would love to see the world, but due to your situation, circumstances prevented. Also, we discussed how badly you wanted to visit Japan. Let's just go. I can plan everything. Leave it to me. I have experience traveling to Hokkaido in the north all the way down to the islands in Okinawa. There are mysterious forests of larch, cedar, cypress and Japanese maple that we can hike in, ancient temples, hot mineral springs that we can bathe in. I don't need to impress upon you on how good the seafood is and…"

Pepina cut me off by stating that if we were to embark on any journey it would be with shared expenses and not in so many words, but she basically ended her speech by saying I did not have to do the *'macho teeng.'*

We were back in the Pedralbes district in Barcelona in no time. Pepina had begun preparation of some food for us prior to leaving for the 'jardin' tour. She also told me that Iker's younger brother had been a fisherman all his life and she was never without the best seafood. Pepina got the freshest catch when the fishing is good. I believed that was a subtle hint as to what we were about to partake in. She also mentioned quickly that after dinner and coffee, Iker would drive me back to the hotel.

Pepina poured me a glass of Verdejo Bodegas Portia, a Spanish white that I have never tried. She told me to feel free to wander while she put the finishing touches on our meal. So I returned to the glass atrium/greenhouse entrance of this unusually styled villa.

I was delighted to see so many floral colors. Lily of the valley, white, contrasted with lush purple lilac, numerous varieties of salvia, gallardia, fuchsia, Echinacea and potted roses. There was a potting table in the middle of the atrium entrance with different size ceramic pots of all Spanish design, gardening trowels, and bags of potting mix. Pepina mentioned that this was Iker's playground. I wanted to congratulate him. However, I took a quick peek out the glass window and Iker had once again pulled a vanishing act and the Mercedes in the driveway was nowhere to be seen. I brushed it off and would quiz Pepina later about good ol' Iker.

I then entered a huge room with classic green marbled floors. It contained a fireplace you could park a couple of Vespas in and what must be some antique furniture, all covered in white sheets. Pepina found me, said it would be ready in ten minutes, and to just relax and wait until she had finished cooking the food.

There were many pictures on the wall of what I took to be Pepina's father Donat in a uniform with many decorations. I found a black and white photo of all five girls, standing in a straight line with hands held, all with their Sunday best clothes in front of a grand church. I recognized Pepina right away as the little squirt at the end holding a sister's hand.

They seemed to be in order of age, oldest on the right, descending down in order to the left. The senior sister seemed to be about seventeen years old and I recognized her immediately as 'chin in the pencil sharpener sister,' who I caught a glimpse of at Donat's funeral. That forehead and chin you could spot all the way from Sagrada Familia. I was still of the belief that she was perhaps from another wife of her deceased father. It was obvious she bore no resemblance to the other four sisters.

Meanwhile, the smell from la cocina was driving me wild with anticipation. My stomach was doing a tap dance on my backbone while I patiently waited for Pepina's invitation. Eventually, my perseverance was rewarded with a sweet siren call from the kitchen.

I followed her voice through two arched doorways into a rustic looking kitchen with all the needed implements for a master chef. Numerous copper pots dangled everywhere above her head. There was a beautiful Viking stove with six burners and a true double see-through glass refrigerator, which seemed like overkill since there was hardly any food inside. The floor consisted of odd indiscriminately-shaped flagstones that looked from another age. The dining table seemed a bit out of place, being half-inch thick tempered glass with four standard what looked like Ikea birch wood chairs.

To start off, Pepina, wearing a kitchen apron fashioned to look like a flamenco dress, served up four sizzling grilled mackerel with huge slices of Meyer lemons that looked mouth watering. We dove into our silent meditative eating mode, totally savoring each bite of the fresh frutta di mare. I looked up once to see Pepina turn off a large pot of boiling water, so I guessed a pasta dish was coming up.

I was halfway through a bottle of sauvignon blanc which matched perfectly with the fresh flavor of the ocean. I was correct in my assumption regarding the pasta, as I saw linguine being tossed into the pot with some olive oil and salt. From another pot I saw Pepina transfer some good-sized clams into a large glass bowl. Fresh chopped parsley which she had prepared prior was added to the clams, along with a healthy dose of chopped garlic. As she was grinding some crushed black pepper I pulled out my mobile and took a photo of her in action. Pepina laughingly protested.

"No Gianni, no fotos, I look bad! Heehee. How you like Mac-Enroe … how you say?"

"These mackerel are the best! You were not kidding when you said Iker gets the freshest fish, huh? I can't wait for the *Linguine con Vongole!*"

"Ahh, you eyes, you nose is good, yes Gianni. I always cook for father. He no like restaurants. Not trust-a. And say my cooking is best. Father very good man Gianni." Pepina sighed, made a short clicking sound with her tongue and continued, "I wish you know Father and he know you. But God brought-a heem home."

The pasta was magnificent, al dente to perfection. The clams were steamed in a buttery garlic sauce and very plump. I appreciated Pepina's nice touch in using the curly parsley for Linguine con vongole, and the flat aromatic Italian parsley for the mackerel. After we polished off the clams, we came up for a breather and I made a toast to our health. I included a toast to the following day, *Diada Nacional de Catalunya,* and to my much-anticipated meeting of the four sisters.

Pepina brought a salad of radicchio, endive and escarole, with *manzanilla* and *castelveltrano* olives to the table. I noticed a bundle of dried oregano next to one of the hanging pots. Pepina snapped off a few branches and then between both her hands she briskly rubbed a good dusting all over the salad. The aroma from the oregano was blissful. Pepina was filled with laughter at my reaction to one of her organic herbs. A simple dressing of olive oil seasoned with a drop each of balsamic and red wine vinegar rounded it off. I winked to Pepina across the table as I popped a castelveltrano in my mouth. She made a special effort to get those Sicilian olives, knowing that they were my favorite.

The salad was very refreshing and after a nice meal it is a 'good belly wash,' as Henri would say. I reached across the table in a gesture for both of Pepina's hands, which she happily extended. I kissed both hands and remained in that position for quite some time. "Bless you and bless your hands for creating such a marvelous feast. You are talented in more ways than I can count."

She smiled that beautiful heart-shaped smile and I believe I caught a glimmer of a little blush.

Pepina mentioned that the 'incommunicado' sister numero tres (Estel) might not make it tomorrow but we would see what happened. I did not want to ask any questions about the meeting, my attempt at keeping the conversation light. I had no idea of the dynamics in the relationships of the five women. Pepina said they would all come separately, expecting them all at around noon the following day. I said that I would grab a taxi from the hotel, not wanting Iker to have to deal with holiday traffic. That would be just as well since Pepina said Iker would be celebrating at home with his large family.

I declined an amaro ciociaro digestivo. As Pepina got ready to make our coffee, she casually walked up to where I was seated, bent over to methodically kiss each one of my eyes, then a loving kiss on my mouth that I never wanted to end. Then she abruptly straightened up with a big smile, did an about-face and marched over to the stove to fetch the coffee. Pepina has the ability to take my breath away (not due to the abundant garlic we just ate). I have to keep reminding myself that this is real and that love has shined in my life after such a long drought.

While we were enjoying our coffee we discussed what our trip would be like in Japan, about what the family would do with this house since Pepina said she did not want to live there any longer and about our trip to her little 'jardin' today. As we finished, I asked Pepina to please come back to Nice after tomorrow with me. We could spend a day or two at my flat, then do some hiking up the coast toward Italy or zip down to Sicily, since it's still very warm, and enjoy the beaches.

As I continued on and on to lay out multiple choices, Pepina interrupted me and said matter-of-factly, "Of course, we go your home aftare tomorrow Gianni, there we can know each othare more, cuz I love you."

I must have stared for longer than I anticipated, for I was caught off guard. I could feel the hairs on my neck. I felt giddy, but there was still half a bottle of wine, which is hardly anything to drink by my standards. My arms and legs were tingling. I opened my mouth to reply, but Pepina spoke in my place.

"We love each othare Gianni, long time, ees good, yes? I know your heart meanzu good. You tell me everything. You are open honest life to me."

That night back at the hotel, checking my email I found a correspondence from Gustavo that gave some subtle hints as to a serious issue. Being so late at night here, it was mid-afternoon in the States. I called Gustavo at work because that is where he practically lives.

He immediately took my call. After some basic formalities, he opened up, asking me if I had heard from Valeria. He had been trying to get hold of her for a couple days, but she didn't return his calls. Finally, today he received a text from her saying that she went with a friend for a few days to Las Vegas.

He wanted to know if I heard from her. Gustavo was, in a way, jealous of my connection with Valeria regarding her drug and personal issues. She was very candid with me on some very intimate matters that I kept in strict confidence, which she could not relate to her father. Gustavo was probing me if I was aware of anything that he should be concerned with. I assured my friend that Valeria had not been in touch since our last chin wag, regarding a three-week tenant rental for my townhouse in Santa Barbara. I promised him that I would be in touch if she communicated. One could never contact Valeria. It was always she that would initiate a call.

The Sisters

13

The following day, would you believe out of the hundreds of cab drivers in Madrid, I grabbed a ride from the hotel to Pepina's with the same smartass as before? He was absolutely mute for the entire drive. When Pepina saw me arrive in my snappy, overpriced outfit, she was in disbelief.

"Dees clothes Gianni. Ah, wha iss dees? Dees is not real Gianni. Real Gianni no dress dees way. You comftablue? Come in, I geev you beera."

My first inclination was to give a firm rebuttal for all the labor I went through to get these finely tailored clothes. But once again, Pepina's no-filter, forthright nature was spot-on. Who was I kidding? I might as well have worn a clown outfit, with a horn for a nose. I spent the afternoon being self conscious, thinking that Pepina's family would be staring at my costume. I worried for nothing; the meeting of the sisters was not a very interesting event.

Just as Pepina mentioned, each sister arrived separately with their husband or boyfriend. Alba arrived first - chin in pencil sharpener sister - in a cherry Jaguar XJ with a young man who could have been her son. They acted as if they were on a honeymoon. After introductions, they both bolted to an adjoining parlor room with the sound of salsa music blaring. I took a peek through a crack in the large wooden double doors to witness them both dancing away like two drunken caballeros.

Pepina gave me an offhanded remark that Alba's (the oldest sister) new friend was a Colombian trumpet player. The third sister (Estel) was a consistent zero communication no-show, so I only met three sisters. The remaining two sisters (Jacinta and Flor) arrived within fifteen minutes of each other. They were non-conversant with everyone but themselves. Jacinta had a neck whose veins popped out when she spoke and looked like un-cooked *capellini*. Flor wore a very tight long blue dress. Her torso slimmed all the way down to a waist that reminded me of a wasp; reminiscent of Jayne Mansfield. One could possibly encircle her entire waist with both hands. It was my belief that Flor could be anorexic.

Pepina forewarned me in regard to Flor: "Gianni, please, Flor is a hypodermic, she claims having ebery known a-kind of sickness. She may say to you to egg-sam her. I'm sorry."

I looked confidently at Pepina, and said, "You know, Pepina, I have had numerous experiences throughout my medical practice with patients over the years who suffer from hypochondria." I repeated the word clearly. "I can handle if she asks."

Pepina's face showed immediate relief. "Thank you, Gianni. Yes, you understand."

After a bit, I was leisurely admiring a painting on the wall that I recognized by the seventeenth century Dutch flower painter Jan van Huysum. Now, to be honest, I don't know crap about art. But many years ago at the Getty Villa in Los Angeles, I had attended an exhibit of some van Huysum paintings. In the gift shop, you could buy a replica print, which I did, but I never bought a frame. I have always been fascinated by the super realism of his flower paintings. In vivid detail, one can see ants crawling in between the petals, some dew falling off a leaf onto a pear, or the hairy fuzz of a kiwi fruit.

While I was concentrating on a particular area of the painting, I was interrupted by a melodic voice speaking in fairly good English. "Very intricate detail, yes?" asked Flor.

A bit startled, I replied, "Indeed, van Huysum is a master of detail."

Flor raised one of her eyebrows and said, "This painting was one of Papa's favorites. He fought very hard to purchase it."

It was now my turn to raise both of my eyebrows. My voice croaked when I answered, "This is an original?"

"Why, of course," Flor replied in a dismissive tone.

Flor immediately changed the subject, saying, "I remember you. You showed up at Papa's funeral uninvited." She paused and looked me up and down, while adding, "Well, at least you are better dressed today."

Let's see. How should I approach this barracuda? Should I bait the hook by making a wisecrack? Or just roll with the punches? For now, I'd select the former. "Why thank you, Flor," I replied. "Yes, my butler selected this outfit today. I was worried about his selection. He can be so gauche."

Flor gave me a haughty look, took a deep breath, and said, "I have an issue in my throat. I am constantly getting small pieces of food caught in my throat. I have to chew all my food so thoroughly and even that sometimes doesn't work. Also, after I eat I receive a tickle in my throat that I am unable rid myself of. What should I do?"

Uh oh! Here it comes. Pepina warned me about her sister's 'hypodermic.'

"See a doctor."

"I thought you are a doctor?"

"Retired doctor. Plus I don't have the proper instruments to look at your throat."

"That's a lame excuse."

"Oh really?"

"Indeed."

Across the room I spied Pepina. Her eyes were beseeching me to 'egg-sam' Flor, to humor her. We spoke without words. My belligerence faded. I felt a lightheartedness wash over me. So I smiled then said to Flor, "Ok Flor, why don't we step over here by the bay window for some more light?" I had a pair of latex gloves in my coat pocket (old doctor habit). I only used one for my right hand. I reveled by snapping it on with emphasis, I witnessed a slight nod of approval from the stoic face of Flor.

Of course, there was no way I could perform an endoscopy for a correct diagnosis. So I attempted the best I could. I peered down her gullet. I gently pushed her tongue down with my gloved hand. I feigned a few "Hmm, I sees." Aside from a mouthful of fillings, crowns and horseshit breath, there was nothing to see.

I said to Flor everything looked in order. "But I wholeheartedly recommend that you have your doctor look further with the endoscopic camera." She gave me a somewhat disdainful look, said thank you then promptly waltzed back to her seat on a fainting couch next to her sister Jacinta. Pepina's eyes tracked me down again from across the room to say 'you are dee best my Gianni, thank you!'

For the remainder of the afternoon, Jacinta and Flor were constantly huddled, whispering to each other, while their elderly gentlemen husbands, whom I'm sure were both worth a boat load of money, talked. From what I could tell from their rapid conversations, which best I could translate, they were seemingly involved in the local politics with a heavy distrust in Madrid.

While Pepina was preparing some hors d'oeuvres in *la cucina*, I casually whispered my observations to her; she gave me a look up and down, nodding her head with a smile of respect.

"Si Gianni, you good translate Cat too, really? You sorprise me again. They both politicians, and maybe-a no much longer. Many things a-change fast in Espana… esu-pecialy in Catalonia,"

The driveway was now hosting a Rolls Royce and Bentley, in addition to the Jaguar.

<> <>

Home Alone

14

The next day, we boarded our quick flight back to Nice. Pepina had a considerable-sized suitcase, which boded well for me. She could move in and stay forever as far as I was concerned. We grabbed a cab to make a short side trip to Jean-Michel at the butcher shop. I had in mind to cook a very simple yet scrumptious dish for Pepina - some delectable, tender veal (Cotolette alla Milanese). It's so easy, but what makes this so tasty is the quality of the veal from Jean-Michel. All you need are a couple of eggs, butter, flour and breadcrumbs seasoned ala Chef Gianni. Rounding off the simple meal would be a refreshing Nicoise salad.

Jean-Michel welcomed us with open arms. He bantered about, heaping praise on Pepina and hoping for future get-togethers with Vivian. Jean Michel said he would make Capretto al Forno (roast a baby goat) when we come. I noticed at a glance that Pepina was smacking her lips at the mention of Jean-Michel's culinary offer. He was eager for another chess match. Pepina got on well with Vivian the one time they met and I could tell they enjoyed each other's company. We departed, sending our warmest regards to Vivian and the two children with a promise to get together, hopefully in the near future. For Pepina and I were anxious to get back home, more than likely for the same reasons.

As our cab was pulling up to the house, both of us were straining our necks to look out the window for any sign of Theadora hanging about. As I brought the groceries and luggage up the steps, Pepina went directly to the little orchard, where she was most comfortable. I felt the same way and joined her. But not before making us both a café con leche. As it was brewing I put on a mix of songs I had recorded quite a few years ago.

We enjoyed our coffee amongst the late season jujube and ripening sapote blanco. Pepina was subdued. She mewed softly as I embraced and kissed her tightly in my arms. I smiled deeply into her eyes. Then I glanced away as if distracted; I was still at the point where I didn't want Pepina to see how deeply my feelings were for her. My fear of rejection is cowardly, and I have come to the realization that cowardice has been the main theme in my life. I kissed her with gusto for one more encore performance.

It became so quiet, even the crickets were dumb. Pepina began to say something, hesitated, then angled her head ever so slightly with the sweetest smile. She first qualified her remark as not a 'jink' with a quick wink of the eye, before a sudden hand movement. She mentioned that Thea was far away now and that it was a good thing for her, because her mission had been fulfilled.

I gazed lovingly at Pepina and felt it was not necessary to utter a single word. I respected her mystery and remained silent. She took my hand. I felt the sensation as if we were gently swimming back to the flat. As we entered, aptly, Bowie's version of "Wild is the Wind" was playing softly. Pepina was giggling with a hint of being nervous. I sensed she was fearful as she continued walking toward the bedroom.

To say I have been with a few women would be factual. And only with Emily did I ever have a meaningful relationship. For all the one-night stands, never did one transpire for an instant replay por moi. All my efforts supplied only a physical satisfaction, which was all that was offered.

Somehow, my life has been rejecting any type of notion of a partner. But that all changed the day I heard a voice giving me sound advice on the pruning methods of fruit trees. Pepina consumed me with a love that was foreign, yet so intoxicating. We made love that early evening. In her embrace I felt a renaissance, casting off the skin of an imposter. Our love was on fire. We melted in each other's embrace. While I was kissing every square centimeter of her body, Pepina abruptly sat up, looked me lovingly and directly in the eyes, and said, in a breathless passionate whisper, "Gianni, dees is first time for me. You only man. Please slow going."

Due to my past medical profession, I am quite familiar with the human anatomy. While I had been giving pleasure to Pepina in many areas which I am particularly fond of, and very familiar with, I confirmed that Pepina was as close to natural as the day she was born. I would be patient and oh-so-gentle with the woman I loved, who had yet to be with a man intimately. I made no attempt to subdue a smile as I heard the music change in the next room - Jethro Tull's "Hot Night in Budapest"…

III

We spent what remained of the summer in love's embrace, whether we went for a weekend hike in the mountains, a swim at the beach, cooking a luscious meal or just an evening out for dinner and off to the theater or concert. Pepina was not a big fan of the cinema, much preferring books, which was right up my alley. She has brought joy into my life by continuous laughter on a daily basis.

The other day she stated, "Gianni, these movies have no real story, bad writing. And these side-effects are too bery much." I just shrugged my shoulders when she said that. I was too preoccupied wondering what possible side-effect she could possibly receive from viewing a simple movie. But a while later the light bulb went on; I figured she meant 'special effects.'

Through all of our activity we looked forward mostly to the evening, when we could fall into each other's arms. I would ravish her; like a thirsty man in a hot desert. We instinctively felt as if we were making up for lost time, but without admitting so.

It made total sense to me that our lovemaking (more times than not) took place in the kitchen, either sprawled on my semi-wonky kitchen table or on the marble countertop. Food was our aphrodisiac and foreplay.

Pepina was startled the first morning I brought her breakfast in bed. I have always been an early riser, while I noticed she sleeps more soundly as soon as the sun rises. However, Pepina definitely fancies breakfast in bed, even though initially she mildly protested. Whether I make her a broccoli quiche, breakfast burrito, buckwheat pancakes with organic mulberries from our mini-orchard or simple toast and butter with cup of Earl Gray tea, her eyes light up with excitement on each and every occasion as if it was the first, consuming each bite with quite vocal pleasure. It's fair to mention that our lovemaking was no stranger during the breakfast hour as well.

THE ADVENTURES OF GIANNI & PEPINA

ADVENTURE #1

Location - Germany

15

"Let mee aska yoo dees Gianni?" said a perplexed Pepina. "Where in thee fuck eeza Karl-Heinz?"

With a dignified air of confidence, desperately attempting to defuse the situation I said calmly, "Ok Pepina. Let's keep a cool head. Winfried said Karl-Heinz would meet us on this platform exactly three minutes ago. Let's give him some more time due to his disability." In all actuality, Pepina took the words right out of my mouth. However, it does no good to have us both pissed off.

What better place to begin than on some obscure train station, somewhere in central Hamburg, Germany. You see, Pepina and I made a pact to see the world. We postponed the Japan trip until springtime when the weather would be more agreeable, avoiding the typhoon season and usual flooding that follows.

A few weeks prior we made our reservation online through AirB&B. We decided on this arrangement due to our love of cooking our own food, and the home we reserved had a deluxe kitchen with all the amenities. We absolutely adore fine restaurants as well. When you truly discover fine dining outside, it's as if you have discovered a diamond. But finding one that fits our strict requirements is difficult indeed. We mutually agreed that there is no worse experience than the disappointment of paying for poor dining (The Ultimate Insult for Two Devoted Epicureans).

Initially, our first adventure was to be in Japan. However, it was vital for Pepina to view the Sakura (cherry blossoms), which usually display their beauty during the month of April in the major cities. Okinawa (way south) and Hokkaido (extreme north) also have cherry blossom festivals at different times of the year. We will visit those locations at some point. So, being that it was heading toward the end of the year, our jaunt to Japan would be postponed until the following spring. We both decided that it would be a good time to do some exploring in Germany, since it was in the middle of Oktoberfest - what better time to eat, drink, and hike through the country? We would have no shortage of striking green forest woods in Germany.

My travel companion and fiancée (Pepina) is a lovely, feisty and adventurous Catalonian Cutie, who possesses a wonderful sense of humor, is an imaginative gourmet cook, a gardener par excellence and makes me weak-kneed every time she turns her smile my way. Our travel interests revolve around areas of the world that have botanic gardens, arboretums, hiking trails, fruit orchards, all farms of the organic nature and dining par excellence. All of the above is headlined by investigating new recipes that the local fare offers.

But I digress... we landed in Hamburg, anticipating a wonderful three days of exploring a prolific botanic garden and discovering some fine dining. So we made our way to one of the most curious arrangements for attaining the keys for our first stay there. We thought it peculiar at the time… and now, a few weeks later, we thought it downright stupid on our part.

Here was the plan: The AirB&B homeowner in Hamburg (Winfried) would be out of the country on business during our three-day stay. So far, so good. However, his instructions were for us to continue on the train for two more stations past his stop, make sure to be in the last train carriage, get out at the appointed station and wait on the platform. At precisely 11:45am - German standard time - a gentleman by the name of Karl-Heinz would meet us and hand over the keys to Winfried's home. It is worth noting that our instructions were that it would be easy for us to recognize Karl-Heinz because he was physically challenged with a serious limp, employing a cane.

It was beginning to dawn on me that this arrangement had all the indications of an episode on the *Twilight Zone*. I kept the thoughts of cancelling this arrangement with AirB&B to myself. If good ol' Karl-Heinz didn't show up in the next ten minutes or so I would just book us in a nice hotel. Pepina was already walking up to strange men asking them if they were Karl-Heinz. One well-dressed gentleman with a brief case in one hand, his other arm in a sling, kept curiously following Pepina, wishing that he was Karl-Heinz. I finally approached, asking him if he wanted a matching sling for the other arm, mimicking clenched knuckles. Once he realized she was not alone he beat a hasty retreat down the platform exit.

When our patience had just about run out, we simultaneously saw a young man at the very end of the platform heading toward us with a cane. Pepina waved with a cheerful call. Together, pulling our luggage halfway, we finally met our AirB&B enabler. I noticed he wore special shoe that had an additional two-inch heel. Karl-Heinz was a handsome young man with perfectly coiffed blond hair, crystal blue eyes and a perfectly shaped reddish-brown goatee. His slacks and shirt were ironed to perfection.

"Ya, hallo, Mr. Giovanni?" he questioned.

"Yes, hello Karl-Heinz, we almost gave up our search for you. How are you?"

Karl-Heinz was breathless. "I am so sorry be late, unt please here is key for door mit remote for open garage your car."

"Herr Karl," Pepina said, "we do not have a car, we leave remote safe in house when we go. How far to walk to house from dee station?"

Karl-Heinz gave a big smile. I could tell he was immediately charmed by Pepina. "Ah, yah, iss is very close, five minutes by walking, yah." He added, "I like to go together, show you Winfried home, but I work now, must get back to office."

I assured Karl-Heinz that we were fine and thanked him. "That's ok, Karl-Heinz, the directions we received from Winfried are very precise. Exact German engineering. Pepina and I deeply appreciate you taking the time to help us. Enjoy the rest of your day."

One item that was not mentioned in the AirB&B listing was the flat was up three flights of stairs, with no lift. Struggling with a suitcase in each hand, I made the journey, conjuring up in that alternate reality mind of mine, to believe that I was Sir Edmund Hillary's Sherpa, making the long trek from Mt. Everest base camp to the summit. Pepina was chattering away with just her jacket in hand, wondering poor Karl-Heinz; whether he was born with a disability or had some type of accident. Meanwhile, attempting to not collapse, I finally crested the last step to the front door of our flat. I yearned to plant a flag on the doorstep to cement my momentous struggle to the summit, while futilely trying not to wheeze, but hey, this boy was winded.

The place was impeccable. Winfried was either OCD, or he had a very good cleaning service. On our short walk from the station to Winfried's our noses gravitated to a Doner Kebab shop that was on the main street, just a couple minutes from the rental. The food looked absolutely fresh and tasty. The hauling suitcases pain in the ass was overriding our need to eat. So we hurried to drop off the luggage at the rental so that we could partake in the Turkish fare. *Note - Germany holds the largest Turkish population in the world, outside of Turkey.*

Free from the burden of luggage, we practically broke into a sprint, elbowing each other to get into the front door of the kebab shop, laughing all the way. I ordered up the Iskender Kebab. The smell was mouthwatering: thinly sliced lamb shanks in a tomato sauce smothered in black pepper with pita bread. A nice dollop of plain Greek yogurt topped it off.

Pepina had ordered up an enormous Doner Kebab, which she had difficulty holding with two hands. It was filled with cucumber, tomato, lettuce and tender thinly-sliced lamb. I tried a bite of hers. The Tzatziki sauce was marvelous. The fresh dill was so fragrant. But that sandwich didn't stand a chance against Pepina. I can't think of anything more pleasurable than to gaze at her in ecstasy over what she sees as God's blessing. I have always been a foodie, enjoying cooking my own food. However,

I realized I was in the minor leagues, seeking to graduate into the big leagues… via Pepina's tutelage.

Fully satiated from a delicious meal, we took our passegiata and our usual post-meal coffee and dessert. However, in Germany, from now till eternity, there will be three words ingrained into our brain, and that's *Kaffee und Kuchen* (Coffee and Cake)! No matter where you go in Germany, it always seems like a good time, morning, noon or evenings, for Kaffee und Kuchen. Some of the most wholesome and downright delicious treats exist in Germany: Bienenstich, Rote Grutze, Kasekuchen and of course, Schwartzwalder Kerschtorte (Black Forest Cake). So Pepina and I always seemed to catch one another's eye on occasion. We would both smile to see who could say the quickest, "Kaffe und Kuchen!"

We noticed on the kitchen table that Winfried had left many brochures regarding places of interest. One of the items was a flyer from an indoor/outdoor *schwimmbad* just outside of Hamburg in a country setting. We both loved the water and immediately set off for an adventure.

According to the flyer and checking Google it was just about a twelve-minute drive, so we grabbed a taxi. When we arrived at the luxurious country *schwimmbad*, we were greeted at the front desk. Or, should I say, we were met and given some curious looks by two quite muscular female, middle aged, blonde-haired, blue-eyed Aryan receptionists, who could have been the German National Olympic swim coaches. They wore all white scrubs which were very form fitting. I attempted to ignore their scrutiny. They seemed moderately surprised when the eleven euro each admittance was paid directly. Pepina and I realized we must have been the first olive-skinned Mediterranean couple to have ventured here in quite some time. We spoke only English to them, so we could have been construed as an out-of-place British or American couple.

In the dressing rooms I noticed I would at least fit in with the Speedo crowd. All the German men wore them and I was always most comfortable swimming in them. Of course, when in the States, if you are self-conscious you need to wear baggy swim trunks, or you end up a laughingstock with everyone pointing fingers at you.

The indoor facility was a top-notch, beautiful full-length swimming pool, salt water with five lanes. The atmosphere was stunning, with impeccable lighting, indoor ferns hanging from the walls and I believe the Brian Eno "Music for Airports" soundtrack was playing ever so gently over the sound system. Nice non-skid pavement with intricate mosaic tiles of German fauna complemented the setting.

Pepina and I set off to warm up with a simple breast stroke for one length of the pool. We were just rapturous with the gliding and ease of wonderful cool water. Suddenly Pepina bounced off the side of the pool to immediately begin a powerful free style that was impressive. This girl was possibly related to the Little Mermaid. After another lap she changed into a back stroke effortlessly, knifing her way through the water. I noticed two women geezers with bathing caps standing at the side of the pool admiring Pepina's gracefully powerful form. I admired her too.

After all, I am President and Executive Director of the Pepina Soler Fan Club.

I attempted to teach Pepina my advanced dog paddle stroke, but she just ignored me and continued her laps. There was a small indoor waterfall. When you swam underneath, you came out into the bright outdoor sunlight, into an Elysian paradise. Here is where all the fine toned patrons lounged under wonderful canopies situated under sprawling beech, oak and spruce trees. Multiple hot pools with cooling baths were situated in a handsome design on expertly manicured turf.

We were overjoyed with the exercise, the sheer exhilaration of buoyancy. We also felt like a pair of sore thumbs, noticing that we gathered lots of looks. Then again, it could have been they were checking out Pepina. She was gorgeous in her smooth-as-skin one-piece Ralph Lauren suit with square neckline. She was the prettiest rose in the garden. The lounge chairs had clean towels provided and you could order a vast array of organic juices at a juice bar set up on the lawn. I must say that I could get used to this kind of life. What a gig!

For the rest of the afternoon we swam to our heart's delight. With all the exercise Pepina and I realized we were developing the appetites of two wolves. I asked the juice bar attendant if there were any fine dining establishments in the nearby locale. A very young, tall Turkish man was rinsing some glasses. He had one of those pencil-thin moustaches which he must take considerable time in front of the mirror to groom. Hatchet nose and an Adam's apple so pronounced, you could use it for an ice pick.

The Turk looked at me amusedly, asking what I defined as

'fine dining?' He may have been just showing off that he spoke English well. He had one of those haircuts that seemed so popular nowadays with all the young lads, very short on top, but with one side in the front long that hung all the way down covering one eye. His smirk was growing larger.

So I said, "Is there something that I am missing in this conversation?"

The young Turk took a step closer and leaned toward me just a little bit, lowering his voice, and said covertly, "There is a bet going on amongst all the inhabitants here today. This is a local crowd of hedonistic rich do-nothings. You and the lady are fair game today. About thirty percent think you are Syrian; surprisingly, about another thirty percent think you are Tunisian." He stopped.

Getting a little impatient with this dunderhead, as well as pissed off, I said, "Well, are you going to tell me what the third nationality is?" I could tell he was having some fun on what would be probably just another boring day at the poolside. I short-circuited his idea of humor by asking again, "So that fine dining place? Any ideas, young man?"

His bubble seemed to burst a bit from all the fun he was having. He said curtly, "Do you have a taste for forelle? It's a local fresh water fish."

I replied matter-of-factly, "Does a Pope shit in the woods? Is a bear Catholic?" It was me having some fun now, seeing that he didn't comprehend my comment. I wasn't sure what kind of fish forelle was but I continued, "If it's local fresh water fish, we are on our way." The tall Turk wrote some simple directions on a bar napkin.

When I returned to inform Pepina, she was just getting out

of one of the hot mineral baths. As she climbed out of the steaming liquid, she was glistening in her voluptuousness. My mind traveled to another dimension; her bosom as she skipped up the last step was reminiscent of the Raquel Welch scene in *One Million Years BC*.

Shaking myself back to reality, I told Pepina the good news about the restaurant nearby. She smacked her lips and said, "Gianni! I can't wait to eat some local truita!"

Shit, really? Trout? I said. "So forelle is trout? I wonder if its rainbow trout or brown trout? You continue to surprise me on a daily basis, my lovely signorina. I should have known that you knew forelle was fresh water trout."

"Si Gianni," Pepina stated matter-of-factly. "Germany has clean water. Truita delish!"

We headed for the showers to meet back in the *schwimmbad* lobby in thirty minutes. The restaurant was just a ten minute drive so we hailed another cab. It was nestled on the banks of a good-sized river. The restaurant itself was not fancy. The emphasis was on fresh food.

The menu had not much variety: Pan-fried Trout, Trout *Schnitzel* with *Spaetzle* with Mustard Caper Cream sauce, Poached Trout in White Wine & Vinegar, Celery, Carrots and Leek. Also, Trout *Meuniere* (typical trout rolled in flour), *Meuniere* meaning (Millers wife). It's served up with loads of potatoes. The only other item on the menu that was worthwhile was roasted duck. We both chose the Trout *Schnitzel* with *Spaetzle*. The Mustard Caper Cream sauce was special and once again Pepina was destined to end up back in the kitchen to charm the staff for the sauce recipe.

We dove into our deep meditative dining mode, where not a word is uttered. Eating is close to a religious experience as far as Pepina and I are concerned. The waiter was offended when I asked innocently if the trout was farmed. This restaurant was definitely going into our memory as a worthwhile establishment. After our meal I ordered up a *donauwelle* – a pound cake with sour cherries, topped with butter cream and chocolate glaze. Pepina ordered a traditional *apfel strudel*. We enjoyed our desserts immensely with a cup of steaming strong coffee. Alternating between bites of her strudel and sips of coffee, Pepina looked up at me to wink and say, "Gianni, what a geeg?"

Pepina and I made a promise before we moved on in our travels we would come back here to polish off a duck, which looked and smelled scrumptious. However, as we were about to wrap it up for the ride back to our rental for a well-deserved rest, Pepina said, "Gianni, we get a duck for later. Maybe you fall asleep forget. We not come back. It smells so good!"

I quickly replied, "Si, si! I concur, my love, no arguments here."

Back at Winfried's flat we collapsed from all the exercise and good food. Pepina was out like a light, gently snoozing away, while I kicked back on Winfried's very cozy leather reclining chair to enjoy a glass of delicious dry *Grauburgunder* (Pinot Grigio). I woke up about six hours later, so mad that I fell asleep in that chair. Pepina was still unconscious. I snuggled up to her for additional rest and relaxation, the whole time thinking, *This is just too good to be true.*

There was a small balcony on Winfried's third floor home that overlooked a handsome part of the city. I found myself staring out into the vast expanse of this sprawling city - Hamburg. I found myself leaning slightly over the wrought iron railing. But what I found most peculiar was that I had no clothes on and was screaming, "I'M KING OF THE WORLD!" Suddenly, I felt as if I was being pushed off the balcony. I began to panic, only to find myself being shaken out of my dream by Pepina.

"Gianni, whas wrong, wake up!

I shook my head and smiled reassuringly at Pepina. When I finally gathered my senses, I said, "No worries, my love; hey, it was a joyous dream. I was declaring, in the nude, to the world how much I love you, screaming at the top of my lungs."

"Really Gianni?" she replied, her mind still muddled from deep sleep.

I sat up and began to massage her beautifully uniform petite size seven feet with pink painted toenails. Pepina melted back onto the bed, purring and stretching like a kitty cat. *Meraviglioso*! I could get used to this with the woman whom I love with all my heart.

Is this the something that was just out of my grasp? Or that I never ventured to seek how to achieve that 'something?' Perhaps it has eluded my grasp because I have always been too cowardly in pursuing that something.

<> <>

THE ADVENTURES OF GIANNI & PEPINA

Adventure *#2*

Location – Germany

16

"Faster, faster Gianni! Come on! Don slow down, keep-a going!"

Yes, that's Pepina exhorting me on to keep going, don't falter. I have learned that my lovely lady Pepina has a good appetite for not only all things considered food, but also for speed! We find ourselves hurtling on the autobahn at unheard-of velocity. I grabbed a Peugeot diesel rental so that we can work our way south and eventually into Switzerland for fun and games. While you fly on these well-built German roads, you must keep the ol' eyeball on the rearview mirror. If you spy lights flashing, that is your cue to move over because a vehicle traveling at warp speed will pass in a flash.

We pulled up our travels for a stop in Freiburg, an international university town at the southern end of the Black Forest. Freiburg was founded in 1120 as an independent town, hence the name *Frei* (free).

We booked ourselves in the middle of the old town in a classic hotel with a Michelin-rated restaurant inside. Pepina was eager to become familiar with the immediate neighborhood after a long drive, so we took a stroll on the cobblestone streets. Gothic Freiburg Munster Cathedral was literally a stone's throw away from our hotel.

During our stroll, by chance we stumbled upon a Persian restaurant that had only been open for two weeks. The smell of roasted meats, coupled with fresh scents of basil, dill and oregano, was simply overpowering. I felt like one of those silly old Looney Tunes cartoon wolf characters that can see the aroma then starts floating in the air toward that wonderful smell! I looked at Pepina for confirmation that we should trust our mutual noses and try this restaurant, but her eyes were glazed already; like a zombie, she walked right past me into the establishment.

Between a smattering of Farsi, a touch of Italian and primarily English, we were able to question the wife of the owner (Farahnoush). She seated and served us, apologizing for the workers who were still busy designing the very large dining area. Farahnoush said, "I am very sorry, these gentlemen are measuring the walls, for we are putting some beautiful Persian rugs, mirrors and various drapery for decoration. We are in process of starting restaurant."

She proceeded telling us their story of struggle to get where her and her husband Jahanbin are today, '*mashallah*' (thank God), she would say. She was very upbeat and positive, even when she explained such horrible circumstances. With each serving, she would share a tidbit of the escape from a war-torn country, then scamper away to give help back in the kitchen.

Pepina and I were anxious to hear each and every episode.

This was taking a turn toward a storytelling entertainment-type dining experience. Next, Farahnoush told us that they lost their eldest son two days before the escape, *'inshallah'* (if God wills it*)*, she would say. They were fortunate to able to bury him because his body was still intact after an explosion. We were impressed at how Farahnoush remained so positive in her conviction that God had put them through such a torturous existence but, because it is God's plan (according to Farahnoush), it is a reason to rejoice.

During one course, she brought us extra lavash bread and slices of lemon. She told us that after a few years of poverty in Italy, they were offered better circumstances in Germany. This explained how she spoke some basic Italian. And her husband (Jahanbin) was an architect back in Iran, so he had skills.

Germany has been God's blessing to them, *'mashallah,'* she said. "For look at me! Do I look like I am starving?" she stated while with both hands she grabbed her hips and began to shake her rather plump torso up and down, laughing all the way. Pepina and I praised Farahnoush for her perseverance against so many obstacles. She mentioned also that the only prerequisite to acquire all the amenities of German citizenship… is to learn German! And learn German they both did, with free state-run classes, coupled with immersing themselves in quite a bit of hard studying.

The meal was nothing short of heaven. The juicy wood-cooked meat was marinated and grilled tender to perfection. The vegetables couldn't have been any fresher. Heaps of whole radishes, with the tasty greens attached (la petit dejeuner white tipped variety), bundles of Genovese basil, blood red tomatoes and cucumbers. The yogurt drink with mint was refreshing. We couldn't quite make out the spices for the meat and Pepina was hell-bent into getting our Farahnoush to let her back in the kitchen to see if she could get some recipe information. I had to laugh at Pepina's tenacity in discovering new recipes for future enjoyment. We will definitely both benefit from finding new ways to challenge ourselves in la cucina. Yes!

"Gianni, Chef tell me it's the turmeric, cumin, paprika and sumac in the soy sauce. This issu marinate. I theenk it not create flavor we had in the meat. I think they no tell me all of a-recipe, but we will try!" That's another thing I love about Pepina... I look forward to all the tasty home cooked food that I shall partake in! Hey, what's that old adage? (The way to a man's heart is through his stomach.)

After we settled the bill, we were on our way for a good walk to digest the feast. However, Farahnoush waved to us to come over to a fresh table she had just finished setting. Farahnoush said insistently, "Look, as my new friends, you have to stay just for a few minutes. I have some tea and sweets for you." Pepina and I looked at each other. We obliged and seated ourselves at the table because we now noticed that we were the only patrons left in the restaurant.

Farahnoush came whisking out of the kitchen with a pot of tea and a good-sized shallow pan that looked like very freshly made baklava! Farahnoush hustled to the table and said in a hurried voice, "Look, I am nervous. I know you two beautiful people know food. Please, I just make this, but I am trying many ways. Give me honest opinion. I will not be insulted if poor, but greatly appreciative for knowing where to improve."

We needed no coaxing, immediately digging in the flaky,

honey-drenched gift from God. I have had baklava far and wide, but this was tops. I heaped praise on Farahnoush, for her work had surely paid off. But I noticed Farahnoush was not paying any attention to me whatsoever; the whole time her eyes were riveted with waiting interest to hear what Pepina had to say. I watched Pepina slowly and methodically taste the sumptuous dessert with her eyes fixed on Farahnoush. Pepina measured her words.

"The pistachio issu quality, bery good, I believe honey issu pure orange-a blossom honey, the light vanilla issu ok amount, and uh cinnamon good." Pepina paused to let the taste savor in her mouth then, said confidently to Farahnoush, "Farahnoush, I theenk you use juss little too much rose water."

With that said, Farahnoush bolted straight up out of her chair with the biggest smile on her face and said loudly, "MERCI! Exactly! All you said is true. I know that you are one to give truth. I did make measure wrong with rose water. Mille grazie, merci!"

Later, as we relaxed back at the hotel, I was lounging on the bed, sipping a bottle of *Weihenstephaner* (German wheat beer). Pepina was intrigued by the name Farahnoush and researched its meaning. "Gianni look," Pepina said while holding her mobile and reading to me. "See what the name Farahnoush means. It says -one who is at all times joyous- How wonderful Gianni! Such beautiful name. And she is so much joy in her talking, juss like her name."

<><>

THE ADVENTURES OF GIANNI & PEPINA

SUISSA:

Adventure # 3

17

With talk of some serious hiking on our agenda, we pushed off south to Switzerland, or as Pepina says, "Suissa." We finished our second week of the Giovanni & Pepina road trip, and I must admit thinking back to when Livia in Vieux Nice read the wine lees in Pepina's cup and she said 'we fit each other like a glove.' It was as if we had always been together, a rendezvous from the past, a familiarity, a comforting love that could never be extinguished. We knew each other's tendencies, anticipating each other's needs.

First would be a brief stop at the University of Zurich Botanical Gardens. One of the features of this botanical garden is the three-domed greenhouses that have separate themed environments: 1) Rainforest, 2) Tropical, 3) Savanna. Also, there is quite a large pond where you can take in one of the most incredible frog choruses. There are about 6,000 plant species. We spent one entire day in total freedom, roaming the property, as well as taking an afternoon siesta for a couple hours under the shade of some large conifers. It was a delightful hiatus before moving onto our next location, Lake Lucerne.

Mt. Pilatus was our goal. The elevation would be a factor for sure. From our wonderful warm flat in Kriens we would wake up to cow bells in lush green pastures. Pilatus sits at an elevation of 6,900 feet (2,130 meters). It would be a challenging twelve kilometer ascending trek. A restaurant awaited us at the summit, coupled with a very unique cogwheel train ride back down from the peak. This particular cogwheel train is world-renowned for its record 48% incline, making it the world's steepest. Our rental flat was outfitted with a couple sets of hiking poles that anticipated the need for our journey, and they proved invaluable.

The vast expanse of forest green countryside was breathtaking. The clear turquoise sky contrasted strikingly against the distant Swiss Alp peaks. The Eiger and Matterhorn were visible along our hike, even though they were at least 100 kilometers away. The crisp, cool air was delicious. We reveled sighting in the far distance, on steep mountain crags, small herds of ibex. We packed plenty of water and some light snacks for our four-hour hike. About halfway through our hike and at about the 4,000-foot elevation, Pepina spotted in the far distance, dropping down a few thousand feet in a valley, a tiny little church in the middle of nowhere. You could see the trails of numerous switchbacks that you had to endure to reach the final destination of this tiny place of worship literally in total isolation.

Pepina cried, "Gianni, look. Iss so far away, iss that a crucifix on top? Iss so small. Can you see? Look."

Feeling jolly, I replied all in good humor while focusing on the object. Being quite irreverent, I was slowly making the sign of the cross. I said in a solemn voice, "Dominus Pizza, Eggs Benedictus, Espiritu Sanchez."

Pepina looked at me with her head tilted questioningly. "You know thas not way to say eet Gianni, eh! Why you joke?"

"Pardon mon cheri! My brief attempt at comic relief," I replied.

A bit off our trail at about 4,500-foot level, we heard the sound of oompah-oompah music coming from a large wooden house with a thatch roof. We decided to investigate and as we approached the music continued to play. I noticed that it resembled more of a large barn than a home. Pepina pointed out a one-lane road behind the structure and a large van parked there. Peeking our noses inside a tall pine door that was ajar slightly, we were consumed by the hearty smell of possibly some hot soup. An elderly couple were busy in a long rectangular kitchen. I noticed on a butcher block table mounds of chopped leeks, carrots, cloves of garlic and potatoes. The couple noticed us with warm smiles. "*Willkommen, willkommen,*" said the old man.

Pepina immediately chimed in. "*Lieber Herr,* the zuppa, what-a iss zuppa you make, minestra? Vegetable zuppa?"

The old man, sensing he could now practice his sparse English, became excited to converse with this lovely visitor. He quickly replied, "Ya, my name is Klaus. This is wife Helga." Helga, realizing she may have just been introduced, forced a smile and halted chopping more leeks reluctantly. Klaus continued. "Festival tonight. 20:00. Uh… please comen. Das ist veggable zoupe, sehr gut…uh very good, Madame."

We thanked Klaus and Helga profusely, realizing we could not carry on an in-depth conversation, so we departed. I was kicking myself for taking this diversion. Pepina also was saying there was nothing more she would like right now than a bowl of hot vegetable zuppa. Irritated, Pepina said, "Gianni! If zuppa was finished, I wanted to eat!" My teeth were sharp for anything at this point. The fresh mountain air, along with the strenuous hike was making us both wish we had brought some real food instead of snacks. "Let's carry on," I stated boldly. "When we reach our destination, warm food awaits at the restaurant!"

We rejoined the trail for another hour or so. More arduous hours of steep inclines with numerous switchbacks. Pepina was a real mountain goat. Her cardio was incredible. While my decrepit lungs (from years of smoking hashish and opium) were working overtime, I gasped keeping up with her. I kept thinking how wonderful the beer was going to taste when we reached Pilatus.

Farther up the trail we met a young Kurdish couple (Jochar and Zhian). They were well outfitted with large Osprey backpacks and top of the line hiking apparel. They were comfortably seated off the trail on a fallen spruce. The tree line was fast disappearing as we gained elevation. They had one of those mini-pocket folding gas stoves with a two cup bialetti mocha pot brewing some delicious smelling coffee. I hailed them.

"Happy trails! What a wonderful idea. Nothing like a little caffeine for the final push to the top!"

Jochar was handsome thirty-ish man and sported a jet-black handlebar mustache. He said that he and Zhian hiked this trail regularly. Zhian possessed stunning brown eyes with long eyelashes and an elegant nose that somehow did not seem to match her face. Her lips were enormous, undoubtedly Botox.

They said they resided in the vicinity at Lake Lucerne. They owned a home furnishings company in Switzerland with three locations and sounded like they were living the dream. They were an extremely kind young couple who seemed very eager to chat once they heard me speak in English. After basic formalities Pepina was asking Zhian if their company carried a certain type of linen or some such. I directed my attention to Jochar to let the ladies carry on. When I told him that we were Americans he stated that they both had a goal of going, some day to New York and California. I smiled and said, "Jochar, we have a saying; it goes like this: Nice place to visit, but wouldn't want to live there." He laughed heartily while he twirled one end of his waxed handlebar mustache and stated that they had something very similar to that saying in Kurdish.

Not wanting to delay our trek any longer Pepina and I said perhaps we would see them up top and invited the handsome couple for a beer later.

As we gradually ascended we were pleasantly surprised at the abundance of color, as we spotted in the scree some of the hardy flora native to this at-times rough environment. We found various lichens glued to the rock face. We came across an Alpine Anemone (Pulsatilla alpine), Alpine toadflax (Linaria alpine) and Mountain Valerian (Valeriana montana).

"Oh Gianni, let's take photos for poor Iker. She would love to seeing these flora that maybe grow here only, no? The colairs are so soft." The toadflax had exquisite small purple and orange flowers. The anemone was a beautiful light yellow that reminded me of hibiscus. The valerian was delightful, with long tall stocks capped off with a bundle of miniscule pink flowers.

Even at the cooler elevation I was sweating profusely. My back was soaked beneath the light weight of my backpack. Pepina was as cool as a cucumber. We both marveled at the panorama, stopping occasionally to breathe in the thin, crisp air. Occasionally, I sneaked in a hug and kiss. Always the joker, I was unable to resist kidding Pepina. I said, grinning, "I would like to take you into the woods and show you where the squirrel buries his nuts."

Pepina replied, "The forest is behind-a us Gianni. No squirrels here, eh? Juss lots of rocks and some flora, we mus be careful, no falling." Her naiveté just made me love her all the more. I felt like jokingly showing her. 'Oh yeah? I gotta squirrel here for you, baby!' But I resisted with a smile, rejoicing in my utter pleasure at being in her company.

We crested the summit in four hours and 20 minutes. We did make a couple of stops. That's not much consolation for me; this venture made it very clear to me that I was way out of shape. My tongue was hanging like an old hound dog. Pepina's face was flushed when we reached our goal. We both gave each other weak smiles with both hands on knees, huffing and puffing. The complex at the top was impressive. I was unaware that there was a 30-room hotel at the summit. There were many passageways through the solid rock mountain; some were natural, some manmade. There was so much to see at so many angles: the sweeping vista of the Alps or the stunning panorama of crystal blue Lake Lucerne and its 80,000 inhabitants in the far distance.

At one vantage point close to the restaurant, there was an outlook, where on a clear day (we were blessed with crystal clear skies) we viewed the Wetterhorn, Mittelhorn, Matterhorn, Aletschhorn and Schrekhorn. Let's face it; all the horns were covered! We both enjoyed reading about the myths regarding

Mt. Pilatus; one was it was named after that infamous fellow Pontius Pilate who condemned Jesus Christ to his tragic end.

Originally, it is said Pilate committed suicide and the Emperor Tiberius chucked his body into the Tiber river, which immediately flooded, rejecting the body, so he had it removed and placed on the Swiss mountain. Centuries-old gossip says that every good Friday the ghost of Pontius Pilate appears to wash his hands of the blood of Christ in a small lake on the mountain. Another legend said it was the home of fierce dragons and nobody for ages dared climb it. A red dragon has become the branding logo for Mt. Pilatus.

The views were so breathtaking that after an hour of wandering about we finally realized we were starving, so we headed to the restaurant. Pepina ordered *Kalbsfilet an Honig-Rosimarinesauce mit sautiertem jungen Lauch und Butterneudelin...* got that? Basically, veal filets in a honey rosemary sauce with butter noodles. I ordered two *Kalbsbratwurst* which were grilled to perfection and drowned in a rich, thick brown gravy that I would like to drown in. A hefty portion of grilled onions complemented the carnivorous meal. I washed it all down with three *Quollfrisch* beers, a light lager which is popular in Suissa. Pepina was not too enthused about her meal, stating that the sauce was overly sweet from too much honey.

We kept our eyes peeled during our meal to see if we would run into Jochar and Zhian for a drink, but to no avail. Pepina was interested in the cogwheel train ride back down the peak, so after coffee and one dessert of '*aux fraises tiramisu*' (Tiramisu with strawberries), which we shared, we headed for the station for our exciting cogwheel train ride. And what an extraordinary ride it was! The 48% steep incline is no joke. First of all the seats in the small single carriage that contains 38 passengers maximum are all offset to equalize the severe downward descent. Otherwise, everyone would just fall into the front of the carriage.

The journey down was information overload as we tried to take in the striking beauty of the high snowy peaks and ibex roaming in small herds, clinging to the rock face. I only was able to take a handful of photos while just taking in the experience slack-jawed. Pepina, meanwhile, was jumping from seat to seat like a little girl who has visited the circus for the first time. Pepina cried, "Gianni! Look! The goats! The wild goats. Take peek-ture Gianni, hurry!"

There were only a handful of passengers besides us. Pepina was so exuberant that the other guests became excited as well. They were snapping off photos and chattering excitedly in a variety of languages. Pepina's positive life force is very contagious. She was actually accurate in her description of the ibex. They at times are also called 'steinbock.' They are a species of wild goat that thrive in the European Alps. The male ibex have the most prolific long curled horns that you will ever see. They develop quite a prolific pitchfork shaped beard as well. Or should I say goatee.

The steepness of the cogwheel train was no exaggeration. At certain points during the journey down Pilatus, you had to remain in your seat or else you would experience firsthand the law of gravity. We were grateful to experience this very unique steep descent back down Pilatus en route to Alpnachtstad; there was no way physically possible that we could have attempted to venture back down by foot.

Right down the street in Kriens, 50 meters from our stay, was a community indoor pool. Pepina and I could not believe our luck. Being too knackered after a long day of labor on the mountain, we awoke the following morning, and after some affectionate early morning lovemaking, we took our time, finding it almost impossible to unwrap ourselves from each other's embrace. With tremendous effort we launched ourselves out of the bed trap. Our B&B had lovely fresh-baked brioche and strong black coffee. The brioche was so buttery rich. We licked our plates clean. Pepina looked at me beseechingly to say, "It's ok for another brioche…" but, thankfully, she answered her own plea by stating, "Hey! What you theenkin Gianni? We go swimming to exercise. No more *Kaffe und Kuchen*. Let's sweem Gianni!"

I responded accordingly. "I just want you to know, my lady, for future reference, I will have the last word … And my last word is - yes, dear."

Pepina threw our bathing suits, a couple of towels and a bottle of acqua minerale in a bag and we were off to the community pool.

There was a young lady, perhaps twenty years old, who had long, silky brown hair that reached the bottom of her back. She was wearing a red lifeguard jacket with a white Swiss cross and big white letters that said GUARD, red shorts and a pair of flip-flops. She met us at the entrance door. When Pepina greeted her the young lady broke into a beautiful smile and began to speak quite fluent Spanish with a halting German accent. She told Pepina she spent one year at the University of Madrid her second year in college and that it was her dream to move to Spain and start a small business. Pepina praised her for her enthusiasm and said that she was confident of her success.

The young lady said her name was Gudrun, but her friends called her 'Goodie.' She also mentioned that the facility was only for locals. However, she welcomed us in and said to please enjoy ourselves. As we headed to the restrooms to change I received a call on my mobile which had a 213 area code, which I recognized as Los Angeles. I hesitated answering but Pepina said it might be important. I told Pepina to go ahead and that I would join her momentarily, after I took the call.

The voice on the other end was masculine. He asked me if I was Dr. Giovanni Pisano. I answered in the affirmative and immediately asked what this call was regarding.

He responded by asking, "Are you the legal guardian of Valeria Vidal?"

VALERIA

18

Unexpectantly I received a call from a drug rehab center in Malibu, California. They asked me if I was Dr. Giovanni Pisano and if I was the legal guardian of Valeria. I confirmed the identification; at a loss , I asked who I was speaking to… I was put on hold. Valeria soon was on the phone and spoke in rapid Italian so that whoever was in earshot couldn't understand. Also, she had to lie about the whole step-father/legal guardian thingy because it was the only way to access the phone in rehab. "Dad doesn't know, don't ask questions…" I obeyed.

In short Valeria related to me that the 'guests' (aka AirB&B Danes) were experiencing some difficulty with the cable system. She informed them that she was unable to go due to a schedule conflict. But she would be able to be there the following early morning to see if she could remedy the issue.

The next day Valeria arrived as promised and while she was fiddling with the remote and cable network, she noticed that the Danes left what she thought was a sprinkling of cocaine on the coffee table with a rolled-up dollar bill next to it. In a moment of weakness, by stealth she fingered just a miniscule amount some of the white powder on the sly, for a quick rub on the gums, only to find out it was cut with a microscopic amount of fentanyl. Having been clean for so long and never ingesting that dangerous drug, she immediately passed out with a barely perceptible heartbeat. Fortunately, the Danes were in the house, panicked and called 911. Hence, she was back in rehab. Valeria admitted what a dumbass move that was and that she regretted that she could make such a bad decision, taking a couple steps back in her life.

My desire was to not panic and show anger toward these Danes, or her. If I said a word or two out of line Valeria would terminate the call. I reassured her all would be well and to take the proper course at the center without any issues. If they referred her to 12-step brainwash meetings or whatever… just go along with the program like a happy camper; it would all work out fine. But I already had plans in my mind to book a flight and take care of those motherfucking Danes and get them packing back to where they came from. Perhaps a year ago, last time they visited, they were supplying drugs to Valeria—who knows? We ended the conversation on good terms. Valeria agreed, surprisingly, that she would contact me the moment she was released from rehab. That was a first. Valeria never promised me shit.

Not wanting to put an entire damper on our day, I snapped on the ol' Speedo and joined Pepina, who was doing an impersonation of a dolphin with her steady, firm freestyle swimming. I gazed at her lovingly as she bounced effortlessly off the side of the pool, transitioning into the backstroke. She spied me leering at her, broke her rhythm and quickly came to the side of the pool to question me in regard to the call. I attempted to pose like the God Neptune - damn! Where was my trident? The pose was impotent.

While I was flexing my musculature, Pepina gazed up at me but was unimpressed. She said, "Iss ok Gianni, telefono iss ok?"

I responded in my most cavalier fashion. "Nothing in the least to worry about, my little mermaid. Let's swim and I'll tell you later, after swimming, ok? No problems."

Pepina laughed and said, "Eh! You call me a fish now? Eh! I no mermaid Gianni. Maybe a shark. I eat you later! Heehee."

In my warped brain I thought but did not verbalize, *Oh yeah! I'll give you something to eat!*

After a refreshing and wonderful hour of swimming, we were ready to return to our B&B. As we departed, Pepina exchanged phone numbers with the young pool attendant with the promise of speaking again if she moved to Spain.

Over a cup of coffee for me and a cup of chamomile for Pepina, I took a bit of time to explain the drug rehab call with Valeria and to detail to her all the history that had transpired so far regarding Valeria and her father Gustavo, making sure nothing was lost in translation.

Pepina was a good listener. She seemed tentative at first, then responded with confidence. She spoke carefully, for now it was my turn to listen fully. She said, "You know Gianni… Estats Units not been in the basket for a-places to veesit for me. Please do not offend. Iss juss too many bad things and… too many guns. Society don need guns. People don need guns. But, in America, you need guns! You do! You say sometime to me, why I don look excite when you say about America. Im excite to be with you, my dear Gianni. You are my angel, I have been told."

I chuckled and said that added to the list of many items that I had been called.

Pepina added, "Gianni, you have a … how do you say? Life connect with Gustavo and Valeria. They are friends of you. They are familia of you. You weel help if you can. No worry about me. I come too. We go."

We had packed enough clothes for a couple weeks' trip throughout Europe. So instead of returning to France, we booked a direct flight to Los Angeles International Airport, from Zurich. I quickly called Henri, briefly explaining the circumstances, asking him to look after the homestead and, of course, to help himself to all the luscious fruit (whether on trees or elsewhere).

Henri knows how I dote on Valeria and the reason why she confides in me, her communication problems with her father Gustavo. Henri also knows Valeria and yours truly are on the same wavelength as far as our predilection for and addiction to drugs. Henri has spoken to both Gustavo and Valeria via phone on a few occasions, but they have never actually met. We ended the conversation by Henri asking, "Gio, you will have your hands full with the culinary situation, no? Pepina has not been to the States. She will be most disappointed with the local fare, yes?" Henri really knows how to cut to the chase.

I said, "*Mannaggia!* That goes for us both, Henri. Do you think I care for the California hot dog, burger and fries culture? After we take care of business, we will be back ASAP."

I phoned Gustavo to let him know we would be on the West Coast and I was looking forward to him meeting Pepina. He said that my voice sounded different.

I said, "It's called happiness, Gus." We would be in town soon and I wanted him to take some time from his busy schedule for a get-together.

Gustavo couldn't believe his ears. He said jokingly, "Hey, Gianni! You lucky *bastardo*! Does Pepina have any sisters?"

"You don't know what you're saying," I replied. "You are better off at work, Gus. Trust me. You're on your own in the ladies' department."

He said that he was more than happy for me and would be more than intrigued to meet this Pepina from Barcelona. I attempted to make the call short but he interrupted me to ask if I had any communication with Valeria. I hated to deceive Gus. However, I couldn't break the bond of trust with his daughter. It was just as difficult, if not harder to break my bond to Gustavo. It was just easier for Valeria to confide in me. I would eventually explain to Gus what a parent needs to know. Hey! How do you like that? Me (non-parent) instructing my pal Gustavo (parent) of what a parent needs to know. Makes sense to me.

Before ending the call, Gustavo said, "Gio, Valeria told me two weeks ago that your rental is booked for almost a month by a returning Danish couple. Where are you going to stay? Did they cancel?"

Thinking quickly, I said, "Uh, yeah, you're right, Gus. My townhouse has customers. However, Pepina and I will be checking out a lot of SoCal, maybe take her over to Santa Anita to bet on the ponies, head up to Big Sur, San Francisco—you know, for Pepina it's her first visit to the States." *Whew! I pulled that one out of my ass fairly quickly. Will Gus buy it?*

He responded, "Oh no, you don't. You both are going to stay with me until you get settled. I won't take no for an answer."

"Look Gus," I objected. "That is too much; there is no need to…"

Gustavo stopped my protest and said, "Signore Pisano, you told me the flight. I will be at LAX to pick you up. Not taking no for an answer."

Knowing very well where Valeria received her belligerent nature from, I decided to submit. After all, the ol' apple doesn't fall far from the tree.

"You win, Gus. I will contact you if the flight is late."

Gustavo was overjoyed. "That's what I want to hear. You two will have the whole house to yourselves for as long as you want. Ciao Gio! See you soon, *una bacio per Pepina.*"

I filled Pepina in on the arrangements with the hope that all would be well, with the promise that as soon as I could evict the damn Danes, we could venture up to Sequoia, Kings Canyon and Yosemite National Parks. Also, Olympic National Park and do some real hiking in beautiful rain forests and take in the many waterfalls. Pepina's eyes gained interest and made me tell her in more detail about the Pacific Northwest. Knowing Pepina's love of eating, I attacked her Achilles' heel and began to boast about the fresh-caught fish in the ice-cold rivers, wild sockeye salmon roasted outside with aged cedar wood from the forest. I was just warming up, when Pepina begged me to stop and just book the tickets, the sooner the better. She asked me to fill her in some other time when she wasn't so hungry.

I booked business class for our flight. Pepina had never been on an 11-hour non-stop flight and I wanted it to be comfortable for her. On my numerous flights back and forth to the States, I always booked economy, but would fork out a few extra shekels for the seats with extra leg space with nobody in front of me. There was no way we would even attempt to consume airplane food. So we put together a couple of killer prosciutto and capacollo panini with provolone formaggio. Pepina made a medley of olives with finely chopped celery, yellow bell pepper and parsley, drowned in olive oil, which we could mop up with our panini. Lastly, a few pears, oranges and kiwi fruit.

As always, I would not be short of various prescription tranquilizers and sleeping pills. When I traveled solo, I usually would tell the airline stewards not to wake me for refreshments because I would be unconscious for about five hours of the flight, thus cutting down the long journey. I would refrain from doing so on this trip with Pepina. Prior to takeoff Pepina had both pilots' avid attention - you guessed it; Pepina was up front in the cockpit, quizzing them on the maximum speed of the jetliner. At what altitude do they cruise? What is the difference in wind resistance at 38,000 feet versus lower altitude and its effects on velocity? When she finally came to be seated she said, "You know? Gianni listen, we can go-a reach Mach 0.86. Do you know how fast that is, eh? I tell you, 1060 kilometers per hour!"

"I'm impressed," I said. "It looked like the pilots were impressed with you cara mia."

Pepina replied,, "Don be idiota man Gianni. Madonna mia! The older pilot, he say Alba, he knows, say to me what a great dancer she is. I no want to ask him details…I knowing Alba."

So, I thought, *the notorious 'chin in the pencil sharpener' sister gets around. What a small world indeed. When I met her formally she was dancing with a young Colombian trumpet player. I said* reassuringly to Pepina, "Good for Alba. She seems to always be having the life of Riley."

"Eh Gianni," Pepina said with a bit of irritation in her voice. "She has sad times. I don know who Riley? I don know she meet any Riley."

Changing the subject quickly, I was figuring in my brain the formula for converting kph to mph. I said enthusiastically, "You know, Pepina, I think in miles per hour the speed this jet liner can reach is 645 miles per hour."

Adjusting her seat belt Pepina said dismissively, "Si Gianni, I know, 658.6. Be exacte Gianni."

I worked out the exact math later, after we were airborne. Pepina's math was spot-on.

<><>

The New World

19

We were predictably a couple of zombies upon arrival to the New World West Coast. Pepina spent a majority of her time reading a book by Nuria Perpinya or she was listening to music from Reggae to Rock. She never once watched any of the movies on offer. She would check the in-flight monitor for velocity, reporting to me each time.

"Gianni 922 kph, Gianni 1009 kph."

I was imbibing a bit too much and Pepina gently reminded me that there was always tomorrow. She was my lovely *designated flyer*.

As promised, Gustavo was waiting for us with open arms and, lo and behold, Valeria was standing next to him with a big smile! I tried my best not to look dumbfounded. I honestly didn't know who to hug first... so I refrained either and simply introduced Pepina. As we were loading into Gustavo's Volvo SUV, Valeria said she drove separately and would give me a call later. I gave Valeria a big hug, and she whispered in my ear to read her messages when I got settled. I gave her a wink and we were off. Pepina and Gustavo were animatedly chattering the whole ride back; 99% was Pepina asking in bullet train Spanish about a wide variety of topics in Argentina, including food, Tierra del Fuego, Patagonia, the tango and politics.

Gustavo has a wonderful home in Encino that is now worth a small fortune. Such a waste, since he is hardly ever there. He lives at work. He must have had a couple of maids come in to clean, because every time I had ventured to Gustavo's the dust was a thick as a brick.

Upon arrival, he immediately excused himself, saying that he had two surgeries scheduled for late afternoon. He directed us to sleep for eight hours. I thanked the doctor for his strict rest prescription and he was off. This was a six-bedroom, five-bath on a fairly large parcel of land, with a covered, heated pool. So Gus told us to take our pick of the rooms. While we were unpacking—actually Pepina was unpacking—I was guzzling a couple of Carlsberg beers from a loaded refrigerator. Ironic how I was drinking Danish beer. Not fifteen minutes after Gus went back to work Valeria phoned.

I answered, "Pronto."

Valeria responded immediately, "Dad's left already, right? Work is his place of worship."

I replied, "Bingo, you got it, Valeria. Ok, what's the news?"

A voice tinged with a hint of guilt said, "Strange timing, Gianni. I would have given you the heads up. But they released me when your flight took off from Barca, and Gianni…"

I replied with feigned loss of patience. "Yes?"

Valeria changed her tune. "I am so incredibly happy for you! Mio Dio! Pepina is a dream come true. I know I just met her at LAX, but something inside me says that you are both meant for each other. How did it happen? Anyway, tell me soon, I want to know."

I changed my tune as well, getting down to the issue. "Thank you for your kind words, Valeria. But what's the scoop with the Danes?"

Right away Valeria responded. "I haven't had time to…"

I interrupted. "When did you get the cast removed from your arm?

As expected there was a delay, and then… "I don't understand, Gianni, what cast?"

Unable to refrain from being a smart ass, I replied, "I figured because you had broken arms you were unable to take time to call the Danes."

Say it was because it was a long flight or I was fed up with the drama. At this point, I didn't care. Expecting Valeria to hang up or chew me out, I waited. There was breathing on the other end, silence, then she spoke.

"Ok Gianni, you got me on that one. Maybe I am not as capable as you think. I was overjoyed when I heard last minute that you were arriving, and not alone. I wanted you to take care of the situation before I made a different mistake."

Now with reassurance, I helped Valeria feel secure and told her not to worry. I emphasized that I was absolutely confident in her ability; this was just a bump in the road. I told her repeatedly how capable she was.

I also mentioned to Valeria that first thing the next morning I was grabbing a taxi and heading to la casa di Gianni. I would take care of this issue. Besides, I needed to get in the garage to put the battery back in the car.

Where would you be in California without a car, after all? You would be fucked. My car was a classic French 1975 Citroen DS23. This car was a pet project for many years and gave me a connection to the Old World when I resided across the Atlantic.

A few years back, I was contacted by a Hollywood agent who wanted to use the car for a scene in a James Bond movie. Unbeknownst to me, I was one of only three owners in all the United States who had this particular model. The movie studio hounded me for weeks, finally giving up after I refused to return their calls. Their final offer was $15K for a one-week rental. The parts are just too hard to come by. No way was I going to let my vehicle be abused by a bunch of film fanatics. Who knows what condition it would be in when returned? I told Valeria I would call her the next day later in the afternoon.

The following day, after we enjoyed a breakfast of plain Greek yogurt, pumpernickel bread toast with butter and a juicy papaya, I called a taxi. I was hesitant about Pepina accompanying me in case I had a run-in with the Danes, But I wasn't about to leave her alone on her first full day in California. Gustavo evidently came in very late last night and left very early, before the rooster crowed. Last night while we snuggled, Pepina mentioned that on the ride from the airport to Gustavo's, the look and feel of America was one of loneliness or a kind of depression; she said in Catalan, 'depressió i solitud.' I encouraged her to cheer up because we were heading to greener pastures, out of Los Angeles County, through Ventura County, and farther north to Santa Barbara.

About twenty minutes into our taxi ride I received a call from Valeria. She informed me that she received an email over a day ago from the Danes, who were already back in Europe. Valeria said the email was in her junk mail because they used some other unidentifiable email address, mentioning that it was a fluke that she caught it the next day. They mentioned there was still more than a week left on the rental but they had to get back due to a family issue.

I told Valeria that I would call her later. I had half a mind to ask the taxi to turn back to get our luggage, but I didn't want Gustavo to think we didn't appreciate his hospitality. Surprisingly, there was very little traffic and we made it in no time. Pepina was impressed with the townhome and the location.

"Oh Gianni, we so close to ocean. That is Pacifico, I want my toes in *el mar Pacifico* Gianni," she said pleadingly.

The place was sparkling clean. The tile and wood floors shined. Not a speck of dust. The bedrooms were made and the bathrooms gleamed, smelling of tangerines. On the butcher block in the kitchen was a humungous basket with assorted dried fruits (dates, figs and apricots), a pack of raisin biscotti and an eight-ounce tin of walnut oil. On the living room coffee table were two bottles of Napa wine (Zinfandel and Cabernet Sauvignon). Just the Cab, a Silver Oak 2013, was at least $125 a bottle. The Zinf was a 2014 Vineyard 29 at about $80 a pop! I cried, "Che cazzo!"

Pepina ran from the kitchen into the living room. "Gianni! What happen, you ok? Don't use that bad word Gianni, not good for you."

I was thinking that these Danes were laying it on pretty heavy with the 'I'm sorry' routine. They must have made quite a few shekels dealing drugs. I was just happy that they were out of the country and I could close the door on this incident. I would have to go over the vetting process with Valeria when we talked, and that would be no time soon. I would let her sweat for just a bit.

Pepina was back in the kitchen, this time making some coffee. I was off to the garage to get the ol' Citroen fired up. I always change the oil, coolant and tune it up prior to a trip abroad. I also disconnect the battery. Like a charm, she started right up. Before backing out of the garage I called Pepina over to check out my wheels. She came holding one of my silver trays with our coffee and a few biscotti. She stood on the landing before stepping down into the garage. She just stared in puzzlement, eyeballing my work of art.

"Gianni? How old you again? Is this a 74 Citroen? Is it one with fuel you inject? How you say? Or one with just carbon (she meant carburetor)."

"Minchia! How the hell?" I reached over to turn off the engine, to get an explanation on how my sapote girl was a classic car expert. Pepina stepped down from the landing into the garage walked over to place the coffee tray methodically on top of the washing machine, picked up her café con leche, took a sip and said with a cool and calm voice, "Father had 19 cars Gianni, I drive them all. Eh! Don say minchia Gianni, bad word."

Just to bust her chops a little bit, I walked around the sleek emerald green front end of the car, came over gradually to pick up my coffee, took two casual sips and said, "You were wrong; it's a 1975. The last year they produced the Citroen D23. Oh, and it's the carbon, not the fuel you inject."

We both were now trying to be subdued while sipping our coffee but, finally couldn't hold back laughing. I said she could drive around the neighborhood if she fancied. "But don't go on the freeway."

Pepina finally said, "She only four cylinder. 113 horses. Iss ok

Gianni. Maybe I drive later. She has good figure, no?"

I grabbed Pepina, warmly squeezing her in my arms, and said, "I know who has a 'good figure,' right here in my arms!"

While I bit her gently on her neck, Pepina squeaked because I discovered a while back that that's one of her most ticklish points. I was guiding Pepina out of the garage, back into the house so that I could give her the private real tour of our house, when my mobile rang. Gustavo. I looked at Pepina, who was able to escape my embrace. She made sign language for me to answer.

I said, "*Hola Dottore*! Wha…"

Gustavo jumped in. "Hey Gio! Look, I have dinner already ordered for tonight. We will dine in, having it catered. Let's say 8pm. Ok?"

Whatever protest, if I had one, would be ignored anyway. I responded, "Yeah, sure Gu…"

"*Va bene* Gio! See ya tonight. Love to Pepina, ciao!'(click).

Gustavo was a real germophobe. He despised restaurants; you had to use their silverware, the tables were not clean, too many people with coughing and sneezing in the dining area, I want to watch the chef's hygiene, etc…. That's one issue that drives his daughter Valeria nuts. Since her childhood, he was always after her with isopropyl alcohol, compulsively washing her hands after she touched a door entrance or whatever.

Pepina mentioned what a nice friend I had and she was much anticipating what food was on the menu. I laughed just a wee bit and mentioned that she could bet that the meal, whatever it might be, would be prepared under the strictest of standards, ultra kosher and sanitized. All vegetables would be top organic. All meat would be halal. Pepina began to giggle, saying because

Gustavo was a sturgeon, he liked to be steroid… (I figured she knew he was a surgeon and liked to be sterile).

With the Danes thankfully back across the pond, home secured and the wine and fruit basket loaded into the trunk of my classic wheels, we took off back to Gustavo's. But not before, as promised, I took my lovely *Signorina* to the beach to dip her dainty toes in il mare pacifico.

It was a cool day with a few pillowy cumulus clouds scattered in a pale bluish-gray sky. There was a slight offshore breeze at the moment. We parked, took off our shoes, rolled up our pants and took quite a long stroll, just enjoying the sound of the lapping waves and watching the little sandpipers sticking their chopstick-like beaks into the wet sand in search of sand crabs.

As we walked and held hands, I would steal a glance at Pepina to witness the pure joy she felt as the breeze gently pushed her thick, wavy chestnut hair back. Her mouth was open, taking in deep breaths of the moist, salty air. She would stop from time to time, moving her feet in the water, as if listening, then continue to walk. She finally said, "The water is in pain Gianni, how does one say? I feel the water here is hurting." I just nodded my head without saying a word. We continued our stroll, breathing in the air. I had a bitter taste in my mouth. Was it from the water that Pepina mentioned?

After about a three kilometer walk, we reached a jagged rock jetty that stretched far beyond the first set of waves. We did an about-face and began to walk back the way we came. Halfway back we spotted something about 50 meters ahead of us. It was lying where the rolling surf met the sandy shore. As we approached, we identified what it was. It seemed delicately wrapped in glistening bronze-colored seaweed: a dead baby bottlenose dolphin.

It was already known to me how tuned in Pepina is to nature and the surrounding world. Her sense of time and space is to be admired. She felt the coming death of that life in the ocean. She made me aware that something was afoot. She stared at the lifeless creature for quite some time, in deep concentration or silent prayer. I stood by patiently. Eventually, we continued walking. Finally, she said, "I want to return that baby boy to the ocean, but the tide is coming in Gianni and it would just wash back up on the beach." She hesitated, then added, "It has poisoned."

She was quiet on the ride back to Gustavo's. It was mid-afternoon when we returned. Pepina said she would like to take a brief siesta. I opted to go for a swim in Gustavo's heated pool, which was refreshing. As I was taking my last lap I heard a splash; a lovely mermaid appeared. I took her into my arms. There was no resistance… only pure love.

The evening at Gustavo's was delightful and eventful. Pepina was excited to meet the catering people, a young British couple with only one helper who hailed from Panama. They took over the kitchen area. Large containers of boiling water sterilized all the cooking gear and eating utensils under the careful gaze of Gustavo. The caterers, it seemed, were very familiar with Gustavo from many past dining events. They were obviously aware of and obeyed his stringent standards for cleanliness.

Gustavo, while holding a glass of wine, said to Pepina, "You are going to love this. The food is out of this world fresh. The menu is…" Gustavo pulled out his mobile and read to Pepina, "We shall dine Mexican! First will be black sea bass tacos, hard and soft, shrimp and chicken enchiladas and quesadilla carne asada. They are known far and wide to make the most incredible pico de gallo, coupled with an incredibly creamy, buttery guacamole. There will be a variety of roasted peppers; sweet red bell peppers, little spicy Poblano and Anaheim green peppers and if you want to get adventurous, the Fresno chili pepper. As you can tell, I have a taste for roasted peppers. Last and definitely not least, the table will be adorned with bundles of fresh organic cilantro!"

Pepina was speechless. In my conversations with Gus I had mentioned that Pepina had taken me to another level as far as enjoyment in the culinary arts. I did not divulge any other areas that we enjoy - that was private.

While I was chatting with the caterer's helper and Pepina was asking the young couple if the chickens they used were farm raised and if they had other chicken friends, I noticed across the hall, the front door opened. As if it was a photo op on the red carpet for the Academy Awards, in walked a bombshell.

She was young, in her mid-twenties, long jet-black silky hair that was draped over her right shoulder down to her waist. Hourglass figure in a clinging green dress that had a slit exposing her left leg all the way up her thigh, and onto her nether regions. Jet black eyes, eyelashes that I could comb my hair with. Full-bodied lips were scarlet red. Green alligator stiletto heels capped off her ensemble. She seductively walked directly toward me without breaking eye contact. My feet were rooted in the floor. She placed one hand on my shoulder and said, "Hola Johnny! Soy Gabriela." She proceeded to plant a kiss on each cheek. She paused while I fumbled to say something. Before I could utter a syllable, she added, "*Donde esta* Gustavo?"

The helper for the caterer yelled across the living room from the kitchen. "Hola Gabriela! Como estas?"

Thankfully Gustavo came running from one of the bedrooms in which he changed clothes. He yelled. "Did I hear Gabriela has arrived? Ah! There she is. Regina Caeli!"

Evidently, my buddy Gustavo had been holding out on me. Before he formally introduced us, they rushed into each other's arms. It looked like either the beginning of a steamy 'R' rated movie or a Greco-Roman wrestling match. During all this, Pepina had joined me by my side to watch the whole spectacle. Pepina whispered in my ear, "Gianni, that can be Gustavo daughter, no? Who is he? Madonna mia! He is beautiful."

They finally untangled themselves. Gabriela was straightening out her dress while rearranging her hair. Before Gustavo said anything, he had pulled a handkerchief out of his pocket and was consciously wiping all the lipstick off his mouth. He missed quite a bit on his cheeks and nose, but both Pepina and I remained mute. Gus regained his composure and said, "Pepina, Gianni, this is Gabriela. Gabriela, these are my dear friends, Gianni and Pepina."

Pepina immediately ran over excitedly to Gabriela, grabbed both of her hands and exuberantly started chatting away in bullet train Spanish, complimenting her on her dress. They shuffled off over to a divan and sat down with their heads so close together, they looked like Siamese twins.

I turned my gaze over to Gustavo and was about to open my

yap when he pulled me back over to the kitchen where the catering helper was making some incredible margaritas. Gustavo told me to remain silent until we had one of the icy drinks with salt around the rims in our hands. After an 'a zalud,' Gustavo winked and said in a low voice, "Look Gio, I can imagine what you are thinking. But allow me to say one thing before you remark. It's an arrangement. I'm not a complete idiot. Don't deny an old fool some enjoyment in life. Gabriela is Venezuelan. We met on a flight from Bogota, Colombia."

"Yeah, I know where Bogota is," I said with a smirk.

"Hey Gio, you think an old bugger like me knows what's happening. That was just a show that we put on. Looks like you fell for it hook, line and sinker. Gabriela needs or, should I say, wants an American passport. I will oblige. It's a mutual understanding. She is a very intelligent woman with a lot of potential. She finished studying law in Los Angeles. Her beauty almost works against her."

I interrupted, "Gus, don't get me wrong. You are like a brother I never had. You know I don't use that word lightly. My circle of friends is miniscule. I don't deny you. I celebrate your happiness. Believe me."

There was a relief in Gustavo's body language as he replied, "Madonna, Gianni. Thank you from the bottom of my heart. I know you, above all, would understand. I have caught a lot of flak from a few directions. She will return to her country before long and find a suitable husband. Gabriela will be a force to be reckoned with in Venezuela. She has big plans to turn that government around."

The catering helper came into the living room area to

announce that the food would be ready in 10 minutes. Just as he did an about-face back into the kitchen/dining room area the front door opened. In came Valeria.

<><>

Let's Dine

We sometimes jokingly complain of our friends as a way of justifying our fickleness in advance.
La Rochefoucauld

20

Valeria casually opened the door, turned and closed the door, did an about-face, took two steps forward, then stood fixed, staring in the direction of Pepina and Gabriela, still sitting on the divan. Immediately I sensed some real family friction here. I glanced quickly to Gustavo, who at once attempted to defuse the situation by joyfully announcing what wonderful timing for the food to begin. Valeria, meanwhile, chucked her purse like a guided missile to the nearest piece of furniture and marched like a drill sergeant into the kitchen. Gustavo headed over to Pepina and Gabriela, asking Pepina if she had time today to go swimming in the pool. I bolted into the kitchen, hot on the heels of Valeria to test her proverbial waters.

I was impressed with the catering group. They were making tortillas from scratch. Valeria was already mopping up some guacamole with pico de gallo with a still steaming hot corn tortilla. She was steaming internally. I gave her a quick hug and before I could open my pie hole, she spun around and said,

"What the hell is he doing inviting that putan here, at this time, at this very special time with you and Pepina!"

I immediately wanted to short circuit an altercation here. "Hey, hey, hey… Valeria, just give me a moment. For the sake of tonight, for me, for Pepina, let's role play. We are on the set for some independent movie scene. We are all actors. This will be a delightful encounter and we all are going to have fine food with stimulating conversation. Can you pull it off?"

Valeria stopped eating and gave me a look as if it was the first time she laid eyes on me. "What the fuck are you saying, Gianni? Ignore that bitch, ignore that knucklehead father of mine? Really?"

I put my foot down. "Let me say this once, Signorina. I have been brought into this scenario just moments ago. You have had some time to chew on this, knowing much sooner than me. Is it possible you don't know the whole story? Or me as well? I would say that's a pretty safe bet. Let it go for now. Trust me. Can we get through this evening without any drama? Valeria, my sweet girl, please enjoy this moment for now. Can you? For me?"

Valeria stared at me for a count of three, turned to stride toward the kitchen counter, grabbed a margarita with no salt on the rim in one hand, one with salt in the other hand, and skipped the few steps back to me with such a brimming smile that I thought she would get saliva in her ears. She said enthusiastically, "I'm so excited about this evening, Uncle Gianni! Aren't you hungry?"

Hmm, didn't expect that. But it was an upgrade over mean, belligerent Valeria… I rolled with the punches. I adopted the air of a British lord and replied in kind. "Yes my dear, indeed! Let us sally forth to enjoy all the evening's fare and libations, shall we?" We waltzed arm in arm into the living room, where Gustavo, Gabriela and Pepina were heartily laughing. I raised my margarita and said, "Here is to happiness and friends. May no glass be empty on this auspicious occasion!" A loud 'Salud' echoed throughout the house.

Pepina jumped up from the divan to come and give Valeria and me a big three-way hug. Pepina had broken out and ironed the one dress outfit she packed for the European trip, in case we went to a concert or opera. It was an all-black ensemble: black short skirt, black short jacket and purple low-cut silk blouse that exposed her lustrous bazookas. I never witnessed Pepina ever wearing real expensive jewelry. But I spied some large sparkling, at least three-carat diamond stud earrings for the first time, which if real made me nervous. She was barefoot, but to me, that accentuated her allure.

Throughout the evening, all attending - even the caterers - seemed to gravitate toward Pepina. She had a personality, a charisma that made one feel that they would be more enriched by her company. I already knew that feeling, as did Henri, Vivian and Jean-Michel, who were entranced by her.

There must have been over fifty candles illuminating the dining area. The setting was buffet style. Gabriela was carrying on a conversation with Valeria that looked friendly. Pepina and I were discussing the schwimmbad experience in Germany with Gustavo. He repeatedly said he was going to take a vacation and join us in Europe. I humored him, knowing that it would never happen due to his workaholic nature.

As the evening progressed Gustavo and I found ourselves back in the living room, kicking back. After Mexican food you feel like sleeping. Contrary to that hypothesis, Gabriela and Valeria were in the swimming pool on a warm Southern California night. Pepina, as always, was grilling the caterers on the recipe for the enchilada sauce. Gustavo and I were enjoying a *Fernet Branca,* mine neat over ice, while Gustavo couldn't help being Argentinean, having his mixed with Coca-cola…Aargh! Fernet is an original Italian digestive, a concoction of saffron, gentian, (which prevents bloating), myrrh and chamomile. This spirit gained such popularity in Argentina that a distillery was built in Buenos Aires in the year 1908.

I told Gustavo, ironically, the truth about how the Danish guests at my AirB&B returned home early regarding a family emergency. So I was able to retrieve my car.

Gustavo was amused and said, "Oh yeah, that relic… Oh pardon, I mean classic car that you have." It glanced off me with a smile.

"Ah! So now you are gonna start busting balls about my car?" We were both laughing now.

Gustavo added, "So, I surmise that your Viking guests left you that lovely dried fruit basket full of goodies and without a doubt, the vino. That vino, Gio, is way too good for your cheap ass palate."

Now that barb stung. I replied, "What's going on, Gus? Is this piss off Gio Pisano night?"

Gustavo straightened up in his chair and took on a conciliatory tone. "Hey paisan, sorry. No offense. Too many margaritas. We have always been straight with each other, right? Well, I may be experiencing just a bit of jealousy. You and Pepina are made for each other."

"That's what people keep telling me," I said. "And I must say, I concur."

Gustavo continued, "I need someone here with me, Gio. I'm tired of being alone. It's just, I'm not sure any woman will put up with someone who is working 24/ 7. Marriage terrifies me. Look what happened with my marriage with Valeria's mother."

Pepina appeared from the kitchen, excitedly informing us that now that she had the recipe for the enchilada sauce, she had many ideas for various meats and seafood style dishes. She was profusely thanking Gustavo so sincerely for his hospitality.

Gustavo stood up and said, "Where are those girls? I have an announcement." We heard the sliding glass door to the back yard open. They were both coming in with towels around their bodies and around their wet hair. Gustavo repeated that after the ladies got dressed to come into the living room. He wanted to say something. They both retreated to the bedrooms to change. Valeria's eyes gave me a quick pleading glance as to what the hell was this 'announcement?' I, without a clue, did not reciprocate. Hopefully, Gustavo didn't have one drink too many.

Gustavo received a call from his Cedars-Sinai Medical Centre concerning a patient. The caterers departed while Gustavo was on the call. The girls returned after their evening swim. I told Valeria I honestly had no idea what was up. Gabriela wasn't catching all the nuances of our talk, so we conversed in Spanish. Gabriela said she had no idea what Gustavo was going to announce; he had mentioned nothing to her in the least. Pepina chimed in, saying that she was sure Gustavo was just going to give out a present or some such. Pepina said in English, "Why so angst? Everybody so much."

Gustavo returned, apologizing that some post-op issue came up with an elderly patient, but it had already been resolved. He was carrying a silver tray with five wine glasses, a bottle of Malbec wine and a small rectangular box with a blue ribbon. He slowly lowered the tray onto the coffee table and poured two fingers of the pigeon blood red Malbec in each glass. He then proceeded to propose a toast to Gianni and Pepina.

"I would like to especially say to my dear friend Dr. Giovanni Pisano, to whom I owe an eternal debt of gratitude. Although he had many serious problems over the years, he never, at any time, would begrudge his time, to give me encouragement, to boldly push me to my potential, even though he may have been suffering himself." At this point, Gus was a bit over the top, laying it on a bit too thick. But I gave him the time and space to finish. "When I first arrived in SoCal, a time which seems so long ago, I felt as if I was a stranger who would never make it in this great land of opportunity. However, Gio showed me the ropes. In all honesty, without his guidance, I would not be here speaking with you today. Anyway! Enough of my blather. I would like to give this small token of my affection to Gianni and Pepina." Gustavo raised his glass once more and said excitedly, "Happy trails, a salud!"

He extended to me the small rectangular box with the blue ribbon attached. I felt like a dolt when he handed it over. I looked at Gustavo, then Pepina, who offered no help by staring blankly in front of her. Valeria was twisting a tassel on one of the divan pillows so much it broke off. Gabriela was self-absorbed, primping her still wet hair. Finally, I opened it. Inside was an envelope, which I had to again open while everyone was on tenterhooks. I rapidly tore open the envelope to end the suspense. I unfolded the letter inside, briefly scanning. There was a simultaneous explosion of … 'READ IT OUT LOUD!' Startled, I cleared my throat and read.

~~~

Courtesy of

Great Pacific America Cruises

Soon you will visiting huge centuries-old glaciers. View ice-capped mountains while navigating ancient fjords that tower far above the Pacific Ocean. Look on in breathless awe at the Aurora Borealis.

You will be in the lap of luxury in your extravagant penthouse suite for two. Your journey to Alaska will feature visits to Kechikan, Juneau, Skagway and Anchorage.

ALASKA IS YOURS!

~~~

Pepina leaped out of her seat and ran over to give Gustavo a big hug. Excitedly, she couldn't speak fast enough. "Will we see pole bears? Do we need shoes to walk in snow? How you say, will many big dogs pull us on sled? How beeg is boat? When we go?"

Gustavo jumped in. "The last question I can answer. You have five days before you both depart from Vancouver, Canada. It's the last cruise of the season before winter sets in. So the time is not negotiable. Bon voyage to both of you!"

Valeria stood up and casually walked over to her father to give him a peck on the cheek. Then she said, "Bravo, Dad. That is very kind and a wonderful gift. I'm so happy and proud that you did that. You are always full of surprises."

I'm not quite sure if that last remark with a bit of irony was a veiled jab at her father. But, I was speechless. I held the paper in one hand and my glass of Malbec (which, by the way, was exquisite) in the other.

Finally, Gustavo felt the need to explain. "Gianni, I know that you have never been on a cruise or had any desire. But, I assure you. From one doctor to another, this prescription is just what you and Pepina deserve. You are going to become a fan, believe me. Two years ago the American Urological Association had their 100 year founding celebration. It was held on a cruise ship for a seven-day cruise to Puerto Vallarta, Mazatlan and Cabo San Lucas. I was hesitant. I was skeptical. I never boarded one of those ships; would I get seasick? Would it be boring? How was the food? I'm telling you right now, it was FANTASTIC!"

I cut Gustavo off while he was on the topic of food. "I can't thank you enough, Gus, really. Tell me what the food was like. I already mentioned to you, Pepina and I are very picky about the food we put in our bodies."

Gustavo was eager to answer that. "Listen, pheasant one night, prime rib the next, Bistecca alla Fiorentina, Duck confit, Grilled Halibut, Ossobuco, Beef Wellington and Carpacio… Merda Gio! What more can you ask for, huh? And, don't forget, you two are going deluxe executive penthouse; so you will receive special VIP treatment."

It was Pepina's turn to weigh in. Any surprise? It was about food! "Madonna, really, Gustavo? Peasant? I have peasant sometime my jardin in Espana. They are sooo delish! They are organico, they eat only my jardin. Gianni, this sound good. I not been on big boat. My friend American Linda, you know, one you make mistake to call Minnie. She always go on big boat and say fantastico too."

I made a point to clarify something to Gus regarding Pepina's 'jardin.' "I haven't told you about Pepina's 'jardin,' Gus. Remind me to fill you in later, ok? Don't forget."

Gustavo nodded his head affirmatively, but I knew he was long gone. The drink was taking its toll. Gustavo was a real lightweight when it came to alcohol. I have more than doubled his booze intake, without even a buzz; that is not a good thing, as I well know.

So it was decided we would depart for the Alaska wilderness in five days. I figured a nice road trip up north through Oregon and Washington would take three days, with a couple to spare for fooling around. Then, we would board our cruise. Gabriela was in the kitchen making us all a fine coffee and three desserts from the caterers: sopapilla, crème caramel and rice pudding. Pepina had already tried all three when she was in the kitchen doing quality control.

While all of us were around the table enjoying our coffee and desserts, Pepina mentioned, "You know Gianni, best we fly, not drive to go to big boat." I was surprised, to say the least, about Pepina wanting to fly again. She was still groggy, I could tell, from the long flight and time change. She added, "Gianni, how does one state? You drive like old nonna."

Gabriela spilled her coffee on the white linen table cloth while laughing, Gustavo burst out howling like a coyote while clapping his hands and cheering. "Brava! Ole!" Valeria was smiling, signaling thumbs-up to Pepina. I sat there, sedentary, in the middle of the table, looking like I had egg on my face.

I gave an even keeled retort. "As some of you may know, I have an impeccable driving record. Do not 'jink' me." I winked at Pepina. "I may at times be accused of driving a bit too cautiously, but it is always with the thought in mind of safety first."

I was now preaching to nobody in particular. Gustavo, Pepina and Gabriela were taking all the remaining desserts from the table to wrap in cling film and put in the refrigerator, which left Valeria and me to chat. I quickly told Valeria, "Listen, Gustavo doesn't have a clue that you took a little vacation to you-know-where. I informed him that the Danes who booked for a month left with over a week remaining due to a family emergency. Which is the truth. It's great that I didn't even need to lie. Or, I prefer to say, I didn't exaggerate the truth. Hence, how I got to pick up the car. Look, as far as I see, all is well."

Valeria leaned far over the table to give me a peck on the cheek. "I can't thank you enough, Gianni. I knew you would fix matters for me; you always do. Also, encouraging me to have a different mindset about tonight was good guidance. Gabriela in most ways is just like me. She just wants to make it in this world. Only, lo and behold, I found out she is really intelligent. I firmly believe she will make a great lawyer if she can finish. She is most passionate about the troubles in Venezuela. I could picture her in the future having some impact from a political sense, really Gianni."

I replied that I was so happy to hear that. "You know, sweetheart, I have always loved you since you were a pipsqueak.

I always will. I'm very proud of you, Miss Valeria Vidal."

The gang was coming back from the kitchen. Gustavo was still chuckling and mentioned that it might be getting a little late for the 'old nonna;' perhaps he should retire for the evening. A smiling Pepina said, "No, no, don't say that Gustavo. We know you do joke only. I joke when I say 'old nonna drive.' I'm sorry Gianni. We having funny laugh, right?"

Gustavo said, "Anyway people, I have an early day at the hospital first thing tomorrow morning. Surprise!" Gustavo continued, "So lights out for me. Heads up, if you hear noise early in the morning, it will be Rosalba the cleaning lady taking care of all this mess. Also, in addition I may add, the pool cleaner Jeff usually arrives early. So if you hear someone sloshing around in the water, it's the pool guy. Buona notte, bona nit, buenas noches and bonne nuit! If I missed any nationalities, tough shit. Good night!"

Gabriela had taken a taxi when she arrived. She asked Valeria if she would mind giving her a lift because she still had some preparation for the upcoming bar exam. Valeria was happy she asked and was glad to oblige. Pepina was woozy from mixing a few sips of margarita, one sip of wine, the huge amount of Mexican food, but most of all the time change. My lady was already heading for straight for the sack. So with the remainder of the evening all to my lonesome self, with everyone retiring for the evening. I wasn't about to let that fine bottle of Malbec go to waste.

With bottle and glass in hand, I found myself in an exquisitely high-back red leather chair in what looked like Gustavo's office or library. The chair was incredible and I wouldn't be surprised if Gustavo didn't somehow appropriate this furniture from the distant past in some Spanish palace during the reign of King Phillip II. The solid fitted oak wood, the craftsmanship, large iron rivets made a secure chair an everlasting one.

With this somehow sacred setting in the quiet of the night, I settled in for a little discussion with that elusive rascal Bacchus. Oh yes, only on solemn and rare occasions does the opportunity arise that I am graced with his presence.

Our discussions never meander, never veer; they are on all things grape: the fickleness of the pinot noir, the dry nature of the 'blood of Zeus' (Sangiovese). Or the luscious yellow/green hue of the Verrdichio. Or, the nasty critters that attack the vine, as well as insects who consume the bad insects. These rare conversations could sometimes take a left turn, like, I could ask him how many centuries it has been since the last time he trimmed his beard. He never cared much for these digressions and before he would beg his leave, I would ask him to not be such a stranger. So, as with all our conversations, when bottle empties our encounter comes to an end.

I was still in the mood for something to do, so I nicked a notepad from Gustavo's presidential style office desk, grabbed a custom Montblanc pen and began to jot down some notes as to how to proceed for the next five days. I felt suddenly compelled to get organized. I wrote:

1) Book flight to Seattle…~~no, Vancouver~~. Fuck Vancouver, let's go Seattle. The ship departs from Vancouver, but we can spend some time piddling around in Seattle first.

  a. Visit Bellevue Botanic Garden.

  b. Pike's Place Fish market, etc…

2) Spend next day or two touring Pepina around SoCal.

  a. Santa Anita, Del Mar races (lady luck with ponies?)

  b. Huntington library

  c. LA Arboretum

  d. Descanso Gardens

3) Just humping at home… which home? End notes. Need sleep.

I was actually looking forward to a good night's sleep. Haven't had any rough dreams for quite some time. I can't begin to fathom how much more incredible my sleep has been (no nightmares, no guilt, no regrets). The last time I actually freaked out was that macabre dream at the Los Angeles Coliseum with Emily.

That unearthly vision shook me to the core. Was Emily trying to communicate to me from the vast beyond? Was it the panic about ever becoming happy? It could have been that I was watching too much English Premier League Futbol during that time. Or was it I discovered that two grams of barely uncut cocaine that I forgot about in a shirt pocket in the closet from over a year ago? I was flying higher than a proverbial kite that evening. So naturally I called Henri to say that I was running late with the Moroccan tagine that I made; it was midnight, Henri - already asleep - agreed with me like it was all so normal until I got there, then, when I arrived, still in hyper mode, he made me some tea and spoke to me like a loving brother, gently bringing me back to the third rock from the sun.

Anyway, what was I saying? Oh yes, Emily. Was it some deep-seated angst from distant lifetimes? I have become a believer in that, tending toward Buddhist thought. My life with Pepina has confirmed that. Instinctively, I have always seemed to gravitate toward the middle way. We are connected, and made the causes to be together. Whatever left turn I took in my life, somewhere down the road it prepared me to be where I am in the present, as well as giving me the wisdom to grasp my past and hopefully, get a grip on the future. Where I am in the present is such a good place!

Santa Anita was at season's end. We would miss Del Mar opening when we were on the high seas. So we ventured to have a day of sun and thoroughbred horses. I have always prided myself on being an above-average handicapper, of course, having had world class tutelage during my youth. Years of training with Zio Gerardo and Melvin were ingrained into my soul.

Everyone who follows the ponies prides themselves on their method, as if their idea regarding the inner workings of horse racing is unique and fail proof. In actuality, since the dawn of history, nobody has solved that mystery; bloodlines of breeding, quality of jockey, turf vs. dirt, how much weight, mud track vs. fast track, five furlong sprint or 1 ¾ mile? So many variables, so many questions. Putting the numbers in a hat and selecting at random sometimes yields the best results. The 'Daily Racing Form' is perched on the altar of knowledge for all horse racing patrons. For those who don't want to shell out the price of the periodical, the daily program will do.

By the time we arrived through the gates, it was already post time for the third race. What did we care? It was a picture-perfect sunny 75-degree, early fall day, and we didn't have a care in the world. Even if I was taking Pepina to a dog show, we would have fun.

We ventured to the paddock area to watch the horses saddle up. The horses then proceeded to loosen up, walking in circles while the jockeys met trainers and owners for last-minute instructions prior to the race.

Pepina was immediately fascinated by the jockeys. She totally ignored the horses. She grasped my arm with one hand and pointing with another at one of the jockeys. She said, "Oh Gianni, I have to talk with these jockeys; they are so interesting. Especially the one in pink silks with blue diamonds on his back. I want to talk with him."

I was at a loss as to how Pepina was going to be able to speak with any of these jockeys; they are very busy with no time between races. I said as much. "Cara mia, there is little chance. They are limited with time in between races and don't have time to socialize."

Pepina took this at face value and did not respond. When the race was getting close to post time I asked her what she thought of the nine-horse field at seven furlongs on the turf. I showed her the odds-on favorite, winner of the last three races, while coming down in class. Also, two turf specialist horses, one from Ireland, the other from Brazil. I showed her the program because the Racing Form was too complex to explain for a beginner.

Pepina wasn't interested in looking at the program. She stated simply, "Don't know that Gianni, boy with pink and diamonds win for sure. She is good, no?"

With the patience of Saint Francis I humored her by looking at her choice. A three-year-old, who had only run in five races total - all in the dirt - going off at high double-digit odds. In reality, the biggest long shot in the nine-horse field. I explained as best I could that that horse had as much chance as her to win this race.

Matter-of-factly, Pepina replied, "Does that cavallo understand odds Gianni? I hear pink boy say to man putting on saddle that his birthday today. He speaking funny espanyol."

I looked again at the form to see that this was an apprentice jockey (meaning rookie, first year riding) by the name of Cedillo. He was a Guatemalan. I relayed that information to Pepina, who replied, "Ah, si Gianni. She has look of some nativa… some-a indi."

I placed bets just in the nick of time; the line at the teller was so long. Everyone behind me was cussing up a storm at being shut out at the window due to the race starting. I played my favorite, who was the class of the bunch, then plunked fifty clams to show on Pepina's refugee from the glue factory with the new Guatemalan jockey. I figured even if it came in at least third Pepina would be excited and get a return on investment.

With wager tickets in hand we ran to watch in person at the finish line. Pepina asked me where the jockeys go after the race. So I showed her the tunnel that leads under the grandstands to the dressing room. She said she would wait there to talk to the jockey. I didn't want to separate due to it being a very crowded, busy day at the races, so we waited by the tunnel entrance.

There was a large screen monitor there conveniently, so we were able to view the whole race with very few people in the vicinity, since everyone was waiting in a crowd at the finish line. Well, kiss my ass… I watched Pepina's 'pink boy' jump out in front out of the six post, proceeding to win wire to wire by two lengths. Final odds were 45-1 ($92 for a $2 win ticket!). Mo#^f@! Why I didn't play that horse to win? Or across the board (win place & show)? Instead of thinking I was doing a favor by just playing to show. Anyway, her horse paid $9.60 to show. For a $50 show ticket investment, the return was $240.00 even. Not a bad return on investment. However, if the same $50 clams was bet to win, it paid $2,300.00

While I was staring at the tote board, mesmerized as to what could have been, I looked to see that Pepina had thrown both legs over the wooden fence and trotted across the tilled earth to intercept her pink boy Cedillo. As most people are, he was charmed by the good-hearted nature of Pepina. I heard her say what a special day it was since it was his birthday. He was so flabbergasted that she knew his birthday. They spoke, they laughed, they hugged. The whole time Pepina was twirling his whip that he let her hold. Finally, he turned to sprint back to the dressing room to prepare for the next race.

As I helped her back over the wooden gate and knocked the wet dirt off her shoes she said excitedly, "You know, I understood half. Pink boy want me to visit Guatemala to marry father. I laugh and say thank you but my Gianni would not like it. We laugh too much."

After losing a bundle in the first race, I recouped my losses the next two races to break even for the day. Pepina asked me to hold onto her winnings for a rainy day, giving me her cute wink of the eye. We were getting hungry and track food would not fit the bill. In Arcadia, just two kilometers from the race track, I knew of a great Chinese Dim Sum restaurant that I thought Pepina would find to her liking.

The place was packed. And packed with Chinese, always a positive sign for authentic Chinese food. I am also a big fan of the dim sum carts that journey around the tables offering hot food straight from the kitchen. They start you off with tea. We chose the chrysanthemum tea, which is believed to calm the nerves and aid digestion.

We dove into a bamboo basket of Steamed Pork Buns. These we ate with our hands, steaming white buns that were packed with pork that was so tender in a soy honey-flavored marination. The top of the buns crack open when being steam cooked.

I asked Pepina this time to pass on going into the kitchen to ask recipe questions. It was so busy I felt the cooks would chase her out with a meat cleaver if she ventured into their space. The stuffed eggplant was next. This particular restaurant stuffed their eggplant with deep fried shrimp paste. It had a sweet and sour sauce that tickled the taste buds. Pepina generally is not a big fan of any deep fried food. She was trying to flag down a waitress to see what kind of oil they used.

Next on the list was Shao-Mai; these one bite buggers pack a lot of flavor. It's kind of an open-faced dumpling with shrimp and pork, garnished with a bit of fish roe on top. Lastly, we refreshed our taste buds with a healthy serving of just-steamed bok choy. Pepina and I love this green gift of the garden and made a vow to plant some when we return home.

Fully satiated from our dim sum experience, we began our drive back to la casa. We packed our luggage when we departed Gustavo's home, leaving a note to thank him enormously for everything and let him know that we have moved back over to my home due to the Danes' early departure. This boy was feeling a bit tired and I was hoping Pepina would like to spend the next day or two just relaxing at home until we departed for our cruise. I was feeling a bit apprehensive regarding this Alaska trip, not knowing what to expect. I have never been on a luxury liner. Pepina was in the same boat (no pun intended).

As it turned out, we were both like whipped dogs. We spent the following days lazing about, piddling around in my modest garden, taking relaxing walks on the beach, making love and cooking our meals (not necessarily in that order).

One day we ventured to the harbor. I wanted to see if any of the boats were bringing in any interesting *frutta di mare*. One of the three game fishing half-day charter boats that ventures out of Santa Barbara was unloading.

Pepina and I were reclining on a dockside metal bench listening to the weekend fishermen boast about who caught the biggest fish and who won the pool for biggest catch of the day. We saw a man and young boy disembark; both looked wobbly-legged and were thanking the sun, moon and stars for being on terra firma. The father looked the worst, still green around the gills. He stumbled a bit on the gangway. I approached them and asked if they needed help in any way. The father was struggling with the fishing poles and gear. He was most appreciative of me asking and said that I was the first friendly face he'd seen all day.

As we were now on the wharf sidewalk they both felt more secure. I figured I would ask casually, "So how was the catch? Any action?" The father replied that he was keen on showing his 13-year-old son the great thrill of sport fishing, but unfortunately, he spent most of the trip down in the galley vomiting from seasickness. Every time he would come up from below to see how his son was doing, the other fishermen would all say, "No chumming on this side of the boat, pal!" then laugh.

However, his son caught two rockfish, a 38-inch barracuda and one ling cod that weighed 12 lbs. He said the captain helped him bring in the ling cod. Speaking of ling cod, it is one ugly as hell fish that has some teeth. They are really not even related to Pacific cod. But oh, they taste so nice. When you cook it the meat is white and it is very tender, flaky and tasty, especially when it is fresh off the boat. I have had ling cod that has been frozen and it just isn't the same. But, hey! Can't go wrong with fresh fish from the sea.

Pepina had joined us now and right away congratulated the young man on his accomplishments fishing. We could see that the boy really enjoyed himself. The father stated that they were just loading their equipment into the car. They had to board the ship again because the first mate was gutting/cleaning their catch. He asked just for the filets on the ling cod and said I was more than welcome to take a couple pounds or so for me and my lovely wife. Pepina was so excited with the prospect of fresh-caught fish.

As the father and son made their way to the parked car, Pepina whispered to me, "What kind pescado is 'Lean God?'" I assured her that she would be licking her lips when I was finished grilling that 'lean god.'

We profusely thanked the father, who ended up presenting us with three pounds of ling cod filets. Then, while the fish was still cool, we raced like two Olympians to zip back home for a feast!

While Pepina was carving up some butternut squash and preparing a quinoa salad with finely chopped tomatoes, parsley and red onions with a light balsamic vinaigrette, I was the master of the pescado! First I made a lemon caper sauce to go on the fish; butter, Meyer lemon juice, Eureka lemon zest, little garlic and chopped parsley. Then, outside I got the grill ready.

I have found that cherry wood, apple wood and red oak are the finest sweet-tasting woods to cook with. I let the wood burn down to red-hot coals. I then place the oiled fish filets for only a moment on the grill, enough for it to sizzle and gather some of the smoke and flavor of the wood on both sides. I immediately then place the filets back on the grill, wrapped in tin foil with some butter and a thin slice of lemon and orange, allowing the flavor from the wood, butter and citrus to steam inside the foil until Pacific Ocean perfection. I had a bottle of *Bianchello del Metauro*, a DOC status white wine that would just perfectly meld with the feast. It's from the Biancame white grape, grown in the Marche, Italia wine region.

Uncharacteristically, while we were in our silent meditation dining mode, Pepina spoke. In between bites of tender, juicy grilled fish with lemon caper sauce, she said, "You know, nice man who give fish? He must be Jewish man Gianni, you know. When he come back from car to get clean fish on boat, he wearing a *'yamaha.'* Did you see that Gianni? On head?"

I dropped half a spoonful of quinoa salad on my pants. I stated that I did see the '*yamaha*' on his head and that perhaps it was around the time of a Jewish holiday.

<><>

High Seas

Ignorance is the softest pillow on which a man can rest his head.
Michel de Montaigne

21

To say the least, we were taken aback by the sheer immenseness of the ship/floating hotel/city. We looked like two peasants who have ventured down for the first time from their remote pastoral village to see the big city. Pepina looked at me with a sense of bewilderment, saying she couldn't believe how something this size could keep afloat. We were directed into the bowels of the ship. Already, long lines of folks, just like at the airport, with luggage were waiting in roped-off lines zigzagging to a couple of reception desks. Just as I was about to start cursing all known deities, a young, well-groomed man presented himself as Alexandru, and so his nametag indicated, with a national flag that I guessed was Romania.

Alexandru had a glistening bald head, piercing green eyes and was extremely thin. His coat looked like it was clinging to a coat hanger. My mind wandered to thinking he must have to jump back and forth in the shower just to get wet. I wondered why such a young man would choose a clean shaven pate? I could see the shadow contrast of a full head of dark closely shaven hair. He said stiffly, as if addressing the Prime Minister, "Dr. Giovanni

Pisano and Ms. Pepina Soler?"

We had no idea why he addressed us so formally. However, I answered in the affirmative and asked how we might be of service. He gave the most peculiar puzzled face and said, "No sir. It is I who will be serving you." He then improved his posture, straightened his tie and replied, "I will escort you both directly to your deluxe executive penthouse."

Two well-dressed bellhops in black pants and white shirts with black bow ties took our luggage and departed. Alexandru pointed the way. After a few steps he turned around briskly and apologized. "I'm so sorry, I am your butler on this journey. I am at your beck and call."

We proceeded to walk past the vast lines of the common rabble. Pepina was nervously asking me why so many of the people were shooting her the fish-eye. I had to laugh at her description. I informed her that these fellow voyagers were jealous that we were getting the VIP treatment. We were now marked passengers. But with that said, I wagered that nobody would even remember us once they checked in and got settled. It's just that we would be settled way before them. Nice!

We strolled through hallways with Alexandru, who pointed out paintings and some amenities. Down a grand staircase we went to the grand reception area, then into what looked like a closet, but was a well-concealed elevator. He handed us the key and said nobody else on the ship possessed one. This was our private elevator to use that went directly up to our deluxe penthouse. He also mentioned offhandedly that we also could employ the standard front door as well. However, if we wanted to go directly to the reception level we could use the elevator.

And what a deluxe penthouse it was. As the elevator opened, Alexandru pointed us directly to our stunning accommodations. It was a two-bedroom, two-bathroom apartment with a whirlwind view of the ocean. The dining area had a table that would seat six. Roomy bathrooms sported white marble and private whirlpool baths. The penthouse even had a quasi-business center with large screen computer with 24/7 wireless Internet, printer, fax and miscellaneous office materials.

The computer with unlimited Internet came in handy because I found Pepina using it throughout the voyage, sometimes in the middle of the night, sending missives back to attorneys in Spain with still-unsettled estate issues. There were still lots of 'i's' to dot and 't's' to cross in regard to Donat's will. Evidently, everything was basically willed to Pepina. However, she was selling off properties and dividing up the proceeds amongst her sisters. She felt this was only fair. All Pepina wanted and cared for was the farm… or should I say her '*jardin.*'

Pepina asked me on a few occasions if I felt that Donat would be upset if he knew that she was going against his last wishes, literally. But she also added, contradicting herself, that since she was doling out a vast majority amongst all the siblings he should not be upset.

I took immediate note when Alexandru mentioned the complimentary spirits. I had already smuggled a bottle of Woodford Reserve Bourbon Whiskey in my suitcase (for medicinal purposes). The two bottles provided for our voyage were a Macallan 12–year-old single malt scotch and Remy Martin V.S.O.P cognac. What a day! I could see that I would be well lubricated for this trip.

Pepina was incredulous. She said directly to me, "Gianni, this is so much Gustavo do, who you keel for him? Where you berry body?" She made sure I saw her wink. She loved this gesture. I thought she was just so damn cute. So, being a dick, I just responded by simply shrugging my shoulders. I was not expecting this level of treatment at all. While Pepina was talking with Alexandru about how many people throw up due to sea sickness, I was imbibing a wee dram of scotch, just to christen the voyage, you know… as one does. A salud!

Alexandru trained us on everything from how to use the remote to operating the whirlpool tub. Last, he handed me a small device like a pager with a single button on it. He explained that all we had to do was push the button and he would appear momentarily to assist us in any endeavor. Thanking him for all his assistance, Pepina and I were guiding him to the door so that we could have some privacy.

As we were closing the door he apologized because in a few hours we were to report mid-deck for the emergency protocol training. "Sorry," he said. "All people on board are required to attend, no matter what." He said not to worry. He would come at the appointed time and accompany us to our 'muster station.' I wasn't in the state of mind to even ask what that was all about. But he did say he would retrieve us at the appointed time. I could see Pepina wanted to ask him what he meant but thought better.

When we were finally alone, Pepina leaped into my arms excitedly. "Gianni, I do whirlpool. What you do?" Settling in with 12-year-old single malt while relaxing sounded just like what the doctor ordered for me. So I reclined on a very comfy sofa. To my left, resting on a small table, was a compact stereo system. I pushed the button 'On' for power. Voila! Bob Dylan's "Like a Rolling Stone" could not have been more appropriate. While Pepina was soaking her Botticelli-like body in the whirlpool, I kicked back and enjoyed the ride.

Pepina yelled from the bathroom with the bath water running, "Hey Gianni! Why we go for mustard … eh, I don understand?"

"I don't know, cara mia," I yelled from the sofa, "but I love a good pungent mustard on a dog-pile of nice lean pastrami, especially on fresh rye bread."

Pepina had already disrobed. She just barely poked her head out of the bathroom doorway corner with a disgusted look on her face, muttering something unintelligible. I could see that she was getting fed up with my lame-ass sense of humor that I found absurdly deranged most of the time myself.

As Pepina bathed in the whirlpool, I thought back to the last couple of leisure days we spent together before departing on this voyage. Going for long walks along the beach, driving to Big Sur, visiting Carmel and loving life. We spoke with Gustavo just before boarding our ship to thank him once again. He was, as always, working and just about to go into surgery. Valeria called the day before we boarded our flight to Seattle, sending us love and happiness. She wanted me to promise that we wouldn't disappear back across the Atlantic without seeing her. I was vague and stated who knew what the future held, or some such blather. I could tell she was not happy with that response, but did not flip her lid as usual, displaying restraint to hold her tongue. I thought, *Brava! She's maturing.*

"Valeria, my dear, I have not thanked you enough for the

wonderful dinner the other evening. You made Pepina feel so comfortable. She told me that she is going to call you personally and wants you to stay with us when we return. She has many connections in Espana in the hospitality industry. She would be more than glad to introduce you to a few of her connections. You are fluent in Spanish. You just need to become familiar with different idioms. I'm giving you a heads-up ok? We did not have this conversation. Anyway, no pressure. This is something that is her idea, ok? Oh, and, she would not get her feelings hurt if you said no. So don't lose any sleep worrying about that."

Valeria laughed heartily. "I really love you two. I can tell together you both are a lot of fun to be around. Listen, don't worry, Gianni, I won't give you away. When Pepina calls me, I will act surprised."

"I appreciate that," I replied thankfully.

Valeria continued, "Other than that, I can't give her those answers just yet. I'm getting it together now, Gianni, because of you. Believe it or not, Dad too. I need to give him a break. I have given that poor guy a real hard time. I made friends with Gabriela. She is super brilliant. I'm attracted to her yearning, her desire, her never-give-up spirit to transform her country in Venezuela. Her intelligence outweighs her beauty. But let's face it, she is super-hot. I believe she will make a difference, either politically or through law reform."

The whirlpool bath suddenly had gone silent,which brought me out of my whirlpool of thought over the last few days. This scotch had a nice tranquil effect. Or was it the bon voyage result of being on a cruise ship? It was great that Valeria and Gabriela, against all odds, struck up a friendship. I would be interested in hearing what Valeria says when Pepina calls her. Pepina cried from the bathroom, "Don't drink all that whiskey, Gianni. We need food before you drink any more." It had been beyond my recollection of anyone ever telling me to not drink any more. Anyway, in the short time since we fell madly in love, it is I who always has the last word. I responded appropriately. "Yes dear!"

Alexandru arrived as promised in a few hours. He was holding two life vests and said it was time to go to our muster station to receive emergency safety protocol training. I explained to him that neither of us had ever been on a cruise ship before, so we appreciated all the information he could pass on. He was delighted at the prospect of teaching us the ropes. After the safety training he asked us what we would fancy for our first meal. Pepina and I agreed that since we landed in Seattle we spent a good portion of our time eating seafood at Pikes Place Market, a one-hundred-year-old market that was famous for its fishmongers. Pepina was moderately impressed with its history, but was stunned by the prices. "Hey, why dees fish so much cost money? They swallow gold?"

We agreed to steer away from the gluttony of the last few days and that a light vegetarian meal, perhaps some soup and definitely salad. Alexandru smiled and said that he could recommend a nice restaurant, or we could dine in the penthouse. We told Alexandru that we chose the restaurant since we wanted to mingle amongst the general population, as well as to tour this vast ship.

Our butler made a veiled attempt to not sound snooty by saying, "Oh heavens, no! I mean, I'm quite sure as the journey progresses, you shall prefer the company of your own and not wish to mingle with the general citizenry."

I let that remark go, thinking that Alexandru was finally warming up to us enough to speak freely.

Gustavo is very aware that I tend to be a casual dresser. He left a very nice Armani suit, pants with a couple shirts and an assortment of ties included in a garment bag hanging in the hallway outside our bedroom the morning we departed. There was a note stating, "Gianni, believe me. You will need this for the cruise. There will be evenings when you need to dress up. We have always been around the same size, but I noticed your gut is expanding. Love you, fratello mio!"

Unbeknownst to me, that whole ensemble in the garment bag definitely came in handy. When I read that note from Gustavo to Pepina, it translated into a green light for her to spend practically one whole day purchasing quite a few gorgeous outfits for the voyage.

We were chaperoned by our ever-present butler for our first meal in a quaint but luxurious VIP restaurant with only eight tables. Pepina pointed to a couple of Swarovski chandeliers. Our white linen table was set next to a pseudo-giant porthole for us to take in the view of the vast ocean. The high-back tuck and roll velvet seats were comfy.

There were only two other couples when we arrived. After viewing the menu, we soon abandoned our initial desire for a light meal of soup and salad (yes, concerning food, we have zero will power). I chose the Coq au Vin. They even asked me to personally select the vino to braise the chicken with. This cruise was definitely off to a good start since Coq au Vin many times depends on the wine you select to flavor the cooked dish. So I selected a California Pinot Noir from Josh cellars that I have had on a few occasions. Pepina selected Honey-roasted Quail with cumin and orange sauce, with steamed asparagus.

Our waiter was an elderly, snappily dressed gentleman, with black suit and bow tie, bald head with perfectly manicured short gray pencil-thin beard. I thought the buttons on his immaculate white shirt would burst at any moment to fly across the room. His belly was a testament to his enjoyment of the food aboard. His name was Domenico and he was pleased to speak Italian, as I guessed correctly that he was from Calabria. Conversely, Domenico made no hesitation to ascertain correctly from my accent that I was American –*touche*!

Since it was not so busy at the moment he told us that after this voyage he will work one more cruise, a 45-day journey to Japan, Korea and China. He would then retire after 26 years of working cruise ships. Pepina congratulated him on his career. While we were informing Domenico this was our first cruise an elderly Asian couple were being seated at a table across from us, as well as two other couples in front of the stylish restaurant. Domenico excused himself to attend to business.

The food exceeded our expectations. So far, since crossing over the vast blue to America, we have mostly prepared our own food. We of course shared each other's meal and were joyous at the prospect of many days of gourmet dining aboard the cruise. I was very much enjoying my cocktail, a Tanqueray and tonic, and having a laugh with Pepina about the butler when the Asian couple across from our table greeted us.

By their manner and grace, it was obvious that they were Japanese. The man was short, very distinguished, with a full head of standing steel gray hair. His wife was polite and graceful in her manner with jet-black, obviously dyed hair tied up in a bun. They reminded me of the emperor and empress.

The gentleman humbly apologized for interrupting us. He said he could not help but overhear us speaking in Spanish and some French. His wife also was bowing and apologizing for her husband's boldness, but he had been studying Spanish since he retired five years ago and always looks for opportunities to practice. Pepina responded by summoning over Domenico so that he could put our two tables together. Pepina right away wanted them to join us.

His name was Mr. Mori. He asked us to call him Ken. His wife's name was Midori. They were a delightful couple. His Spanish was atrocious and we had a hard time keeping smiles pasted on our faces trying to fight through his brutal accent. Pepina was a good instructor and corrected him in obvious places. I noticed she snuck a few Catalan words in there out of boldness. These few words had ol' Ken scratching his head. I'm sure he already downloaded the entire Spanish dictionary by now in his Japanese engineered brain and was wondering how these words slipped by.

After a while, over a few drinks we gingerly moved into English, which was much more comfortable for all concerned. I knew one basic phrase in Japanese that I learned from Henri's Japanese lady friend years ago. I was looking for an opening to see if I could slip it in the conversation naturally to impress our dinner guests.

Midori and Pepina were talking about Midori's company in which she designs handbags. She was displaying a very petite leather handbag to Pepina, who was in awe over the quality.

During the same time Ken was telling me that in the 80s he was president of a bank that was forced to merge with another, which demoted him. By 2000, that bank was swallowed by another that led to his ouster. However, within the same year that bank merged and became Japan's second largest financial group, of which he was elected CEO. Midori broke off briefly from her conversation with Pepina to apologize about her husband's non-stop talking. I saw my opening. I stated, "Midori-san, his story is most interesting and showed that he had the determination and perseverance to ultimately win in such a difficult business. After all, *ano ne, nana korobi yaoki. Ne…*" (literally- if you fall seven times, you get up eight times). Their faces both simultaneously froze. Then, in unison they bowed in their chairs until I thought they would bang their heads on the table.

Pepina looked at me and said, "What you say Gianni, don't be not nice to our friends."

I instantly said not to get the wrong impression; that is the only phrase in Japanese I know that I learned by rote, long ago.

After coffee, we said our goodbyes to the couple with the assurance that we would continue our stimulating talks throughout the voyage. They were veterans with cruise ships and said this was their 32nd trip aboard a luxury cruise liner.

We were in dire need of an evening passeggiata for our digestion. We retreated to our penthouse for a quick change from our formal clothes into something more appropriate. We commenced to stretch our legs and investigate this huge vessel. We elected to depart out the front door as opposed to the elevator. As we opened the front door, Alexandru was standing at attention like a cigar store Indian. Startled, Pepina said, "Ale, what happened? Why you stand here at door."

I jumped in as well. "We give you the night off. Only tonight."

"I knew after dinner you both would want to walk the ship, so I thought I could give you the tour," Alexandru said.

"Not needed, old man," I objected. "We quite like to encounter the mystery of the layout. It's part of the fun for us."

Not quite knowing how to respond to that, he hesitated, started to say something, then fell mute. I could see his dilemma. "Look Ale, if we need anything, I have this beeper thingy you gave me. I shall employ it if needed by all means."

I was unsure if he was satisfied with my reply or disgustingly pissed off at my patronizing manner. But he nodded his shiny cue ball head yes. Then, he said "As long as you use the device to call me for any small reason at all."

I think this cruise ship adventure shall be quite agreeable!

Our first stop was Ketchikan, Alaska. Besides the lovely walk along many scenic river views, the main event was Pepina getting into a lumberjack axe-throwing contest. I was bewildered, to say the least. I was in awe at my sapote girl's talent in heaving a double-edged axe overhead with both hands at a huge block of pine with a target circle on it. Perhaps, some distant marauding Viking horde in the eighth century passed their genes in the vicinity of northern Iberia? She was quite prolific in her axe delivery. However, when all was said and done, she came in second place out of nine women contestants who were twice her size. The first prize winner was a red-headed Teutonic giant who identified herself as Imogen Von Rensler from the Netherlands.

It only took two days for me to realize that this cruise ship was just a floating modern-day Roman Saturnalia: the constant feasting, a perpetual dessert landslide. Basically, 'Kaffee und Kuchen' on steroids; an onslaught of cream puffs, blueberries in whipped cream, cheesecakes, chocolate mousse, strawberries dipped in chocolate, bread/butter pudding, Black Forest Cake, crème brulee, ice cream and unlimited cookies. I stopped only because I ran out of breath. The only thing missing from this Roman orgy was peacock tongues glazed in honey. Oh, the obligatory vomitorium too.

We found on our walks that we passed many other eating venues. Pepina and I were astonished at the amount of buffet food that was available. We stopped at one event where there was cooking outdoors with a band playing. It was located just outside one of the huge buffets. Pepina said, "Dees is Roma Antica. Gianni, they eating and celebrating 24/7.Only everyone is aristocracia."

As we walked around the large gathering of the general population we observed far off in a corner, across from a large swimming pool, by some lounge chairs, the Japanese couple Midori and Ken. They had two young people cornered and Midori was exhibiting her small handbag, extending the expensive item into the hands of the young lady. They looked like a newlywed couple. Pepina, with her head cocked sideways, gave me a questioning look.

"Gianni you no think that…"

"That's exactly what I think," I said. "Mr. Ken and Ms. Midori may be financing their voyage by fencing perhaps counterfeit luxury handbags. By the way, cara mia, did Midori offer you to purchase one?"

Pepina looked at the ground quickly, then back to me, and said, "Yes, yes Gianni."

"Well…" I said. "How much did they think they could chisel us for?"

Pepina gave me that cute grin and wiggled her pixie nose and said. "They are eleven thousand dollars in Japan. But she could get for me eight thousand dollars. Why I want handbag? I no need."

I thought about what Pepina said. It's true, I have yet to see her with any type of purse or handbag, ever. As time passed on this voyage, I believe Ken and Midori had the sagacity to realize that Pepina and yours truly were not fair game; it seemed as though they made a point to avoid us, knowing that they were unlikely to hoodwink us.

When we reached Juneau we had no plans, so we just walked into town. Many of the ship's passengers were queuing up for taxi service about 100 meters from where the ship anchored. Pepina asked a couple where everyone was going. The couple said to Sitaantaagu, as it was called by the native tribe, presently known as Mendenhall Glacier, situated in Tongass National Forest.

There was an option besides a taxi; you could charter a plane and fly over the vast icy wonder with lake and waterfall, or take the local bus. We elected bus. Not because I'm a cheapskate - which I am - but because we wanted to elbow in with the locals to see the daily life. A majority of the bus passengers, we noticed, looked to be native Tinglit. We found out during the ride that the closest drop-off to the glacier was a three kilometer hike, which ended up just fine because all the feasting was beginning to make us lethargic. We needed exercise!

It took 45 minutes before the bus dropped us off. The driver pointed his finger down a wide trail through a dense forest. He laughingly added that it was just a short stroll and if we were lucky some bear might spot us on the way. I believe I counted a total of five tobacco-stained teeth remaining in his grinning mouth. I thought to myself, *Either he has very bad hygiene, or most of his teeth have been knocked out for being a smart ass. Probably both.* The bear remark grabbed our attention.

It took us thirty minutes to cover the three kilometers. The air was crisp and fresh at an elevation of 5,200 feet. Hand in hand we made it to the entrance of the visitor's center. In the far distance we could see a waterfall at the side of the glacier. We were told that the Mendenhall glacier was 14 miles long. We asked a park attendant how to get to the waterfall and we were directed toward the trail head.

Nugget Falls is a two-tier waterfall that descends a total of 377 feet. It was situated so it looked like a giant slide at a waterpark for Titans. We made it to the base of the deafening waterfall that cascaded down the side of the mountain. We could stand literally a few meters from the continuous thunder of the rushing water. If there ever was a location worthy to videotape or photograph, this was it. To communicate we used hand signals. We had the whole area, which was comprised of a sand bar created by the waterfall, to ourselves. To get some perspective we walked back off the sandbar, back onto the trail to capture sheer scope of the cascading water.

As I was framing Pepina in a photo, making hand gestures for her to move, I heard a sound off to the side of me. Out of the thick bramble and bushes stumbled a rather gangly young female park ranger. She was at least six foot two. She appeared to have been living rough. Pepina came jogging up to say hello. She said her name was Sandra, pointing to her park badge. Sandra had what appeared to be long ginger hair tied back hastily in a club. Small pieces of branches and leaves seemed to be tangled and interwoven in her unkempt hair. Her uniform seemed as if it was due for the laundry. She had a Motorola walkie-talkie attached to her heavy duty belt. Her thick soled boots were caked with dried mud. The large backpack she slung off her shoulders was old and had been sewn together in many places. She asked us how we were enjoying Nugget Falls.

"So what do you think? Pretty awesome, isn't it? I still can't believe what a gift from God this place is. I'm from Boston, but I always wanted to live in the great northwest since I was a child. Alaska is God's country! When I was seventeen I took a bus, hitchhiked and finally made it. This is where I belong."

I mentioned that she came from off the trail through some thick forest. Was that safe since this was moose, mountain lion and bear country? Sandra smiled and for such a young person she also revealed a set of very crooked choppers that were in dire need of an orthodontist. She happily replied, "Oh, I sleep out here all the time. Sure, there are lots of bear. In this area we rarely see caribou or moose. Possibly an occasional puma. But hey, they don't bother me. I know all the bears by name; they wake me up all the time. They just smell, being curious, and then go on their way. If they have cubs, that's a different story."

Pepina had her hands up to her mouth in disbelief listening to this brave young lady who we wholeheartedly believed. She seemed a throwback to an earlier age of living in the wild and not having it any other way. Her sincere nature and passion when she talked about the seasons, how the ever-moving glaciers make music throughout the valleys and canyons—Sandra was living her dream life. Pepina said, "Sandra, you are brave woman. Don't Alaska give you place to sleep? Dangerous and cold. Your job is most difficult, no? Maybe you write book?"

Sandra just smiled adoringly at Pepina. She said in mid-winter she did stay in a cabin that the Parks Department provided. But for the most part she preferred the outdoors. She gave her backpack a tug and said she had a small portable mini-stove and everything she needed was inside her backpack. Sandra also added that she was a vegetarian. She mentioned that just moments ago she cooked her breakfast: brown rice.

I looked at Pepina, who looked back at me and said to Sandra. "What did you eat with the brown rice?"

Sandra said, "Why nothing, just brown rice. It's so delicious and the water here cannot be beat. You know, even the natives here say that the water is blessed. This glacier is very old and the snowfall each year is deep. I bathe in the freezing lake. In the winter I cut a hole in the ice to take the plunge nude. It reminds me that I am alive!"

We both warmly invited Sandra to accompany us back to the visitors' center. We spied a restaurant there and offered to buy her lunch so that we could continue talking with a most interesting Ranger. She thanked us both very graciously a few times, but turned down our offer, stating that she stayed away from there and would only go there if they radioed her for an emergency. Sandra stated that she much preferred to stay in the forest and meet kindhearted people like us. She mentioned that from the woods she saw a brilliant yellow aura by the falls, which meant there was positivity, and that meeting us proved her point. She referred to the visitor center as civilization.

Walking back on the trail en route to the center, we spoke in awe of this young lady who found her calling. How she knew from a young age that a wild and still untamed land was her true destination in life. Pepina said she would pray that she remained safe, because it was hard for her to fathom sleeping in the wilderness with creatures who could do her great harm. Pepina added. "Sandra found true life Gianni. Makes her happy. It took me too long time. But I find you, eh? Why it take long… I don know. But we happy too, right Gianni?"

I stopped in my tracks, grabbed the woman I love with all the gusto I could summon, and we kissed - right there in the middle of the trail - as if for the first time.

"Yes, we found each other," I said holding her at arm's length, smiling at her heart-shaped face, her pixie nose all red from the chilly, thin air. "I vow here under this glorious turquoise sky that I will never let you go!"

<><>

SKAGWAY
(UPPER DEWEY LAKE)

If there were no God, it would be necessary to invent him.

Voltaire

22

The only agenda item we had actually researched was the Upper Dewey Lake hike in Skagway. It was definitely on our 'to do list.' We would have eight hours to make the intermediate/hard rated hike, then, be back before the ship departed for the last leg of our voyage to Whittier, for the long bus ride to Anchorage for our return flight. Alexandru, our ever-present and devout butler, wholeheartedly advised us against it. He said, "Oh no, you are not equipped for that strenuous hike, just walk around in the forest by the stream for a couple hours. Go to lower lake, then go back into the town saloon for beer and pizza!"

I was a bit taken aback by his bold direction as to what we should do. However, I brazened it out by inviting him along, if he could get away from work. He begged off, saying that he never hiked it himself. But others aboard the vessel had, and they said it was most arduous and demanding. From Skagway proper, it was an 11-mile round trip hike with 3,000 feet of climbing.

Hey, we scaled Mt. Pilatus, Suisse! Let's see if we rise to the challenge here, in the last great frontier. Alaska!

The rating of that trail should be hard/very difficult. We had no hiking poles, so we made do with some branches found along the trail. After three hours of the most taxing climbs, thoughts crept into our minds that we bit off more than we could chew. We were about to turn back, satisfied that we had endured a most difficult hike even without making it to the Upper Dewey Lake. We were taking a water break and catching our breath when we encountered two young men sliding down a very steep switchback. They were laughing, but it was frightened laughter. They were very friendly and most effeminate. I asked them if they were locals.

One of the young men, whose eyebrows were shaved very thin with earring and a lip ring, said, "Oh no darling, we flew in from White Horse 110 miles on a hydroplane just for the day. First time here. We live in Portland, Oregon."

I mentioned we were just thinking of turning back because we were on a cruise ship and would have to return on time.

They both objected in unison. "No, don't stop!" Then, lip ring said. "You only have about another hundred yards to go. But go slowly. It's difficult. The view is worth all the effort!"

His partner was a youth, who was shorter and just a wee bit chubby. He sported an incredibly long, braided jet-black pony tail. He smiled at us mischievously and said, "Oh my, you must make the extra effort. The vista is beyond awe-inspiring." He paused bashfully and added, "It's very romantic."

We thanked them both multiple times and were reinvigorated to proceed, knowing that we were just moments away from reaching the climax of our hard-fought journey.

Although we made it to Upper Dewey Lake, the last bit is steep and grueling. I was ready for the knackers for sure. My breathing was extremely labored. Pepina held her own, but I could tell we overextended ourselves. It was a slam-dunk that we would not continue a few more kilometers to scramble up to Devils Punchbowl. But the vista that we enjoyed was stunning. The snow-capped mountains, alpine terrain, waterfalls and rushing streams made this hike a dream come true.

What I witnessed on this particular hike gave me a personal determination that I would study more about the life of fungi. I took enough photos so that I could research later. The varieties I encountered for the first time were numerous. The environment was wet and lush. The lake itself was a remnant of a receding glacier from time out of mind. Our only regret was that we couldn't spend more time just taking in the majestic beauty and serenity of the lake. We were in accord that there would be only return from this point onward. What a great decision that was, because the return down was time consuming and treacherous, while wreaking havoc on both our knees and ankles.

Alexandru's counsel to us for our adventurous hike was that we were 'ill equipped' and 'just walk around in the forest by the stream for a couple hours, then go back into the town saloon for beer and pizza!' Well, let me tell you, he was wrong about one thing for sure. We were NOT going 'back into the town saloon for beer and pizza.' We were headed directly back on board to shower and soak our weary bones in our whirlpool. Screw the pizza and beer!

It became apparent to us that life on board a cruise liner can be most addictive. There are many activities. Pepina was always heading to the library to do the Sudoku for the day, utilizing the gym, going to the spa, Zumba classes and whirlpool. We made a solemn promise not to sneak off to Kaffee und kuchen without each other, for the cruise made all these delicious desserts available around the clock. It took the restraint of an aesthetic yogi to keep from finding an excuse to devour them.

I was in constant search of a skilled foe to challenge me at table tennis. I became bored with all the blue-collar, amateurish chowderheads who thought they were good. I easily dispatched them all. I believe it was on the third day of the cruise when I met a Chinese old man with a slight humpback. He proceeded to wipe the floor with me. I may have had one or two points only by his mistake. He thanked me for the game, stating, "Thank roo. You rich man, no? I saw you we boarding ship."

So much for getting the 'fish-eye,' as Pepina remarked.

There was a basketball court as well. I'm not that much of a geezer yet. I can still shoot some hoops, especially deep from the three-point line. I had a good time one afternoon with a group of guys shooting horse, which became nice and competitive. Everyone introduced themselves, but then during the shoot around everyone called me VIP.

"Ooh nice shot, VIP. Hey, VIP for a long three… yes! Nice hook shot, VIP!"

The men were just having fun. But I got tired of that crap after a while. Pepina said nobody ever mentioned a thing to her the whole voyage. The deluxe gym, spa and sauna would have been sufficient for the whole voyage, but we spread our wings aboard the colossal ship to get a real feel for this cruise business. Personally, I could see why some people, who have the financial resources, practically live on these luxury liners, hopping from one voyage to the next. There was one family being honored in the daily newsletter from the ship, stating that it was their 100th voyage with this cruise company. Bottom line, it's a different type of luxury with the variety of activities, entertainment, food and ports of call. However, we both agreed that this was just a tad bit decadent for our taste.

On the last night aboard, I woke up in the middle of the night to find that Pepina was not in bed. I thought perhaps a trip to the loo, but I heard the gentle tapping sounds of a computer keyboard. It was no problem for me to get up since I had to take a leak. I made a bit of noise to alert her that I was up as well. When I approached her I asked if all was well.

Pepina took a deep breath and said, "You know, Gianni, my seesters, they are making arguing with each other. I try to be fair. They say I am bad. Gianni, I want to share to give everything. So each can be happy. But, they call names to each other. I am sad Gianni."

I didn't know what to say, but I needed to say it fast. I got down on one knee beside Pepina, who was sitting at the desk in front of the computer. I responded, "I am at a loss for words, my dearest. But I know this for sure; I can tell you this. I am with you all the way. I am here, my love. Whatever you decide, I will support you. I found you and I will never let you go! I love you infinitely!"

We gazed lovingly at each other, hands clasped. We stayed that way for a while, comforted in the knowledge that we were one.

Eventually, Pepina whispered, "Gianni, let's go home. We

can always return soon. I have to make sure seesters, Gianni…"
Pepina was unsure; she wanted to speak but remained silent.

"Yes my love, I'm here; what is it?"

She opened up. "Flor is getting another divorce. And husband is making hard time."

Ah ha! Flor. Good ol' horseshit breath, hypodermic, Van Huysen expert, anorexic Flor. Hopefully, I didn't say that out loud..? Did I? WHEW! I don't think I did. I replied with utmost care. "*D'accordo, mi amor* (we are in agreement, my love). We will catch a flight from Seattle since we are already booked. Then, on to LAX to say goodbyes and then back for a direct flight to Barcelona." In an attempt to cheer her up with something regarding food I said, "Look, I have been preoccupied with returning to Pasquale's place in la Barcenoleta. Ever since you treated me to that feast, I've always wanted to return."

Pepina gave me a look of suspicion, then smiled and laughed as if I just handed her the crown jewels. She cried, "Oh, you theenk you are cute, no? You theenk of good juicy food make me happy, huh? Gianni, you know, you right! Hahhee!"

Well, that seemed to do the trick. I hate to see the woman I love be all depressed about family issues. I said, "Let's go back to bed, my love. We can sleep in and we shall have room service breakfast catered in for once. After all, you are my VIP!"

As we were returning to bed our in-house phone rang for the first time. I looked at Pepina and said it must be important from the ship, perhaps an approaching storm. I answered. It was Alexandru. He hurriedly spoke.

"I'm terribly sorry to call at such an absurd hour. I am actually standing at your front door. I felt calling would be more appropriate. I wanted to present you both with a rare opportunity. It has only happened as many times as I can count on a couple of fingers. We are in the right place at the right time. I know it's freezing outside because we are now at our farthest north venture. Go out onto your balcony. Gaze starboard, slightly to stern, and you will be able to behold the Northern Lights. I say good night." He promptly hung up.

Pepina was worried. "Gianni, did ship hit iceberg? What he say?"

Without saying a word I grabbed all the blankets off the bed and told Pepina to follow me asap. I zipped through the living room area to access our sliding door onto the balcony. It was indeed freezing. I grabbed Pepina and wound us up in a cocoon of sheets and blankets to look into the far dark distance. Holding my girl tight I whispered, "Let's see if we can be blessed with the Northern Lights."

As Alexandru had instructed, I looked directly starboard with a slight angle to stern. Slowly, we witnessed what first appeared as a green, round gaseous ball. It was light green in color which became a much darker hue of green. It began to swirl in a circular motion, like a green whirlpool. The circle of spinning gas became larger. To the left of the whirlpool, Pepina cried, "Mira! Gianni!"

Yet another similar swirling round gaseous ball appeared. There was quite a space between these two separate but like entities. We were silent. Witnessing this wonder of nature could be defined as a religious experience. The two swirling balls then began to leak thin rivers of green gas racing toward each other to join and become one. Once joined the intensity of the color pulsated slowly between light and dark until running out of steam to dissipate into nothingness. Shivering in the vast darkness, we shuffled back into the penthouse without making it as far as the bedroom. Like a tigress, Pepina attacked me on the sofa and we made love that evening as if in a dream.

I woke just before dawn to the sound of the whirlpool. I was tangled in knots on the carpeted floor with an assortment of pillows, sheets and blankets. After untangling myself, I crawled over to the libations cart just for a wee dram of that VSOP cognac, just to understandably clear the cobwebs in my noggin while contemplating the incredible lovemaking. Did we actually witness the Aurora Borealis, or was that a dream? Well, I recalled vividly Ale's call in the middle of the night. So it was real. Gonna have to thank that bald-headed bugger before we depart. I do recall telling Pepina we would have breakfast catered in this final morning. I ordered Eggs Benedict, double order of bacon, veal sausages, buckwheat pancakes with organic blueberries and a goat cheese quiche, orange juice, assam tea and a carafe of hot coffee. After all, we needed our vitamins after a long night of cardio....

<><>

Appreciation

Don't think money does everything, or you are going to end up doing everything for money.
Voltaire

23

The journey back was delightful. Anchorage airport is one of the more fascinating experiences for flying, with an array of stuffed moose and grizzly and polar bears throughout the lobby. I was told on the bus ride to the airport we just missed an icon of Anchorage – Boozewinkle, an eighteen hands at the shoulder moose who hangs out at a large billboard advertisement along the highway. There happens to be a large orchard of crabapple trees in the area, which Boozewinkle has an insatiable appetite for. Consequently, the digestive system of a moose contains the juicy apple mixture for quite some time, which in turn, begins a fermentation process. Hence, poor old Bullwinkle becomes belligerent, unpredictable – Boozewinkle! The local folk just love him and put up with all the shenanigans he gets into in his inebriated state (kicking stray dogs, peeing in resident's driveways, head-butting street signs and sleeping in the middle of an intersection). He sounds like a grand old fellow who I would like to sit down and have a chat with.

I called Henri to let him know to expect us within the next week or so. Henri laughed, stating that he dreamed about us the other night. He said Pepina and I held a racing contest; she was on a mule and I on a jackass. She won. Her prize was a nice Capretto al Forno (roast kid). She spoon fed me the prize while I rowed a boat in the middle of the ocean. I asked Henri how long it had been since he decided to start taking hallucinogenic drugs.

When I told Pepina my conversation with Henri, she was intensely curious. Pepina said she would speak with Henri in detail when they met next. She said she needed to ask him some specific questions regarding his dream.

Some time ago, Henri, in an inadvertent way, inspired me to scribble some notes called 'The Piddler's Guide to Gardening.'

On occasion when Henri would pay a visit, he preferred to sit among my postage stamp size mini-orchard of fruit trees. I have a cedarwood bench that serves as a pseudo-potting platform for my herbs. It was Henri's favorite spot to sit and watch a tiny warbler snatch an aphid off a tree branch, or gaze at a centipede crawling amongst the rich dark humus soil.

The deep down subtle simpleness of his happy time among nature compelled me to jot down a few ideas. Those ideas 'mushroomed' into some blossoming scenarios. Those scenarios formed into short stories.

Henri would report to me in an adolescent playful way how he would spy a speedy lizard snatch a mosquito while he was trimming some dill, listen to three finches singing a delightful trio or watch the slow flight of a hawk soaring beneath the clouds. His exuberance somehow obliged me to grab pen and paper. It is a project that to this day I enjoy visiting when new adventures arise.

I also needed to tie up some loose ends with Gustavo and Valeria; I didn't want to pull a disappearing act and seem ungrateful after being indulged by our friends. Pepina had purchased a large two-carat marquise emerald ring, set in white gold, for Valeria. I don't know where or when she acquired that gem during our journey, but it was a beauty. I was hypnotized looking at it. Pepina said that emerald was Valeria's birthstone, as it was mine. When Pepina asked me what I got for Gustavo I informed her that that was not a good idea. Whenever in the past I had done Gustavo a favor or bought him some article, he would immediately feel a compulsion to pay back, overcompensating in the extreme. I made my case to Pepina.

"Look, my love. It's not worth the stress we will cause Gustavo by getting him a present. You have to believe me on this one. He will always feel that he owes me for some bizarre reason. Perhaps it's because, as you may recall, you mentioned before. Nobody knows 'where I berry body.'"

Pepina paused for that to sink in, then said, "Ok Gianni. I let you and Gustavo be friends. I only want to show a big thank you, you know?"

Right away I responded, "And you have, cara mia. Look at what you have gifted Valeria. Gustavo could not have wished for a greater gift than you showering his beloved daughter with such a beautiful emerald. He will be most impressed and thankful, but mostly impressed."

We were able to transfer right away from Seattle to an LAX flight with no glitches. I texted Valeria to see if she could pick us up at the airport and if she could not, we could grab a taxi, no problem. No sooner had I sent the text, than she replied before I could put my mobile back in my pocket. She said she would be more than glad to pick us up. I was so fortunate this worked out because I could drive while the girls could chat in the back seats all the way back.

It looks like fate, destiny, providence or whatever label I place upon it, has indeed shined upon my life with Pepina. I stopped asking why it has taken so long for me to share my life with a loving woman who has accepted all my foibles and directed me away from the destructive tendencies that were in my orbit. That 'something' in my past dreams that always seemed to elude my grasp has disappeared into the ether. This trip was a benefit. It has made me come to the realization that I am a stranger in a strange land here in America. I believe it will be quite some time before we make a return trip.

As I expected, I was the appointed chauffeur on the drive home from LAX. Valeria and Pepina were both huddled in the backseat, laughing and scratching all the way back. We stopped off in Encino before driving on to Santa Barbara.

Believe it or not, Gustavo was home awaiting our review of the cruise. There was a spread of assorted cheeses, fruit, bread and drinks for us. We showered Gustavo with the best of judgment and praised the level of service we received. Pepina wisely waited to give Valeria her present. We discussed our adventures regarding Pepina's axe-hurling prowess, unbelievable hike to Upper Dewey Lake, Nugget Falls and of course, our butler service. As we sat around the table enjoying the snacks and one another's company, Pepina announced that she picked up a little something that Valeria might like.

"Valeria, this catch my eye. It would be something that

matches you, cara mia. I hope you like it."

Gustavo and I were sampling a fine bottle of Cortese di Gavi, a vino bianco that was superb with the cheese. I gave a chin thrust nonchalantly at Gus when Pepina made her announcement regarding Valeria's gift. He immediately shifted his attention to the clamshell-shaped box Pepina had just handed to his daughter. Gustavo stood up from the table and skipped over to stand behind Valeria's chair to witness her opening the present. I hate to trot out the old adage that states 'a picture is worth a thousand words,' but they were both floored. Valeria said while crying that she had never seen anything so beautiful while Gus, with a solemn face, kept shaking his head back and forth in disbelief.

The girls were busy hugging and chattering away. Gustavo was pouring us another glass of that beautiful light, fruity nectar from the Piedmont region. He said, "Well Gio, I didn't think you had good taste. I know you don't have good taste. Uh, correct that, except with women. Pepina is a treasure. I already said it once. I will say it again. You are one lucky bastard! Before your next reply on why I'm giving you a hard time? Don't forget. Peace, brother. It's ok if we pick on each other. That's what good friends are for, right?"

Changing the subject I said, "Gus, Pepina has some legal matters that she has to attend to regarding the recent death of her father Donat this summer. It was unexpected - the legal matters that is, not his passing; he had been ill for quite some time. She has four older sisters - do I need to say more? Get the litter box out for the cat fights. We have already booked a flight back to Barcelona. I am so glad we made this trip, really. You may want to take a break from the grind, Gus. I know you won't. But if you ever decide to, you are welcome to come, even if you just want to bust my chops, ha!"

I did not want Valeria to drive us home. I said we would take a taxi. However, both Valeria and Pepina protested. Pepina said Valeria could spend the night at la casa di Gianni. I was fine with that. No sense in arguing.

I guess the girls wanted to spend some more time together. I was getting the feeling that Valeria was thirsting for some motherly love. She never knew that feeling due to her biological mother abandoning her while she was just a toddler, being raised by Gustavo in a single parent home. And who better to fit the bill than Pepina for some motherly love. My guess was Pepina had already spoken with Valeria on the long ride back regarding coming to Spain for a career opportunity in the hospitality industry. They probably needed more time to discuss.

Both Pepina and Valeria had hit the sack. Meanwhile, I was in the process of nursing my second beer. It was a lager that was bitter. I grabbed a tried and true Guinness stout. It tasted like medicine. They both were not pleasant. I was not tired in the least so I settled down to transport myself for a good read with Gore Vidal's *Julian*. After about 50 pages Valeria appeared, standing beside me. She spoke softly.

"Gianni, why are you still up? It's late." I smiled at her sleepy eyes; she looked like the little girl I remember taking to the beach to give her her first surfing lesson.

I replied, "No worries, sweetie. I'm just decompressing with a good book. Why don't you get back to sleep?"

Valeria eased herself sidesaddle on the soft armrest of my comfy chaise lounge chair. She paused for a while in thought… then said, "Without sounding too clichéd, I guess I am looking for guidance… as usual. The drugs—how have you survived?"

I immediately interpreted that as *how has a drug-addled old fool like you made it this far?* I plastered a smile on my face to be as consoling as possible and said, "Valeria my dear, if a dedicated druggie like me, mind you, former dedicated druggie, can give away his vast cornucopia of pharmaceuticals to a free clinic in Ventimiglia with all my years of addiction compounded, then why can't a young person, with a young body, adapt and say farewell to that nasty beast that keeps rearing its head? For me it has been a crooked road and no bed of daisies but it's fucking better than waking up not knowing where the fuck you are. Right?"

"But how did you do that, Gianni?" Valeria said pleadingly.

I sat up as straight as possible after being burrowed in my chair like a pocket gopher. I had switched gears to my best bourbon after the nasty beer, but even that tasted like turpentine. I looked Valeria directly in the eyes and said as sincerely as possible, "This is very personal that I will tell you. There is a something that has always eluded me, consciously and subconsciously. I could never unveil that something, either because I was too chicken shit, or I just didn't give a damn. Now, because I found that… that something I truly want, I am resolved to attain it! In the final analysis, drugs just don't fit in my future. With that said, my dear Valeria, I fight it every day. You think that I don't still want to go score some fine coke at the shipyards?

I am so fortunate to be enjoying my life with the woman of my dreams. Our meeting was very mystical. I will explain that to you at a future date when I get a better grasp on it myself; there is still so much I don't understand."

"You know why I have always trusted you Gianni? Valeria placed her hand on my shoulder and was directly looking into my eyes. "Because you have never fed me any bullshit. I totally relate to what you just said. You know what you are talking about regarding the drugs. I guess I just don't have the confidence yet to trust my judgment. I know I am weak. I will tell you, though, Gianni, I will fight it as best I can."

"Go to back to bed, young lady. We will always be there for you. *Buona notte, sogno di oro.*"

"Love you, Gianni, *buona notte.*"

Valeria had stocked the refrigerator in anticipation of our return. After a restful night's sleep, Pepina and I woke up to a wonderful spread for breakfast. Asparagus with scrambled eggs on olive bread toast, organic strawberries, blueberry muffins, fresh carrot juice and a pot of steaming coffee. Valeria had already departed. There was a note on the table, written in her flamboyant cursive style. She wrote:

Thank you for making me part of your lives. Dad and I eagerly await for your return, and who knows? Maybe we will surprise you one of these days with a visit....

I love you, holding you both close to my heart...
oxoXOoxox

V

<><>

RITORNO

There are joys and sorrows greater than we can feel.
La Rochefoucauld

24

The one-way direct flight from LAX to Barcelona cost a small fortune, especially business class. But I tell you, I would pay it all over again. The absolute comfort I was experiencing after flying with the lemmings all these years in economy was quickly becoming a habit. Pepina dove into another book, a Caterina Albert collection of stories (*Jubileu*) written in 1951. Also, she polished off listening to all the Rachmaninoff piano concertos.

I brought along the first book in Jean-Claude Izzo's trilogy. It has been about ten years since I last read those noir crime novels about his hometown of Marseilles.

For the first time ever on a flight I was able to have one short informal pow-wow with my elusive pal Bacchus on the flight back; he told me very briefly that he was headed to Capri for the baths. He added it may not be necessary for us to meet any time soon. He always impressed me as a gentleman. I felt deep down it was his way of saying goodbye, forever. Words to express my grief would not have been sufficient; I respected him too much. I responded with just a solemn bow… and then, oblivion.

I was blessed with the sweet sleep of youth at that point. I woke up six hours later. Pepina said she kept checking on me because I was so sound asleep. She said I repeated very softly the word 'oblio' from time to time. I cannot recall ever sleeping so well without the aid of some tranquilizer, barbiturate or booze. Perhaps it was my old friend's way of saying thank you for all the years of our intimate chats.

Ever-faithful Iker greeted us as we arrived at El Prat Barcelona airport. His eyebrows by now had returned, taking on a life of their own. They must be quite handy for storing the odd spare sandwich or keeping the car keys, which are always so bulky in your pocket. Iker's job was secure due to the fact that it was decided that the soon-to-be divorced Flor was moving into the family villa permanently. There was one thing all the sisters including Pepina agreed on; they all loved Iker. He could continue overseeing matters for the ladies and continue to piddle around in his lovely atrium. Just like my lovely Pepina says, *'what a geeg!'*

In the following days Pepina was working with multiple lawyers on finalizing paperwork that the home would be in all the sisters' names (sans Pepina). There was also a leased property in Madrid included. Donat's elaborate car collection would be auctioned to the highest bidders, with the proceeds going to the four sisters. All nineteen cars with the exception of one—a 2005 Maserati Quattroporte that had only 8,000 kilometers on the odometer. Pepina made an arrangement with Flor that Pepina would keep that car at the villa for her own personal use whenever she was in Barcelona. It would be Iker's responsibility to take care of the car maintenance.

There was no argument over Pepina's 'jardin' and the revenue it brought in, since the siblings had no interest in actual work. Pepina said every single cent of her earnings from years at her former job went directly into an annuity. She was at peace with these arrangements. Pepina confided in me that she will sleep very soundly knowing she provided for her sisters unselfishly.

Before departing for our flight to Nice airport, Pepina made a visit to her father's grave to pay her respects. I felt deep down she hungered for some closure. Her regret for not being with Donat at the time of his passing was still heavy in her heart. Her only consolation was that he did not suffer; the stroke was massive and he passed quickly.

We went straight home from the airport. All of our mini-orchard trees were in the dormant state. I noticed in the refrigerator, there was a cardboard box full of jujube that Henri harvested. On the side of the box I recognized Henri's script, which looked like an enebriated chicken with ingrown toenails had scratched out '*bon appétit!*'

The jujube were in their date stage, chewy and full of flavor. Pepina and I snacked on them while relaxing with a café con leche. Just as we were settling in there was a knock at the door. It was Carmelo with the post. He was startled when I opened the door.

"Monsieur Gianni, I did not expect you. Henri said you were out of town for a while. How are you?"

"Sa va Carmelo! What is that large package you have there? Is that for me?"

"Oui Gianni, it is insured. I have no idea what it is. What have you been doing? You have lost weight, no? You look so good, Gianni. What happened?"

At a loss for words, I just told Carmelo that I had been exercising al lot.

To that he replied in exasperation, "Physhhhh, exercise—hah! I walk my balls off for the last seventeen years delivering post as courier, I look like merde."

"Carmelo, when you bring the post tomorrow let's have a drink together. I have a nice bottle of reposado tequila I have been waiting to crack open. Gotta go now. See you tomorrow, ciao!"

I brought the parcel in, leaning it against a cabinet in the kitchen. Pepina was unpacking some clothes and had changed into some casual sportswear. She looked at what the postman had delivered and asked if I was expecting anything. To solve the issue I retrieved a pair of scissors and began to unravel the well-fortified and expertly wrapped item. I abandoned the scissors for a box cutter to slice through the top layer of thick cardboard. I saw a frame inside the box. Holding the bottom of the box with both feet, I pulled the frame out of the container to behold the original Van Huysen painting that I so admired at Pepina's villa. A note from Flor was attached.

===

Dr. Gianni Pisano, you have good taste in art. Thank you for taking the time to examine me. I followed your direction and saw a doctor who informed me that I have 'gastroesophageal reflux.' At least I know now what I am dealing with.

On a different note — take good care of our Pepe! She is very dear to us; you have been warned. We are happy she is happy.

Flor-

===

I stared dumbfounded at the original painting by that seventeenth century Dutch painter. The front of the painting was protected by a clear, sturdy sheet of Lexan polycarbonate plastic. I gave a look of dismay at Pepina, who returned that look with a grand smile and said, "This make me happy that Flor thank you Gianni, believe me."

We agreed to remain in privacy for a while, relaxing by the shore, swimming in the azure sea and stretching our legs in the hills before venturing into Nizza. For any additional legal issues left unresolved, Pepina asked her attorneys to email her or contact her via mobile phone. She also provided them with my fax number at the flat if necessary.

It was a lazy morning when we had no inclination to rise up from bed. I was holding Pepina in my arms. She whispered, "You asleep Gianni?"

"Yes." I feigned sleep with my eyes closed and voice mimicking a dream state. "I am having the most marvelous dream that we are in a cozy bed and that I am holding you close. I feel as if I could stay like this forever."

Pepina ignored what I just stated and said enthusiastically, "You know, let's visit Vivian and Jean-Michel. I would like to see the children."

I began to laugh, seeing through my sapote girl's clever ploy. I exposed my Catalonian cutie. "I know you, my dear!" I opened my eyes and was now leaning on one elbow to face her. "You are licking your chops, anticipating Jean-Michel's Capretto al Forno! Haha! Right? I got you! Haha!"

Pepina gave it her best shot with a look of incredulousness on her face, but she couldn't hold it for over two seconds; she burst out in laughter with me as we rolled back and forth on the bed, resulting in being tangled up in the warm comforter. She kept laughing while tomahawking me with her pillow. I blurted out between blows, "We …know each other…all… too well – food first! Haha!"

As we settled back down for a wee nap, due to our tussle in the sheets, I whispered to my girl, "Hey, screw waiting till spring for *sakura* (cherry blossoms), let's head to Japan now. We can tour all the spots for *rotenburo* (outdoor scenic hot springs)."

Pepina sat up and began to shake me vigorously. "Less do it. Gianni, reeely! I want to see Japan!"

"Leave it to me, my love. The arrangements are as good as done.

<></>

New Beginning

Once we are able to confess our faults, we should find them easy to bear.
La Rochefoucauld

25

Our visit with Vivian, Jean-Michel and their two children, Sofia and Kevin, was joyous. Henri was his usual philosophically affable self. He brought a wonderful bottle of D'Usse Cognac which Jean-Michel and I were nursing all day. Pepina purchased a couple of backpacks for the children's school books. She also gave Vivian an elegant Alhambra scarf that she picked up in Seattle, Washington. Vivian was hesitant about accepting such a gift. However, Pepina reassured her that it was not expensive.

The Capretto al Forno was roasted over red-hot wood coals on a rotisserie that Jean-Michel devised. When the kid was about half-cooked Jean-Michel threw some dried white sage (Salvia apiana) over the coals. The smoke lent a special flavor to the already delectable milk-fed juicy meat which deliciously melted in our mouths. Pepina assisted Vivian in preparing rutabagas and parsnips in olive oil with crushed black pepper. It matched well with the meat dish. They also roasted some red bell peppers on the grill.

Jean-Michel and I were in no shape after the feast to partake in a chess match, so we postponed our rivalry for another time. Henri never participates in any competitive activity but is a willing spectator. His interest lies in conversations regarding the human condition, and of course, women.

Our little group's revelry continued on into the evening. Pepina heaped praises on Jean-Michel and Vivian for creating such a lovely family. A good portion of the time she spent with Sofia and Kevin, playing games and asking them what their interests and dreams were. Pepina had mentioned to me on a few occasions that she never regretted not having children but took great pleasure in enjoying the company of young people.

Late that evening, back home, Pepina told me what a wonderful group of friends we have. Also, she was still confident that Valeria would eventually gain the confidence to join us here. I just smiled adoringly as I held her in my arms, while Gustavo's voice kept popping into my head about what a 'lucky *bastardo*' I was. After all, not everyone gets a second chance.

Early the following morning we were just sitting down to enjoy a crustless quiche lorraine we had made two nights before. As we were digging in, enjoying it with fresh croissants and coffee, while discussing our itinerary concerning the Japan adventure, Pepina stopped eating suddenly and said, "Gianni, do you hear that?"

I stopped munching for a couple seconds... silence. "No cara mia, don't hear anything."

As soon as I said that we both heard a tapping sound on the

side window by the mini-fruit orchard. I walked over to the window but did not see a thing. Pepina began to walk outside and I followed her.

When we arrived at the trees Pepina stopped immediately. Her eyes pointed the way. I looked to the top branch of our sapote tree. There, perched with her back to us, was Theadora. She spun 180 degrees to face us and began to screech, chirp and squawk up a storm. She spun back around and continued with a Eurasian jay opera. There, up on the roof, another jay bashfully poked its beak over the roof's ledge to give us a quick peek. Theadora was encouraging him to pay his respects but he was too shy. Theadora gave us one quick glance, coupled with a high-pitched squeak. Then, off she went, up and up and over all the homes, with her elusive boyfriend following her in hot pursuit.

"Thea found her Gianni, just like I found you," Pepina said with tears flowing endlessly down her beautiful heart-shaped face.

I replied, "Just like we found each other, my love." I held her tightly in my arms, our hearts flapping against each other in a rhythmic beat. "Now let's go back inside to finish our breakfast."

<center>~~~~~</center>

Another Chance:

The Adventures of Gianni and Pepina {Book II}

Join Gianni and Pepina in their new adventures as they travel to Japan, Korea, the archipelago of Okinawa and India. Why has Henri surprisingly appeared in Osaka, Japan? Has he re-united with his former love and intellectual match, Michiko? (Japanese Ambassador to United Nations)

Copyright@Giulia Ebrahimi

Giuseppe Scarpine is the author of Second Chance-The Adventures of Gianni & Pepina.

When the author and his lovely wife are not growing organic produce or cooking and dining gourmet food, you can find them hiking in the Pacific Northwest, the extensive California coastline or the challenging trails throughout Spain.

In his spare time Giuseppe relaxes by grafting fruit trees whilst piddling around as Director of the forty-one acre Conejo Valley Botanic Garden in Thousand Oaks, California.